MY NAME IS AURORA

A novel by

ERWIN BUCK

Library and Archives Canada Cataloguing in Publication

Buck, Erwin W.
        My Name is Aurora/Erwin Buck

ISBN 978-0-9811459-5-2

Also by Erwin Buck

Fiction
Angels Landing
Veneer
Deadly Music
I, Aurora

Children's Book
(with illustrations by Larry Routliffe)
The Boy Who Swallowed a Lake
The Boy Who Wouldn't Kick

Poetry
I Could Long Love You
Fearing Angels...and Others

May you be half an hour in heaven
before the devil knows you're dead.
                              -Irish saying

For Nancy

CHAPTER 1

If you're lucky enough to be Irish,
then you're lucky enough.

- Irish Proverb

"My name is Aurora. Aurora Weeks," said the female caller at the other end of the phone line. Her voice had a strong Irish accent, and she sounded to be in her late twenties or early thirties.

My first instinct was to hang up. Someone pretending to be me was not something I found funny anymore. I stayed on the line, though; her Irish accent intrigued me. But I honestly didn't know how to respond. After all, I was Aurora Weeks. Was there really a genuine other Aurora out there? The one who had stolen my identity a couple of years ago didn't count, since her real name was Tatyana. And she was dead.

"I'm calling from Galway in Ireland," the caller continued. "Do you have a moment to talk?"

"You're not putting me on, are you?" I asked, my guard still up.

"Oh no, not at all. You see, I found you on the internet. I read your bio and the co-incidences were just too much, so I tracked down your phone number."

"What coincidences?" I asked, a little less guarded.

"We have the same name, we're both writers, and we're both Leos. But the most amazing coincidence is that your grandparents are from the same county in Ireland as my grandparents - Kilkenny." She paused, and I heard static on the line.

"Are you still there, Aurora?" It felt weird to call her by my name. I'd never met another Aurora.

There was more static and crackling, as if the wind had a direct opening into the telephone cable.

"Yes, I am. I'm having a problem with this telephone, and I need to replace it. It keeps cutting out on me. The storm outside isn't helping, either."

"Can you give me your phone number? If we get cut off, I'll call you back."

She gave me a number, which I wrote down.

7

"How did you know about my grandfather's county?" I asked, my curiosity aroused. I didn't have the faintest clue where my grandfather had lived before he came to Canada. I just knew it had been in Ireland.

"I read about it online. Your father's name came up when I googled the Weeks name. On one of the websites, there was an interview your father gave while visiting Ireland on a trade mission. In the interview, he mentioned that his father was born in Kilkenny. When I read that, I thought that it was all too uncanny. We surely must be related."

I didn't dare tell her that as far as I knew, my parents had named me after a city just north of Toronto. Okay, they would never admit to it, but I could have sworn I'd overheard them tell that story to one of their friends at a party. Regardless, I began to wonder if, in fact, this caller with the same name was indeed genuine. I sure hoped so. I disliked phonies with a passion. Or phonies without a passion, for that matter.

"That's a really interesting question," I said. "I don't think I've ever seen a family tree, but I'd be happy to ask my dad. Unfortunately, right now my parents are hiking the Camino Real in Spain."

There was more noise and crackling on the line.

"The reason for my call," she said loudly, punctuated by lots of static, "is that I'm coming to Toronto next week on business. Can we meet for a cup of tea?"

"I'd love to. Let me give you the number of my cell phone. Best to call me on that, and I'll also give you my e-mail address." I gave her the information.

"I'll be in touch. I'm really looking forward......" With that, the line went dead.

How very strange. I'd just been disconnected from myself.

CHAPTER 2

Don't give cherries to pigs, or advice to fools.
- Irish Proverb

I pondered the phone call as I sat at my desk. Were we really related? I knew that I was part Irish, at least on my father's side, so I supposed it was possible. And if I wanted to, I could probably find out online. The internet had made our world very small and was full of sites devoted to genealogy. But to be honest, family history had never been of any interest to me. I knew people who spent inordinate amounts of time making up complicated family trees and tracking down long-lost relatives. With all the databases available on the web, it was becoming much easier to do. No more traipsing around church cemeteries or civic registry offices; now much of the information was available at the click of a mouse. Yet I couldn't imagine phoning up someone halfway around the world whom I'd never met and introducing myself as a distant cousin twelve times removed. What exactly would you say after three minutes of explanation, other than 'how are you?'.

I hadn't planned on being at work today, but a sudden small emergency had cropped up. The executive producer of my show had asked if I could come in and do a bit of voice-over work. It seemed that some new, energetic trainee sound editor had accidentally erased part of a soundtrack on the latest, and last, segment of my bi-weekly television show.

My show had been on the air for almost two years. Now the network was revamping its programs, and I was one of the casualties. Which was fine by me; I'd never been comfortable being an on-air personality. I did it well, but my inner self was always in turmoil. I was more of a behind-the-scenes person. That was why I enjoyed writing so much. I could do it at my own pace and schedule.

My television show dealt with political affairs and ran on the local CBC channel. The content ranged over a variety of current political issues on which I was a supposed expert. Politics was my main love, and having grown up in a political family, I was pretty good at it, if I do say so myself.

Unfortunately, the show didn't pay enough to allow me to make a full-time living at it, so I also wrote books and columns on a variety of subjects. My last book was about identity theft, a topic that I had quickly become an expert on when it had happened to me. In fact, it had almost gotten me killed. The book before that had been about greed in the financial community. And that had almost gotten me killed, too. What was it with me? Did I have a bull's eye on my forehead?

My latest project was a series of articles about the Canadian Senate. A recent controversial appointment to the Senate by our Prime Minister had again raised the issue of whether the Senate should be abolished. Fortunately, I had about six weeks to do the articles, so I didn't really feel too pressured.

I pulled out my cell phone to make sure it still had power. Dave was calling me between lectures to confirm our plans for tonight.

Dave Fullerton was my boyfriend. Or should I use that word at my age? It made me sound like a teenager, yet I was closer to 40 than I was to 20. I couldn't call him 'my partner', since we didn't live together. I couldn't call him 'my man', since I wasn't Tammy Wynette. Maybe I'd just settle for 'my Dave'. As far as labels went, that was probably as good as any.

He hadn't exactly been my 'anything' on our first encounter. You see, he had been a detective at the time, and he'd arrested me for murder, which wasn't exactly the best way to start a relationship. It all got sorted out quite quickly, though, and eventually I saw Dave in a new light. We'd been seeing each other for two years. He had taken a leave from the police force and was studying to be a lawyer.

We'd developed a good routine in our relationship. He did his student bit during the week, and we got together on the weekends. You could say that we had a long-distance relationship, even though we lived in close proximity to each other. We talked often on the phone but, not wanting to be a distraction to his studies, I tried hard not to call him too much. Come the weekend, though, it was a different story.

We both lived in condos. Mine was rented, at Avenue Road and Bloor. Dave owned his, a small one-bedroom on Sherbourne Street, not that far away from where I lived.

One of these days, we would probably have a conversation about pooling our resources, but neither of us was in a hurry, or so it seemed. And that was just fine by me.

Dave was studying at Osgoode Law School. I admired his courage in changing careers in mid-life. Granted, he was just going from one side of law enforcement to the other. Nonetheless, he was giving up a good pension and a fairly solid career so far, my arrest notwithstanding. The bottom line, though, was that if you weren't happy in your job, you weren't happy with your life.

While waiting for Dave to call, I googled my name. I'd done this many times before, usually when I was bored. All kinds of links came up about books and articles I'd written. I even had a Wikipedia entry; my publisher had arranged that. After scrolling through two pages of links related to me, I saw a link to an Aurora Weeks in Galway, Ireland. I clicked on the link, and it took me to her home page. Her business was ancestral research. The telephone number listed was the same as the one she'd given me. So there really were two of us. All of a sudden, I'd doubled in size. I looked to see if there was a third Aurora out there, but no such luck.

My cell phone chirped. Really, it had a bird chirp as the ringtone.

"Hey, Dave," I said, "you'll never guess what."

"Hey, Aurora," he replied, "what?"

"There's two of me."

"So we can do a ménage a trois?" Dave had a good sense of humour. I often thought that was why we got along so well.

I briefly told him about my phone call from Ireland. He was mildly interested, but I could tell that he was preoccupied, so I asked him if we were doing our usual dinner thing at Angelo's. He said yes, which was the right answer, and hung up.

Before shutting down my desktop, I sent Dad a quick e-mail asking if he had a family tree or any historical information on our family. Who knew, maybe Irish Aurora and I were in fact distant cousins. I told him, of course, that it could wait until they came home. If, in fact, they ever did. I also sent my brother Barrie a similar e-mail, but it struck me that he had even less interest in our ancestry than I did. I thought that it might be the west-coast air that made him so laidback. He lived in Vancouver with his wife and two children.

As I headed out, I reflected that the chilly September air definitely signaled an end to summer. What was it about Labour Day that always caused the weather to change? It was like we went from summer to autumn overnight.

My soon-to-be vacant office was located in a trendy new waterfront area on Queen's Quay. It was right beside Sugar Beach, a man-made sandy oasis with pink umbrellas and Muskoka chairs. Face one way and you'd see the harbour and the Toronto Islands. Turn sideways and you'd get a glorious view of the Redpath Sugar refinery.

Public transportation to this wasteland was still rather sketchy, so I usually walked there and back. Today was no exception. I needed fresh air and some exercise.

I went east to Lower Sherbourne and then up to the Distillery District, which had become a popular destination for dining, art, and coffee. But the city, in its wisdom, had allowed it to be surrounded by high-rises, looming at the back of every building. Soon the cobblestone streets and brick buildings would seem like a besieged fort.

From there, I meandered along King, up Church, and through Ryerson University's grounds, finally ending up on Yonge. It was my favourite street in the city. It had everything from porn to prom outfits, from glitz to ditz, from trendy to retro. And restaurants of every kind, size, and ethnic variety.

At College Park, I noticed a store called 'The Irish Shoppe'. With my newfound potential distant relative from Ireland, I must have been more conscious of the shamrock today, and I could have sworn I could hear the store calling to me.

Taking my life in my hands, I crossed Yonge Street in mid-block. This was the kind of activity that would have a subtitle on the bottom of the television screen saying 'Don't try this at home'. Fortunately, St. Patrick must have been watching over me, because I was able to avoid the speeding taxi that nearly ran me over.

Reaching the opposite sidewalk safely, I studied the window of 'The Irish Shoppe'. There were Irish calendars, picture books, sweaters, caps, walking sticks, china, and numerous other themed items. I decided to go in and have a look.

An older woman with a very pronounced Irish accent asked if I needed any help. I told her that I was just browsing, and she went back to unpacking some boxes.

I looked at the woolen goods, the placemats with pictures of the countryside, the calendars with pictures of smiling Irish children, the fridge magnets of leprechauns, and a vast assortment of personalized coffee cups with every Irish name imaginable, except Aurora.

A wool scarf caught my eye. It was hand knitted by Mary Tully of County Mayo, according to the tag affixed to the back of it. The price was a bit steep, but as I ran my fingers over it, I liked the feel and the texture. I wondered who Mary Tully really was.

The storekeeper, noticing my interest, asked if I wanted to see any other scarves.

"Do you source these from a wholesaler? Is there really a Mary Tully?" I could be very skeptical at times. Maybe even bordering on the edge of cynical. For all I knew, 'Mary Tully' was the nickname of a computerized sewing machine in Taiwan.

"Aye, yes," the woman replied. "There really is a Mary Tully. In fact, I know her personally. I make three buying trips to Ireland a year. Anything in this store that is hand-made or hand-crafted, I picked out myself."

"Is it all from the Republic?" I asked. "What about the north?"

"Oh, it's from all over Ireland, north and south. I don't draw a line," she said with a wide grin. "We're all Irish. The rest is just politics. I take it you're not Irish. Are your parents?"

"My grandfather came from Ireland. Kilkenny, I believe."

"Aye, I know it well." She went over to a counter and pulled something out from the back. It was a tea towel with the image of the county of Kilkenny printed on it. "This is a very popular item. I sell at least three or four a month."

"Really?" I said, genuinely impressed. "I'll take it then, as well as this scarf. And the next time you see Mary Tully, tell her that she knits lovely scarves."

"I will. She'll be pleased. She's 86 years old, and knits twenty-five of these a year. Not to mention the ones she does for her family. She has twelve children, thirty-five grandchildren, and fifteen great-grandchildren. She's a local legend in her county," the storekeeper said proudly.

'What for? Procreation?' I wanted to ask, but I didn't dare.

I decided to wear the scarf as I continued my trek uptown. It felt very cozy around my neck. The texture of the wool reminded me of a sweater I'd had when I was young. Perhaps it too had come from Ireland. Note to self: ask Mom who gave it to me and what happened to it.

Mary Tully's scarf gave me a new impetus to follow my Irish roots. Or maybe it was the phone call from my namesake in Galway. Regardless, I suddenly had this irresistible urge to trace my ancestry. If there was ever a perfect time to do it, it was now. Nothing else was clamoring for my attention, except for my articles on the Canadian Senate. And who knew, maybe I could document it all and write a book, I thought. Then I remembered Alex Hailey's "Roots". Somehow I was lacking a bit of substance. All I had was a woman with the same name who could be a distant cousin, and a lovely Irish scarf. Hardly the stuff novels were made of.

CHAPTER 3

A friend's eye is a good mirror.
- Irish Proverb

As I neared Bloor Street, my cell phone vibrated. Although the ring tone was on, the loud construction nearby made it impossible to hear. I answered with little hope that I would actually understand the caller.

"Aurora, it's Wendy. Can you hear me?"

I ducked into a retail store. "Hi, Wendy. Sorry for the noise. Construction here is unbelievable. How are you?"

"I'm great, absolutely great. I just closed a deal that came from out of the blue, and I feel like a glass of champagne to celebrate. Want to join me?"

"Sure. Where are you .... at the office?"

"No, I'm at the Four Seasons."

"I can be there in ten minutes. Where will I meet you?"

"I'm in the lobby bar."

"Ok, see you shortly. Order the champagne."

I first met Wendy Sherwood during my identity-theft crisis. She was the leasing manager of the new Trump Hotel, where the evil Aurora had purchased a condo using my name. In the course of straightening it all out, Wendy and I had become good friends. Wendy had moved on in her career since then; she now handled office leasing for one of the larger commercial brokers.

Wendy was sitting on one of the couches in the lobby bar, talking on her cell phone. As soon as I walked in, she waved, said goodbye to her caller, and put the phone down. She stood up, clapping her hands, and then gave me the biggest hug. That was Wendy. You'd think we hadn't seen each other in years, yet it had only been a couple of weeks.

"Oh, Aurora, I'm so happy to see you. Look at you," she gushed, standing back a bit to take me all in. "You look like a movie star."

Here was the thing about Wendy - she actually meant what she said. I was sure some people would immediately think she was a phony, or someone who had perfected the fake-nice persona so common these days. But not Wendy. There wasn't an insincere bone in her body.

"Have you ordered?" I asked her as we sat down.

14

"No, I just had to make a quick phone call," she said, still beaming.

"Well then, let's get that glass of champagne to celebrate your deal."

"Oh, goody!" she exclaimed. I didn't know anyone else who would use that phrase except for my five-year-old nephew. But with Wendy, you really knew she meant exactly that - "Oh, goody!"

I motioned for the server, who was busy polishing the brass on the bar rail. I ordered two glasses of champagne, and he wondered if we might be interested in a bottle. There was a promotion going on. Wendy looked to me to make that decision. Champagne sometimes makes me stupid, so I tossed the ball back to her.

Wendy didn't give it any further thought. "We'll take the bottle," she said. And then quickly added, "It's not every day that a deal like this comes along. You'll love this story."

She moved to the edge of the cushion and leaned close to me. "I was at a house party a few weeks ago, and a man I had just met was telling me about his job. He's the CFO of a large company located in Don Mills. His company was booming, and they were looking for space downtown. I asked him if he was using a real estate agent, and guess what he said?" she asked breathlessly.

"What?"

"'I hate real estate agents. They just try and sell you something.'" Wendy did her best to imitate his gruff voice. "Those were his exact words. Can you believe it? And he's the CFO. And here's the neat part. He didn't know I was an agent, and I didn't tell him. I asked him for his business card, which he gave me without even asking why. Then we were interrupted, and I didn't go near him again for the rest of the evening."

The waiter arrived with our bottle of bubbly.

"To your success," I said as we raised our glasses.

"Mm, this is so good," Wendy exclaimed, after taking a sip of the champagne. "All right, so the next day I did my homework. I found out how many employees there are in his company and how much space they currently have, and I reviewed all of the inventory downtown that might be suitable. It didn't look good at first, but then I was talking to my boss, who mentioned that we had just been awarded a contract to lease space in the new World Bank tower. BINGO. I knew that it would be perfect."

She picked up her champagne glass and took another sip. Then she leaned back in the sofa, a big smile on her face. "Let's just stay here all afternoon," she said happily. I do believe she was serious.

"I did some number crunching," she continued. "I knew what the landlord wanted, so I structured a deal that had some leeway in it. I called the CFO, introduced myself again, and asked him to meet me for a coffee. I told him I had a business proposition for him. He still didn't know I was an agent," she gushed, with an impish smile. "Well, you should have seen the expression on his face when I handed him my card. For a second, he looked like he was all set to bolt out of Starbucks. And then I hit him square between the eyes."

I looked at her, startled. Did she mean that literally?

"I gave him a business pitch and the only thing I used was a paper napkin. No Power Point, no glossy brochure. Just a napkin, telling him what it would cost to move into this prestigious building. Let me tell you, I blew him away. And best of all, he hadn't even started his coffee yet."

The waiter came back and refilled our glasses. If Wendy didn't finish this story soon, we might have to get another bottle.

"I think I really caught him off guard. He asked me some questions, which I answered easily. Then I looked at my watch and told him I'd kept him long enough, and that I had another meeting to go to. If I were to describe him at that point, I'd say that he was truly speechless. I left him sitting there, staring at the napkin."

"That was taking a chance, wasn't it?"

"Not really. He wasn't dealing with an agent yet, so what was he going to do? Besides, I dazzled him. I really did." And I believed her. When Wendy sounded enthusiastic, it was hard not to have the same feeling yourself. She just radiated it.

"Later in the day, I got a call from him inviting me to come and meet with his boss, the CEO. The meeting went well, so well in fact that by the end of it, they gave me exclusivity to act on their behalf. Within the next week, the deal was worked out in principle, and a month later, we formalized it."

As she finished the story, I thought for sure she was going to get up and do a little happy dance. That was another thing about Wendy. She was happy for herself, but equally so for the landlord and the new tenant. "Good karma all round," she concluded, draining the last of her champagne.

The waiter came by again and refilled the glasses. The bottle was getting dangerously low.

Wendy asked what I'd been doing, and I told her about Irish Aurora. When I finished, she looked at me very seriously, her brow furrowed.

"Be careful of the Irish," she said in a most serious tone. Not like Wendy at all. In fact, I didn't know if I'd ever seen her so serious before.

Just for the record, Wendy wasn't one to ever say anything bad about anyone, as far as I could tell. She was the proverbial example of someone who wouldn't say shit if their mouth was full of it.

"I love the Irish," she said, leaning forward confidingly. "My favourite aunt, Linda, is Irish, and she is delightful. Absolutely delightful." Wendy paused and had another sip. I could tell that she was trying to find the right words. Then she sat upright, as if to steel herself, and said, "But the rest of the family is just nuts. Talk about dysfunctional. It's all about religion and the British. They are fanatics on every level. They want nothing to do with England, they want Northern Ireland to be reunited with the South, and they want all the Protestants shipped off to Scotland or Wales, or London. Poor Aunt Linda. She is totally apolitical, but her husband Brendan is so polarized that he can't open his mouth without offending everyone within earshot. The older he gets, the more entrenched his ideas become. No wonder the Irish have had their Troubles." She shook her head. "Isn't that a lovely way to describe bloodshed and ruthless killing?" It was a question that didn't need an answer, and I was a bit shocked. I'd never seen Wendy so agitated.

"Let's talk about something happier," I offered, trying to find the Wendy I knew.

"You're right. I get very worked up about them. I don't know why. They are such stubborn, narrow-minded people. Thank God they live in Ireland and not here." She had another sip of champagne, and that seemed to calm her down.

"How's Dave doing?" she asked, and I got the feeling that she too wanted to change the subject. Fine by me.

Our conversation became light-hearted again. We finished the bottle, by which time Wendy was even more effusive, if that was possible. We rolled out of the bar by 5:45. Thankfully, my condo was just across the road. After several hugs, Wendy kissed my cheek and said, "You're the best." And off she went. I watched her walk down the street, and I was reminded of Dorothy in the Wizard of Oz, skipping down the yellow brick road.

Since I had agreed to meet Dave at 7:30, I had less than two hours to mitigate the effects of the champagne. I quickly downed two glasses of water, did half an hour of pilates, and then had a hot bath.

Despite all of that, I still felt a buzz when I left the condo. Thank God I wasn't driving.

17

CHAPTER 4

Honey is sweet, but don't lick it off the briar.
- Irish Proverb

Dave was already at Angelo's by the time I arrived. It had become a bit of a game with us to see who would get there first, and he always beat me. I never planned to be late, honestly. Events always seemed to conspire against me.

Angelo's had become a second home for both of us. It was close to both of our condos, the food was really good, and the ambience suited us. Not to mention that Angelo himself was a real sweetheart .... to me, anyway. Funny how things worked out; if it hadn't been for Tatyana impersonating me, I would have never gone there. But I did, and Angelo and I hit it off right away. Now Dave and I ate there probably once a week. And why not, I said to friends of mine who thought I was unimaginative in going to the same restaurant time after time. If you liked a place, make it yours!

A glass of Peroni was sitting in front of Dave, and he and Angelo were caught up in an animated conversation. Probably about the Premier League, as always. Angelo's team was AC Milan, while Dave's team was Bayern München. Don't ask me why. Dave had never even been to Europe. Somehow, though, when he was born he got soccer genes instead of hockey genes.

They stopped talking as soon as I walked in.

"Hello, nice lady, let me take your coat," Angelo said, bustling around the corner of the bar and whisking my jacket away. Once it was hung up, he went back behind the bar and poured me a generous glass of Vino Nobile wine from his hometown of Montepulciano, deep in the heart of Tuscany. His cousin was the vintner, and Angelo imported the wine by the caseload. For my part, I helped him make a good dent in his inventory.

Dave and I made small talk about daily stuff. That is to say, I made small talk and he politely listened. He seemed a bit preoccupied, or maybe it was my lack of scintillating conversation. I brought up the call from my Irish namesake.

"Can you find out if you're related? Do you have a family tree?" he asked half- heartedly.

"Not that I know of. I sent Dad an e-mail asking if he had one, but I probably won't hear from him until they come back. Here's a funny thing .... sending the e-mail actually made me realize how little I know about Dad's relatives. And it reminded me of a conversation I had with Emily Mitchell at the office. She's in her early fifties and has lived in Toronto for thirty years. Her father lived on the west coast all his life and died unexpectedly. At the funeral and a celebration of his life, she listened to his friends and business associates and relatives pay tribute to him, and suddenly she saw a whole different side of him. It shocked her to realize how little she actually knew her father. I think I know Dad pretty well, but I know very little about both of my parents' backgrounds. I only had grandparents on Mom's side, and they both died before I went to university. I know nothing about Dad's parents, who died before I was born, other than the odd thing that's slipped out in conversation."

Dave was quiet, thinking of something.

"I remember my Nan," he said finally, in a wistful voice. "She was my mother's mother. She lived close to us, and I saw her a lot when I was a kid. I loved her, she doted on me, and we had such a strong bond. Then, when I was eleven, we moved away, and I was crushed. After that, we'd only see her once or twice a year. I missed her so much, and I think she missed me too. And here's the sad part, I didn't care about losing Grandpa. He was always a grouch who treated us kids as if we were a nuisance. How they ever raised children on their own is a mystery to me. But I cried many times over her."

"Imagine how hard it must have been for Nan when you moved away."

"I was mad at my parents for a long time after that. I didn't really understand why they moved. Dad got a better job, but so what? Why didn't he just get a job here? That's what kept going through my mind. It took me a long time to get over losing her." He turned around on the stool and signaled to Angelo, who was clearing off a table. "Let's get some food, I'm starved."

Angelo escorted us to our usual table. I looked at the dark mahogany wainscoting, but there was still no little gold plaque to designate this as our table.

As we ate, we talked about Dave's law course and my Senate assignment. I had the feeling that he was still distracted by something, and I gently prodded him to open up. But Dave was the type to take that kind of prodding as a sign to retreat even further. So I didn't pursue it.

19

Back at my place, we had a quick nightcap and then went to bed. Much to my chagrin, Dave said that he was really tired and would I mind if he just went to sleep? What an idiot. Of course I minded. What, were we an old married couple now? But before I had a chance to make a case for a romp in the hay, he was peacefully asleep.

CHAPTER 5

Time is often a great storyteller.
- Irish Proverb

I was lying in bed the next morning, wide awake, listening to 'Mr. I-Don't-Snore'. I thought about Wendy's uncharacteristic outburst about the Irish. I was probably as guilty as the next person of equating the Irish with the potato famine, drinking, and lots of blarney. And, oh yes, fighting with each other.

But they were a charming people. I mean, why else would everyone pretend to be Irish on St. Patrick's Day? Other than for a good excuse to tie one on. I will confess that in my early twenties, I spent quite a bit of time in Irish pubs drinking and singing. There was nothing quite like an Irish pub with a band belting out "The Black Velvet Band" or "The Wild Rover".

Of course I knew of my Irish heritage, but Dad never made a big deal about it. He was a first-generation Canadian and never dwelt on his family's Irish past. As far as Dad was concerned, he was Canadian and so were we.

I did know about Ireland's economic boom, nicknamed the Celtic Tiger, thanks to research I'd done for a segment on my show a few months back. It had roared loudly in the mid 90's, and Ireland had gone from rags to riches. Jobs were plentiful, the future was bright, and real estate values soared out of sight. Then, ten years or so later, amid the growing global financial disaster, the Tiger had all but died. The banks found themselves on the verge of collapse, thanks to Iceland and the murky Wall Street junk bonds. The country was saved when the Eurozone bailed it out, but the rescue came with a price: Ireland lost control of its finances. The fall was swift and painful, and it brought on years of hardship, economic decline, and a level of emigration reminiscent of that of the potato famine.

The snoring beside me didn't show any sign of letting up, so I quietly rolled out of bed, wrapped myself in a robe, and made some coffee. When it was ready, I picked out the 'I' volume from my World Encyclopedia set and flipped it open to Ireland. Granted, I probably could have gotten better information from Google, or at least more current information, but once in a while I liked to resort to paper.

Somehow it just seemed more credible. Besides, my parents had paid a lot of money for our set of encyclopedias, so I used them whenever I got a chance. It was like comfort food.

Wendy's comment about the Troubles kept coming back to me. I was familiar with the expression, but I'd never fully understood or comprehended what it was really all about or what its origins were. I just knew that it was Northern Ireland's term for the sectarian strife that had plagued it in the 1970's and 80's.

After an hour of reading, I felt that my brain wanted to go back to bed. Yes indeed, the Irish had experienced their Troubles and that was a quaint way of describing it, as Wendy so aptly put it.

I closed the book and reflected on the fact that the British Empire had left a sad legacy behind of colonial rule. Just look at India and Pakistan. Or Palestine. South Africa. Ceylon. Israel. In fairness, though, so had the French, the Spanish, and the Portuguese. Even the Dutch had engaged in colonial exploitation, as had the Russians, the Chinese, and the Germans. The list was endless. Since the beginning of recorded history, countries had been exploited, carved up, divided, and then abandoned. Closer to home, look what we had done to the aboriginal people! When it really got down to it, war and injustice was as constant as the setting of the moon or the rising of the sun. Ireland had its Troubles, but it was not unique.

The smell of coffee must have finally lured Dave out of bed. It was close to nine, and I was on my third cup. Our Saturday morning ritual was to go out, pick up the weekend papers, and sit at Lettieri's in Yorkville, reading them from cover to cover, accompanied by calorie-laden croissants and bagels. I liked doing some of the puzzles, and Dave would devour the sport sections.

I was ready to entice Dave back to bed to continue where we hadn't left off last night when he asked if I wanted to go for a run first before going out for breakfast. We did that sometimes, to justify the bagels and cream cheese. I could see that he really wanted to go, so I agreed.

Before long, we were heading down Philosopher's Walk on the U of T campus. It was a cool morning, and I was beginning to wonder if I should have put on an extra layer. I didn't need to worry, though; we were sweating in no time.

We always ran at a pace that let us carry on a conversation. I often wondered about couples that I saw running together without interacting with each other in any way, each of them listening to their own music. "Is it that hard to talk to each other?" I want to ask them.

"Did I ever tell you about my days on the drug squad?" Dave asked as we turned onto Harbord Street.

"I don't think so. Was that part of the training?"

"Not really. I thought it would be good experience and a way to get ahead. I was working at an OPP detachment outside the city at the time, and my supervisor told me about the opening. So I put my name forward and had three or four interviews with a variety of officials, including the head of the drug squad, a guy named Harry Schulz."

Dave stopped and bent down to re-tie his shoe laces while I jogged on the spot.

"Is it hard to get on a squad like that?" I asked as we resumed the run.

"Yes, it is. They're very particular about who they pick. Mainly because the guys on the squad are very tight with each other. They have to be, because a lot of time they're undercover together and are always putting their life on the line."

"Must be hard to have a family life."

"It takes its toll, let me tell you. I think they spend more time with each other than they do with their families. That's just the nature of the job. You know how they hired me? I spent the weekend partying with Schulz and the other guys on the squad. It was their way of interviewing me and making sure that the chemistry was right."

We stopped at a red light at Queen's Park Crescent. A police car went by and honked. Dave waved, and we crossed the road once the light turned green and picked up our pace.

We resumed our conversation again once we were on the running path at Queen's Park.

"So what was it like?" I asked.

"At first, it was really exciting. Doing undercover surveillance work, just like in the movies. But a lot of it was mindless, too. Let me tell you, surveillance work can be very boring. I mean, you're tailing a dealer and he's meeting people for drinks. So you sit in the car for hours and hours, waiting for him to come out. We did bust some pretty big drug rings, though, and that was satisfying."

"Was it a good experience?"

"Yes and no. Yes because I learned a lot, and no because I never cracked their inner circle. Schulz ran the squad very tightly, as if it was his own little kingdom. I never felt that he trusted me. It wasn't anything that I could put my finger on. We always got along well, but I had the sense that he kept his distance from me."

"How long did you stay on the squad?"

"Two and a half years. Then I got transferred out."

"Why? Were you pushed?"

"No, I asked for the transfer. I couldn't see myself doing that kind of work for much longer. I mean, for those guys the squad came first; their family lives were practically non-existent. I didn't like that. Besides, I never felt that I was part of the team; I was always kept at the edge. If there was a takedown, I'd be stationed outside, making sure no one got away."

We stopped at a drinking fountain. The cool water felt surprisingly good.

"How many more loops do you want to do?" I asked. My stomach was sending me signals that the food gauge was low.

"Let's do one more," Dave said. Good enough for me. That would take about fifteen minutes.

Dave told me some stories of the more dangerous busts he was involved in.

"I can see why you'd want to get out," I said when he finished. "Writing is a safer occupation."

"Uh-huh," he said, "and how many people have tried to kill you?"

He had me on that one.

We got to the end of the run and, as we always did, walked for about five minutes to cool down. I was glad he'd suggested the run, if for no other reason than it got me out from under the shadow of Ireland's Troubles.

"Did you tell me all this for a reason?" I asked, because it wasn't like Dave to talk so much about himself without any prompting.

"Sort of," he said. "I've been hearing rumours about an internal investigation into that drug squad."

"Really, why?"

"There were a lot of whispers after I left about guys on the squad confiscating drugs and re-selling them, or taking cash and valuables from the drug dealers."

"Really? Did you ever do any of that?" I asked without thinking.

Dave looked at me sharply, offended that I would ask such a question. "No, I didn't."

"Sorry, I meant, did you ever see any of that?"

"Still the same answer. No." Now he sounded put off.

"Are you worried about this?"

24

"Not really. I'll know more next week, though. I'm going out for a beer with some guys who were also on the squad."

"I thought you said they didn't like you."

"No, that was just Schulz. But if he didn't trust you completely, then the other guys picked up on that, regardless of whether they liked you or not."

"By the way," he said as we were going up in the elevator, "there's a law conference I want to go to in a couple of weeks at Memorial University in Newfoundland. Will you help me get a cheap flight?"

"How long is it for?"

"Two days."

"Sure. I'm an expert at this. My middle name is Expedia," I said, tongue-in-cheek.

As we walked down the hall towards my condo, I suddenly remembered my Aunt Fionola, in Trinity, Newfoundland. And her daughter, Paula McKerr, who, if I remembered correctly, lived on Fogo Island.

I stopped Dave. "Would you like some company on your trip?"

"For the law conference?"

"No. I want to visit my aunt. I haven't seen her in so long that I'm feeling guilty."

"Great idea. Maybe we can do some quick sightseeing."

"How about some slow sightseeing? Hey, maybe we can make it a mini-vacation." 'And get married while we're there,' I almost said jokingly. Then I thought better of it. Look what happened the last time I'd tried to get married!

CHAPTER 6

Better good manners than good looks.
- Irish Proverb

The rest of Saturday morning and afternoon went by quickly. After we had brunch in Yorkville, Dave went off to buy new skates. He played in a pick-up league with police buddies once a week at some ungodly hour of the night.

I went off to get my hair cut. Most of the time my hair was shoulder-length, but lately I'd had this urge to buzz it. I wasn't there yet, but one of these days I would be. I almost took the plunge today, but my hairdresser, Andre, talked me out of it. Instead, he gave me a nice trim and put in some highlights.

On my return, I called Aunt Fionola, who was delighted to hear from me and even more delighted when I told her I was coming for a visit. I asked her about our family history, and she said she had some documents that I might be interested in. Then I sent Paula a short e-mail telling her the dates of my impending visit. Before I knew it, the afternoon had slipped away and I was on my way to Dave's. When I got there, he offered to make a curry dinner.

I had to hand it to Dave .... he did make good curry. Maybe a bit too spicy for my liking, but I wasn't one to complain when someone cooked me dinner. He had the spices neatly lined up on the counter, like little soldiers: Turmeric, Garam Massala, Ground Coriander, Cumin Seeds, Ground Cumin, and a couple of unlabelled jars. He also made a cucumber raita and rice pilaf. To complete the mood, he played a CD by Ravi Shankar.

Dave liked drinking beer when eating curry, so I had one as well.

During dinner, I brought up the subject of the drug squad.

"How does an internal investigation actually work?" I asked, between sips of beer to quench the fire on my tongue.

"Well, the police chief will appoint someone, usually a senior investigator who's on the force. He'll review the allegations and talk to a wide variety of people, including lawyers, other police officers, and even the criminals."

"Are there many internal investigations?"

"I'm not sure how many, but when you think about the fact that the force employs thousands of men and women, there will always be a bad apple or two in there somewhere whose actions spark an investigation of some kind." Dave took a long sip of beer. "I think maybe I added too much cayenne pepper. Let me get some water for us."

"Should members of the police force really be investigating themselves?" I asked, after eagerly gulping down some of the water he handed me.

"No, they shouldn't, which in itself is a problem. There's too much baggage involved, and too much pride. No police chief is going to come out and publicly admit that members of his force are corrupt, much less charge them."

"So what happens?"

"Oh, they may reprimand an officer, maybe transfer him to different duties. But rarely does it become public. Unless you get a pissed-off lawyer who may leak something to a newspaper because he's got a client who's been a victim of the squad."

"A victim?" I asked skeptically.

"Of course. Drug dealers are the perfect victims. Say a drug dealer is busted and the police seize a large quantity of cash. The dealer knows how much cash he had, but when he's charged, he finds out that about two hundred grand is missing. And that some of the charges against him have been fabricated, like resisting arrest, assaulting an officer, and so on. Now, who's he going to complain to? Nobody's going to believe him, so he doesn't have a hope in hell of getting anyone to even take an interest in his allegations."

"So do you think the drug squad you were on did things like that?"

Dave took a long time in replying. "Maybe yes, and maybe no."

I waited for him to expand on that, but he didn't and I didn't press him. We finished the curry, and both of us nearly had tears in our eyes.

"Maybe I got the measurements mixed up," he said a bit sheepishly.

"Don't let that stop you from making another one, though." I said, between gulps of water.

"I won't."

We quickly cleaned up and headed to the movie theatre.

The romantic comedy was neither romantic nor much of a comedy. Throughout the movie, my mind kept wandering between Ireland, perfect victims, and the lingering fire in my mouth. Thus, the time passed quickly.

CHAPTER 7

Where the tongue slips, it speaks the truth.
- Irish Proverb

Now that my television show was over, it felt strange in the mornings not to have to head off to some production meeting or planning session. I'd naively thought that I would have all the time in the world to read and write. Yet it amazed me how quickly the time evaporated. I didn't get up as early, I took longer to read the paper, and on some days, the hours just seemed to disappear into a black hole. I was getting much more exercise, though. I went for a run most mornings, and I made a point to walk everywhere I went if I could. I was also getting more conscious of what I ate. Over the years, my weight had slowly crept up. It wasn't enough to be of real concern, but I wouldn't have minded going down a couple of sizes. And now seemed like a perfect opportunity. Mom would say, 'Make hay while the sun shines.' So I was taking the opportunity to make hay.

When I came back from my run, I looked at myself in the mirror before stepping into the shower. Overall, I was pleased with what I saw. My butt might be sagging a bit, but who the hell could fight gravity? My stomach could have been a bit flatter, but I hadn't noticed any tightness when I did up my jeans, so I was sure that it was just my imagination. Anyway, I didn't see Dave complaining, so who was I to worry?

The first e-mail in my inbox was from Paula McKerr.

Hey cousin, how wonderful to hear from you. I can hardly wait to see you. Of course I'll come to Trinity. I try to make it at least once a month, if not more often. Mum still lives in the same house, alone, and sometimes we fear it's too much for her. But she won't hear of moving into Trinity proper or with us on Fogo. She's getting close to 80 now and slowing down a bit, but she still drives to church. She's still very independent, and I'm glad. I want to see her stay in the house as long as she can. Saw you on CBC not long ago being interviewed about a book. You looked the same, but you were sober and not singing. Wasn't that a lark we had in St. John's? Lol. You seem to have done right well by yourself. See you soon. Paula.

I hit the reply button. *Hey, Paula. Looking forward to seeing you too. Is there a George Street in Trinity? If not, is there a pub we can close, or are we too old for that now? Yes, it was a great time. It will be nice spending time with you and Aunt Fionola. See you soon.*

I vividly remembered the last time I'd seen Paula. I was still in my teens, and Dad was going to Newfoundland, partly on government business and partly to see Aunt Fionola. Mom couldn't go and neither could my brother, but I was free, so he took me along.

Paula was eight years older than me. At the time, she was 25, and I remembered thinking that she was so old. She worked in St. John's, and we hung out together quite a bit at night in the few days I was there. One night, when Dad was at a meeting, Paula took me to George Street. I was still underage, but no one noticed or cared. By the end of the evening, I was very drunk. Point in my favour, though. I was a happy drunk. We went to several pubs, and the last one had this amazing Irish band. That's where I learned the words to "The Wild Rover". We sang it all the way home at the top of our lungs. Paula was pretty tipsy herself, but it was clear she knew how to hold her liquor a little better than I did.

I leaned back in the chair, allowing the flashback to linger for a few moments. I softly sang *"And it's no nay never, no nay never no more...."* When I stopped, I wondered if maybe there was more Irish in me than I'd let on.

My inbox signaled a new message. It was from Irish Aurora, telling me that she'd arrived in Toronto and to give her a call on her cell when I could. I dialed the number with the strange area code. Her Irish accent was unmistakable when she answered.

"Hello." Her sing-song voice stretched that simple little word to three syllables. At the end of the third syllable, her voice went up at least an octave.

"Hi, Aurora. Great to hear from you. Are you in town?" I asked, realizing as I did that it was a redundant question.

"I am indeed. Sorry I couldn't write before I left, but the storm knocked out all the power, including my internet. Then I got caught up in a bunch of things, and so here I am in your fair city."

"Well, I'm glad you made it. Where are you staying?"

"It's a hostel on Church Street. I really don't like spending lots of money at a fancy place just to sleep there. It's close to the Eaton Centre."

My mind pictured the hostel she was staying in. I knew it by sight and often wondered what it was like inside. I always thought of hostels as being at the bottom rung of the accommodation ladder. Could I be wrong?

"Can I take you out for dinner?" I asked.

"Oh, I shouldn't put you to all that trouble. A cup of tea would be grand."

"Nonsense. How about I meet you outside the hostel at 6:30? My favourite restaurant is nearby."

"That sounds great. I'll see you then," she said, and then added, "Are you sure this is no trouble?"

"Not at all," I replied. In fact, it was a welcome diversion.

CHAPTER 8

You can always tell an Irishman,
but you can't tell him much.
- Irish Proverb

I had no idea what to expect, and in an odd way, I was really looking forward to meeting my namesake. It was an unexpected surprise in my rather dull life at the moment.

For once, I actually arrived on time. A young woman was waiting outside the front entrance of the hostel. She couldn't have been more than five feet tall with curly red hair that cascaded over her shoulders. She wore a long coat that was accented by a purple scarf wrapped around her neck. The shade of pink lipstick she wore matched the colour of her cheeks.

Her face lit up as soon as she saw me.

"Aurora?" she asked as I walked up to her. I nodded, and she gave me a hug. Friendly people, these Irish. We made small talk as we walked toward Dundas Square, which was only a few blocks away.

The square was jammed with people. There was a free concert in progress .... something about a battle of the bands. The music blared out in every direction, rendering conversation useless. The garish neon billboards on the buildings around the square added to the excitement. We paused for a moment on the crowded sidewalk to take in the spectacle. The band was good, and I started to sway with the rhythm.

After a few moments of listening, I led Aurora up Yonge Street to Elm. It was slow going; the sidewalks were filled with young people heading for the square. It felt a little as though we were fish swimming upstream.

Finally we reached Elm Street, where the sidewalks were less crowded.

"Is it always like this, then?" Irish Aurora asked.

"Not really, although I must admit I don't spend a lot of time in this area. I live in a more genteel part of the city."

"Well, it certainly looked exciting back there. It was what I imagined Times Square to be like."

I hadn't made that link myself. Times Square was unique and defied comparison. But I felt a touch of civic pride to think that a tourist would make that connection. Wait a minute. What was going on here? I was from Ottawa. Had I gone over to the other side?

We reached Angelo's, and I led her inside. It was still early, and we had no trouble being seated. Angelo was nowhere to be seen, but his niece Giovanna showed us to a quiet table.

Irish Aurora looked around with great interest. "What a charming place," she said. Her Irish accent was beginning to grow on me, but it seemed a bit out of place in an Italian restaurant.

Just then, Angelo appeared and came over. I stood up and he gave me a big hug. Angelo and I had graduated to that; I was practically family now.

I introduced him to Irish Aurora, and he gave me a puzzled look. Angelo was very familiar with my previous namesake. She had stiffed him for a big dinner bill - so I could understand his confusion. This was the third Aurora Weeks that he'd met. I hastily explained who Irish Aurora was, and how I'd met her.

After welcoming my guest, he promised to bring over some wine and appetizers and left us alone.

Conversation wasn't hard for Irish Aurora. In fact, once she got going, it seemed as though she would never stop. I sat there trying to absorb it all, but it was coming at me so fast that I would get lost at times. And once in a while there would be an Irish phrase thrown in that was beyond my level of comprehension.

Thank God we were interrupted periodically by our server, or by Angelo himself. Only then was I able to catch my breath and maybe ask a question. But that was all it usually took - one question, and off she went again. Mostly it was about life in Ireland and her family. She had so many stories about various family members that I began to envy her for her large and seemingly close family. One story that really intrigued me was about Auntie Bridie, who had thirteen children. The last was born out of wedlock, and Bridie kept the child, a girl, indoors for the first two and a half years. She didn't want to incur the wrath of the local priest or the gossip by the neighbours. Finally she concocted a story about adopting a toddler whose parents had been killed in a tragic accident. Mercifully, Bridie's other twelve children led less colourful lives; otherwise we would have been there all night. Irish Aurora did talk a lot about her two siblings, Neil and Catherine. I stifled a laugh when she mentioned that Catherine talked non-stop, while Neil hardly opened his mouth. I wondered what the two sisters would be like together. Who would have the last word?

I was curious about her job and managed to get a question in about it while she was sipping her wine. "I understand you do ancestral research. I didn't even know that was a business, much less one you could make a living from. Tell me about it."

"Aye, yes. I've been doing it for a few years. I help track down family relatives all over the world. For a price, of course," she said, with an impish smile on her face.

"Including me, it seems," I said, draining my glass of Vino Nobile.

"I didn't actually set out to find you. That was just a fluke. And you have to admit, it was a pretty amazing coincidence. I mean, after all, two weeks ago I didn't even know another Aurora Weeks existed, and now I'm sitting here with you on an another continent. That's pretty remarkable, wouldn't you say?"

"It's quite remarkable. What made you look for me in the first place?"

"Actually it was quite simple. I was talking to one of my relatives, and she asked me about the origin of the surname Weeks. I really didn't know, and so I did a little digging. As part of that, I googled the name Weeks and you popped up all over the place. And I ran across the article about your father. That's when I knew I had to contact you. Beyond that, I never did get any further in the family research."

"This is your business, though. Is there really enough money in it?"

"Aye, there is. You see, I specialize in estate work. Tracking down long-lost family members, or distant relatives. There aren't many who do this line of work, so I have little competition, and besides, I'm pretty good at it, if I do say so myself."

"So, are you here to find someone in particular?" I asked quickly, before she started again.

"Indeed I am. A law firm hired me to track down an heir to an estate. A rather large estate, I might add. I found him living here in Toronto. However, the law firm wants me to interview him and make absolutely sure that he's the right heir. Chances are he's never met the relative in question, or is even aware of him."

"Are you a private investigator, then?"

She laughed. "I'm not, but I sometimes feel like one. I just use genealogy databases and public records to locate people. Most of the time, I'm successful at it. But once in a while, it does become impossible. I had another case in Canada several years ago where a man was trying to connect two branches of a family. He had done years of work, but was stymied by one missing person. I still remember the name of the missing man .... Julius Ruttle. He was a United Empire Loyalist who had just disappeared. We couldn't find any record of him anywhere after a certain date. And so, much to my client's dismay, because we couldn't find Ruttle, no connection was ever established between the two branches of the family. But he did pay me handsomely for my efforts."

"Does your work involve a lot of travel?"

"Not normally. Mostly I do it from my home in Galway. I'm up in Dublin quite a bit when I need to check some records, and when I'm there, I usually stay with my sister. Once in a while, though, I have to make absolutely sure I have the right person, and that usually involves an in-depth interview as well as some proof of ancestry. Once, we even had to do DNA testing."

"So, this individual doesn't know you're coming?"

"He does. I have had contact with him. But he really doesn't know why I want to meet with him. It's a long story, though, and I won't bore you with it," she said with a smile. For a moment, I'd tensed up. I was afraid that she was actually going to tell me the long story. Knowing her tendency for blarney, we could be there all night.

But I liked my new friend, or should I say distant cousin. She had a good attitude, and she'd probably make a great journalist. But if she was, then we'd have two of me.

I was not sure if I could stand the competition.

Aurora and I almost closed Angelo's. There was only one other couple left, who looked to be engaged in a serious argument. Angelo was hovering in the background, waiting for their heated discussion to end so that he could present them with the bill.

I couldn't remember when I'd ever met a person who talked as much as Irish Aurora. Really, I mean non-stop. Give her a topic, and within ten seconds, she'd be off on a variety of tangents. I just sat back and marveled at her skill. Was it an act, or did it come naturally to her? I'd heard that the Irish were great storytellers, and Aurora was certainly Exhibit A in that regard. Dad wasn't; in fact, he was the opposite. In the end, I came to the conclusion that Aurora was just a natural talker. Actually, what I enjoyed most was her Irish lilt. It was as if I was listening to music.

I paid for dinner. Thanks to Angelo, it was fairly reasonable, despite the two bottles of wine. I think Angelo only charged me for one. I often wondered how he stayed in business when he seemed to give so much away. I suspected that the Montepulciano wine was fairly cheaply priced. After all, it was all in the family, and I was probably their best customer.

Irish Aurora promised to stay in touch, and that if she ever established a family connection, I'd be first person she'd tell.

We parted in front of the restaurant with a big hug. She started to walk away and then came back.

"By the way, my family and friends all call me Rory. I hope you do, too."

"Good night," I replied, giving her another impromptu hug. "Are you sure I can't walk back with you?"

"I think I can manage just fine," she said with a big smile, as she threw her scarf over her shoulder.

I poured myself into a taxi.

CHAPTER 9

If it's drowning you're after,
don't torment yourself with shallow water.
- Irish Proverb

The next morning, I was lying in bed wishing that I hadn't had so much to drink the night before. I felt totally drained and made myself promise to never touch wine again. Or, at least, to drink a bit less. From somewhere in my condo, I heard the chirping of my cell phone. I looked at my watch. It was just past eight. It must be an emergency of some sort, nobody ever called me this early.

I found the phone in my purse, and the blessed little thing was still chirping away.

"Hello," I said, in my best early-morning hung-over voice.

"Hi Aurora. You sound as groggy as how I feel." It was Dave.

"Is this an emergency?" I asked.

"Uh-huh. A caffeine emergency. I am in need of caffeine, and it sounds like you could use some too."

"When?"

"How about in fifteen minutes? At Starbucks, on Bay."

"Fifteen minutes? Are you crazy? I'm not even dressed. And I look like hell."

"I love it when you're not dressed and look like hell. Come as you are. See you there." With that, he hung up.

If nothing else, his call woke me up and galvanized me into action. Although that might have been a bit of an overstatement. I wasn't exactly moving at warp speed. It served him right that I was ten minutes late.

Dave had a coffee waiting for me when I arrived. He looked at me with an impish   smile and said, "I'm so disappointed. You're dressed, and you don't look like hell."

"I always rise to the occasion," I replied, taking a sip of coffee.

Much to my surprise, Dave looked pretty chipper. And dapper as well.

"How was your night out with the boys?" I asked out of self-defense, because I really wasn't in the mood for talking.

"It was okay. You know what it's like when guys get together."

"No, I don't .... I'm not a guy."

"Well, you order beer, maybe a basket of chicken wings, and you talk about anything and everything that's not important. Then you order some more beer, tell a few off-colour jokes, make stupid hockey or football predictions, and before you know it, it's time to go home. How was your evening?"

"It's too early to talk about it. I have to remember it first." I took another sip of my coffee, hoping it would clear away the cobwebs. "Oh yes, it's coming back to me now. I couldn't get a word in edgewise the whole night. But otherwise, it was fun. Too much wine, though. I must have made a really bad impression."

"Are you kidding? The Irish love drinking."

"I guess I'm Irish, then."

"Me too, I guess. I was drinking Irish beer all night."

"So seriously, how was your night with the guys? Did you find out anything about the drug squad investigation?"

"Well, yes and no. They confirmed that there were rumours, but they didn't know any more than I did. Or if they did, they didn't let on."

"Was your buddy Schulz there?"

"No, it was just Miller and Francona. I always got along well with them. Nice couple of guys, basically, but they're very loyal to Schulz. Maybe too loyal," Dave said, his voice trailing off.

I got the feeling that he was trying to convince himself that they were, in fact, nice guys. I just sat in silence. Sometimes it would take Dave a while to say what was really on his mind. His eyes were focused on his coffee cup, and he was running a finger along the rim.

"Actually, I got the feeling that there was a hidden agenda to our get-together last night," he said finally. "But I couldn't quite put my finger on what it was. We talked a lot about some of the drug busts we'd been on together. But they kept coming back to one in particular, almost as if they were pumping me for information."

My ears perked up. "What kind of information?"

"About what went down on that bust. I hadn't thought about it for years, so my memory was a bit hazy. They kept trying to get me to remember stuff, and I found that odd. Finally, I changed the subject just to get them off my back."

"Do you think it's related to the police investigation?"

"I wouldn't be surprised. Supposedly a couple of Toronto Star reporters have been nosing around. Knowing The Star, they'll do some big story with screaming headlines."

"And what's wrong with that?" I quickly jumped in. As a journalist, I was always ready to defend other journalists. Even if they were reporters from The Star.

Dave looked at me with a startled expression. "Nothing, I guess," he said quietly. "As long as my name isn't in it."

The way he said that made me wonder if there were things he hadn't told me yet.

"Would it be?" I asked, trying not to sound anxious.

"You never know, do you?" he replied, not making eye contact.

We had finished our coffee, and I finally felt clear-headed again. I wanted to talk some more about all of this, as it was starting to worry me, but Dave said he had to leave and attend a lecture.

I walked home slowly, trying to decide how to spend the day. Should I do research on the Senate, or should I do research on Ireland? By the time I reached my condo, I still hadn't made a decision.

So I went for a run instead. Sometimes I did some of my best thinking when I ran. It was almost like being in an altered state. My mind would float from one thing to another, and by the end of the run, I usually knew exactly what to do.

In this case, I decided that I needed to start on the Senate story. It would pay me money. Ireland wouldn't.

CHAPTER 10

Lie down with dogs and you'll rise with fleas.
- Irish Proverb

One of my morning routines was to scan the different newspaper headlines. I had an app on my computer that let me look at the front page of any newspaper I wanted, and had it customized to include fifteen newspapers from across the country and elsewhere. I got all of the major papers in Toronto, Ottawa, and Montreal, as well as The Vancouver Sun, The New York Times, and The Wall Street Journal. If I saw an interesting story, I could click on a button and it would me to the paper's online website.

The Toronto Star's front-page story was about six drug dealers who'd been arrested several months ago in a police sting. They'd been in jail since then, awaiting a preliminary hearing that had finally started the day before yesterday at Old City Hall. There was a sketch of the six, all unsavoury-looking characters, sitting in the prisoners' box. I knew from what Dave had said that such cases were a bit of a nightmare for the Crown attorney, because each accused might have a different lawyer and, in some cases, an interpreter, which could become a logistical nightmare.

I clicked on The Star's icon in order to read the entire article.

The Crown had just begun presenting its case. An undercover police officer was on the stand giving evidence when suddenly, without giving any reason, the Crown attorney asked for an adjournment. The motion was denied by the judge hearing the case, Judge Montgomery.

When it was the defense's turn to question the detective, the lawyer, James Goldman, asked the officer if his unit had ever been investigated by Internal Affairs. The Crown attorney objected to the question.

He then asked permission to approach the bench. Permission was granted and there was a conversation between the two, at the end of which the judge adjourned court for the day.

The following morning, when all six prisoners were in the box again, the Crown attorney read a prepared statement to the effect that the Crown was staying all the charges against the six drug dealers.

Judge Montgomery declared that the accused were free to go.

At first, there was a lot of confusion. Some of the accused didn't speak very good English and needed translation. Finally, in shock, the accused started walking out of the courtroom. Some actually ran. With police looking on, the drug dealers streamed down the central stairway and straight out the front doors. To them, it must have felt like winning the lottery.

The Crown attorney didn't give a reason for the decision to stay the charges. The Star speculated that it was related to the ongoing investigation into the drug squad, and that the Crown no longer trusted the reliability of evidence produced by any member of the squad.

I went back to the other Toronto papers. None of them had this story on their front page.

I sent a text to Dave. *Did you see the lead story in The Star?*

Within a minute, my phone rang.

"I was just reading it," Dave said.

"Does it mean what The Star says it does?"

"I think so. Whoever the officers were that made the bust are probably under investigation, and the Crown knows it will never win the case."

"Is it the same drug squad that you were on?" I asked.

"Looks like it, but I didn't recognize the officer on the stand. Nonetheless, I can see why the Crown stayed the charges."

"There is something inherently wrong when drug dealers are handed a *'Free Pass - Get Out of Jail'* card," I said indignantly.

"That's why the police have to be squeaky clean. How can you convict someone on the word of a corrupt cop? By the way, did I tell you who's been leaving me voice messages? Harry Schulz."

"What does he want?"

"I don't know. But my tummy tells me to stay away from him."

"Go with your tummy. I always do."

"Got to run. How's your head today?"

"Much better than yesterday."

"Mine, too. See you soon."

CHAPTER 11

*You've got to do your own growing
no matter how tall your father was.*
- Irish Proverb

Several days later, my parents flew into Toronto, en route to their home in Ottawa. They'd timed their flights so that we could have an early dinner before they caught their last plane. 'Very nice of them,' I said to myself, with a hint of sarcasm. It seemed as though they'd been away more than they'd been home lately. But I was happy for them. If you couldn't have fun in your retirement, could you ever?

Both looked amazingly healthy, tanned, and in good physical shape. I could have sworn that they looked five years younger than the last time I'd seen them. But even more interesting was the fact that they seemed to have grown so much closer to each other. There was a fondness between them that I'd never really seen before. Not that they'd ever had a bad relationship, but they'd always kept their feelings for each other private up until now. There had never been any outward shows of affection between them other than perfunctory kisses or hugs.

Now they walked around holding hands, and the odd time I'd caught them nudging each other playfully. At times like that, I'd started to get embarrassed. Couldn't they have toned it down a bit? But, come to think of it, I was a bit like that with Dave. Actually, I was worse .... I'd just drag him off to bed. I hoped I wouldn't see Dad doing that with Mom. That would be the last straw.

I was happy to have dinner with them, and they were too. Mom really wanted to stay overnight, but Dad was anxious to get home. He wanted to attend some social event back in Ottawa with his political cronies. That surprised me. Not that long ago, he had categorically stated that he'd had it with politics and politicians, and now preferred the company of mere mortals.

Unfortunately, Dave couldn't join us. He had a class that he couldn't miss. It was too bad he couldn't come. He got along well with my parents, although he'd only seen them three or four times, if that.

We met out by the airport, at *The Keg*. When I lived in Ottawa, the local Keg was my favourite hangout. I was a creature of habit, and if I couldn't eat at home, I liked to eat in familiar surroundings. Otherwise, I felt as though I was sitting in some stranger's house, wondering if I was going to like the food. There was a Keg close to the Parliamentary Library where I'd spent a lot of time writing and researching. It was always open late, and I'd closed it many times. I had fond memories of the waiters noisily stacking chairs around all around me, trying to give me a hint.

Our conversation was far-ranging, much of it about their travels and my brother Barrie and his family. We talked about the current state of politics, which, despite Dad's outward claims, he was still pretty sharp about. He'd spent most of his career as a politician serving under four prime ministers and had never lost an election. When I was young, I was convinced that one day my father, John Waverly Weeks, would become prime minister. And that would put me in the spotlight just like Amy and Chelsea. Okay, so I was twelve then, going on sixteen. But he never had those aspirations; he was happy as a backbencher.

Dad asked about my job, and I told him that the television show had run its course.

"You mean you're unemployed?" Trust Dad to tell it like it was.

"No. I'm still writing articles. Maybe I'll come up with another book. Right now, I'm doing a feature article about the Senate and whether it should be abolished."

Dad looked at me questioningly. "Have you come to a conclusion yet?"

"No, not really. Although it seems pretty obvious. Were you ever asked to become a senator?"

He didn't answer right away, and I could tell that he was formulating a reply.

"I was. And I turned it down. Too many strings attached. Besides, I didn't want the lifetime commitment of attending meetings and putting the taxpayer on the hook for my welfare."

"Seems to be a lot of that, from what I see," I said. After all, senators were appointed for life.

"Well, don't stay unemployed too long. You're not getting any younger." I saw Mom give him an elbow, which made him flinch.

"I'm sorry," he said. "I know you always do well."

I told him about Rory and how she'd found me. He found it very interesting, and recalled the trip he'd taken to Ireland so many years ago. But no, he didn't remember any other family member with the same first name as mine.

"Did you ever think of moving to Ireland when you were young?" I asked.

"Not really. There might have been a small pull, but honestly, life in Canada was too good. At that time, Ireland was third world. It had very little industry, and people really lived hand to mouth. Canada was, and probably still is, the land of opportunity."

I swore I detected a wee bit of an Irish accent as he spoke. Had I never noticed that before, or was it just something that I was used to and hadn't thought about?

"You never talk much about your father. Do you know much of his background? Are there a lot of relatives?" I asked.

Dad gave me a resigned look, almost as if this was a topic he really didn't want to talk about.

"Da was a stout Irishman from Kilkenny who could charm the devil. And he did, many times. I do believe he came from a large family. I met some of them, but that was a long time ago. He met my mother after her father was shot by the British, and they decided that they didn't want to raise a family in such a troubled place. Both really wanted to get away from the oppression and bigotry so prevalent in those days. More so my mam, especially after what had happened to her father. Some of my father's mates had emigrated to Canada and wrote letters telling him what a wonderful country it was. That's all he needed to hear, and they were gone. Fionola was just a baby then, but I was born in Canada. There were three others as well, all born here."

"Three others? I thought there was only you and Aunt Fionola."

"No, but the three were all stillborn. Da desperately wanted a male heir, someone to carry on the family name, so they kept trying. Finally, on the fifth try, they got lucky. That's why there's such a gap in age between Fionola and me."

"Did you say that your mom's father was shot by the British? Was that in a war?" I asked.

"I suppose you could call it a war. He was murdered by British soldiers," Dad said matter-of-factly. His tone took me aback; he was talking about the murder of his grandfather, but with no emotion in his voice whatsoever. It was almost, if I hadn't known better, as though he was giving a weather report.

"What do you mean, murdered?"

"To be honest, no one ever talked about it much. Either it brought back too many painful memories, or they were in denial. What I know is that my grandfather ran a hotel in Castleconnell. British soldiers raided it one night because they suspected it was an IRA hangout. There was a shoot-out in which a couple of Royal Irish Constables were killed. When the shooting stopped, the soldiers executed my grandfather for being an IRA sympathizer. It was a terrible tragedy, but not unusual in those days. Fionola knows the story better than I do."

"So what happened afterwards? Was any one charged?"

"Not that I know of. Times were different then."

"But I'm sure the British just didn't go around executing people willy-nilly."

"Perhaps I've oversimplified it. I take it that you don't know about the British soldiers in Northern Ireland, who were known as the Black and Tans. It was a brutal time, and they could be as brutal as the people they were there to police. Talk to Fionola - she'll know more about what happened." His tone had changed, and I recognized it to mean that he wanted to change the subject.

"Well, I'll get a chance to do just that soon. Dave is going to a law conference in St. John's in two weeks, and I'm tagging along. I called Aunt Fionola and told her I was coming for a quick visit. She sends her regards, by the way."

Dad's face brightened at the mention of her name.

"Why don't you come, and we'll have a real family reunion," I said hopefully. "Paula is coming down from Fogo."

"That would be nice, dear," said my mother, "but we'll be on the cruise then."

"Cruise? I didn't know anything about a cruise," I said, feeling abandoned again.

"Oh, it's just a short one. Only twenty-one days. Your Dad gave it to me as an anniversary present. We're flying out to Vancouver, staying with Barrie for three days, and then we board the boat to Alaska." Mom leaned over and kissed Dad on the cheek. Note to self: find a man like Dad.

"You said that your parents came here to escape bigotry and oppression. If so, why did your father go back?" I asked Dad, his family history still on my mind.

"You know that my mother died of a brain aneurysm, right? I was 13 at the time. Da took it really hard. He had no family here other than Fionola and me, and as bad as it was in Ireland, he missed it. It was Mam who was the driving force behind them coming to Canada. She was quite happy here, but the fact that Canada was so staunchly British really rankled my father. He refused to apply for Canadian citizenship because he would have had to swear allegiance to the Queen. So he made his mind up to go back to Ireland, and be part of the Irish Free

State. Fionola was 25, and I was 15. She was already on her own, so I went to live with her until I finished my schooling. I hardly saw Da after he left. He never wanted to come back, and I really didn't have the money to visit him."

Dad looked away, and I sensed real regret in his voice.

"But you did see him again, didn't you?" I asked.

"That I did, but only once, and I didn't stay long. He had remarried, and I felt like a stranger in his house. His new wife, who had been an old friend, was nice enough, but I just didn't feel any connection to her or to the life they'd created for themselves. When he died, Fionola and I went back for the wake," Dad said, staring into his coffee cup, uncharacteristically quiet. "Charlene, his second wife, arranged everything, and you'd swear that Da had no life before he married her from the stories that people told. Both Fionola and I were almost outsiders." I could see that this was painful for him. Mom must have thought so as well, because she leaned over and took his hand.

"So you don't know if there's a family tree for the Weeks side of the family?" I asked, not really knowing what else to say.

"I suspect there is somewhere. If Fionola doesn't have it, then you'd have to contact some of the Weeks clan. There's quite a few."

"Maybe I should take a trip to Ireland," I said, half-kidding.

Dad gave me a sharp look. "Shouldn't you be looking for a job?"

Once a dad, always a dad.

CHAPTER 12

Anything that keeps a politician humble
is good for democracy.
- Irish Proverb

I'd always felt pretty savvy about my knowledge of the Canadian political scene. That was until I started to do research on the Senate. The good work that the Senate did was always overshadowed, it seemed, by one scandal or another. Take, for example, Liberal Senator Andrew Thompson. He was appointed to the Senate at the young age of 43. When he turned 65, he moved to Mexico. For the next eight years, he attended the Senate for only fourteen days and still collected his full pay. Embarrassed by his absence, the Senate gave him a deadline to appear or lose his job. When he failed to appear, he was suspended, and six weeks later, he resigned and immediately became eligible for a $48,000 pension. That was one of the more blatant abuses of the position, but there were many, large and small. The list was almost endless, with new ones cropping up all the time.

Just as blatant were the appointments themselves. The Senate had always been used by prime ministers to reward their supporters. Many of them had never held a public position and had been appointed as a reward, or to do a specific job, mostly partisan fundraising.

Sadly, the Senate had been a comfortable retirement home for political organizers who lived on taxpayer money to further their party's fortunes. I could see why Dad didn't want to become a Senator. It would be a lifetime commitment, and with his integrity, it would be an all-consuming endeavor.

The negative side of the Senate began to depress me. Not only that, I felt hampered by being in Toronto. I needed to go back to Ottawa, back to the Parliamentary Library. I could probably stay at Mom and Dad's; they were never home, anyway.

I stopped my research. It was too frustrating doing it from a distance. A recent event came to mind. Not long ago, Malcolm Overton, the executive producer of my soon-to-be defunct TV show, had invited me to a retirement dinner for an executive at the CBC. I could hardly say no, since it would be a good opportunity to network. With unemployment looming on the horizon, I needed to keep in circulation.

After the dinner and obligatory speeches, I'd met the guest of honour. He knew of me, which had me at a disadvantage, since I knew nothing of him other than what I'd heard in the speeches. We had a five-minute conversation, at the end of which he'd handed me his new business card. On it was a picture of him as a 16-year-old boy. Under his name was his new job title: 'Lunch Companion and Drinking Buddy'. At the time, I'd thought it was cute, and I'd even kept his card. I remembered thinking that I must show it to my friend, Walter Osborne, who had worked as a private investigator and was now semi-retired.

I looked at my watch; it was almost eleven. I dialed Walter's number, hoping to arrange a lunch date.

The phone rang for a long time, and I almost hung up.

"Hello," the voice on the other end said, sounding out of breath.

"Walter, it's Aurora. Have I caught you at a bad time?"

"No, not at all. I couldn't find the phone. Doris had taken it to the den, and she never returns it to the cradle. How are you?"

"I'm good. How about you?"

"Can't complain. Nobody will listen anyway, except the cat, who I think is deaf!"

We both laughed.

"I called to see if we could arrange lunch. It's been a while."

"Is today too soon?" Walter said with a chuckle. "I have to go downtown as it is. But we can make it another day if that works better for you."

"No, no, today is fine. How about 12:30 at Milestones, where we ate last time?"

"That's a deal. See you there."

Walter and I first met four years ago when I was doing a political expose on high-ranking politicians, including the Prime Minister and the Minister of Defense at the time. Walter had been hired by a woman to track down a mysterious man in a photograph. In the course of his investigation, he'd unwittingly stumbled across a government bribery scheme involving millions of dollars. That was when our paths had crossed. We'd pooled our resources, and it had nearly got us both killed.

Then, a couple of years later, I involved Walter in the disappearance of my cousin Robin's boyfriend. I'd offered to help Robin find him, and with Walter's help, we did. What neither Walter nor I knew at the outset was that the man had been leading a double life for some time, defrauding investors of millions of dollars and eliminating anyone who got in his way. In the end, I got in his way too. Fortunately, the boyfriend's plan was thwarted, and he fatally shot himself at The Pilot Tavern, right in front of me, Walter, and a hundred stunned patrons.

Since then, Walter had retired, but we still kept in touch from time to time. Lunch with Walter trumped Senate research any day.

CHAPTER 13

A light heart lives long.
- Irish Proverb

Walter was already seated in a booth when I arrived, halfway through a cup of coffee. He rose to greet me and gave me a hug.

"I got here a bit early, so I had a coffee," he said. "You're looking great. I like your hair .... those highlights suit you."

"You don't look so bad yourself, Walter. Retirement must be agreeing with you."

"It has its advantages. Doris and I can do a lot more travelling."

"Is she retired, too?"

"Officially, yes. But she still does temp work. She's not one to sit around doing puzzles all day."

The server, a bubbly young woman with a name tag that said Kat, gave us a lengthy list of specials for the day. By the time she reached the end of the list, I'd already forgotten the first item. We each ordered a glass of red wine.

"When I remember," Walter said, "I make a point of watching your show. You're so good at it. Are you doing anything else?" Walter was a great ego booster.

"Actually the show is coming to an end. New management, new direction. So I'm at a crossroads right now. It's called unemployment."

"Any books in the hopper?"

"No, nothing there either. The only things on the horizon are researching the Canadian Senate and my Irish roots." I told him about Rory and my sudden interest in Ireland.

He smiled and finished his coffee. "When I was on the force, I worked with a guy who was Irish. Michael Ronan Fitzsimons was his name. I remember him very well because he insisted that everyone call him Michael Ronan. Nobody dared call him Mike. Doris used to laugh at how I picked up some of his expressions, like shite and eejit. He'd been in the country twenty-five years, and you'd swear he'd just gotten off the boat. Man, could he drink, and sing. Shame I didn't know about your interest in Ireland. We could have had lunch at the Irish Embassy."

I looked at him questioningly.

"It's a pub, not far from here. Great Irish stew."

49

Our wine arrived, and Kat seemed surprised that we hadn't made a luncheon choice. 'Do we look that starved?' I wondered. She promised to come back shortly.

We talked about a variety of things. Walter was a good listener, and he always had interesting stories to tell. I guessed that when you get to be 70, you should have some interesting stories. Kat kept hovering in the background, so I succumbed to pressure and picked up the menu. I found a nice healthy little salad, and Walter settled on the beef dip sandwich. Kat assured us that we had made good choices. Phew.

"Walter, did you ever get involved in investigating misconduct within the RCMP?" I asked, once Kat had finally left us alone.

"Oh, once or twice. Usually it was for using excessive force during an arrest. Why do you ask?"

I told him about Dave being on the drug squad and the rumours of an internal probe.

"Those are always the hardest investigations. The credibility of drug dealers isn't exactly high. I remember one lawyer who used to file a lawsuit of excessive force on behalf of his client, a well-known drug dealer, each time he was arrested. They were always thrown out in the end."

"Were any of the officers ever convicted?" I asked tentatively. I thought I knew Dave; he was as straight as an arrow. At least from what I'd seen. I hated to think, though, that he's been involved in things that could be construed as illegal, perhaps unwittingly but nonetheless outside of the law.

"Rarely. When you're trying to subdue somebody who would like nothing more than to bash you over the head, it's pretty hard to decide what's excessive force. Sometimes if it's a personal issue between the officer and a perp, then it can get out of hand. But still, such cases are rare."

"Dave said that the police should never investigate themselves, that they'd be too biased. Is that true?"

"Absolutely. In the end, they do stick together. If there were serious allegations from a local force, we'd usually get called in, or the OPP. Better chance of an impartial investigation that way. Did Dave say who was doing the investigation?"

"I think it's just the Toronto Police."

"Well, if he's clean, which I'm sure he is, he's got nothing to worry about."

"I'm sure he's clean," I responded, but I might have crossed my fingers when I said it.

50

Our food arrived. The beef dip looked positively delicious, not to mention the frites. I asked if Walter wanted to trade some cherry tomatoes for some frites. He just smiled.

"So, how serious are you and Dave?" Walter asked between dips.

"I'm not seeing anyone else, but we don't live together. Right now he's preoccupied with his law course. So I guess you could say we're leading separate lives together."

A little boy, maybe two or three years old, suddenly stopped by our table. He had blonde hair, a dimple in his chin, and a killer of a smile.

"May I have a chip?" he asked sweetly.

"Of course," said Walter, and handed him one.

"Thank you very much. I have a new truck, but it's at home."

Just then, a young woman came to retrieve him. She looked a bit harried.

"I'm so sorry," she said, rather embarrassed. "He just walked away when my back was turned, and it was hard to find him in here. I hope he wasn't any bother."

"I have a chip, mama," the little boy said, holding up the frite as if it was a trophy.

"Did you say thank you?"

"Yes, I did, and I told them about my new truck. Can we show it to them?"

"Maybe some other time. We have to go now. Say goodbye."

"Bye-bye." he said, giving us his best smile.

His mother led him away, but every few feet he'd turn around, look back, and wave.

"What a delightful little boy," I said.

"He was, wasn't he? Have you ever thought about having children?" Walter asked. Now there was a question that caught me off-guard.

"With Dave?" I asked, hiding my surprise.

"No, just in general," he said, and then quickly added, "I mean, have you ever wanted children?"

"Yes and no. For a long time I thought I did, and then the urge went away as I got wrapped up in my career."

"You might have noticed, Aurora, that you're not getting younger."

"I'm not? You mean my theory of 'I'm going to be young forever' is a lie? And you might have noticed that I'm not married."

"These days, that doesn't seem to be an issue anymore."

We laughed, and I silently pondered the issue while I finished my salad.

"I hope you didn't mind me asking," Walter said apologetically. "I saw how you looked at that little boy. In hindsight now, I wish that Doris and I had children. There's something missing in our life. I mean, we have each other. But that's just it, we only have each other. There's no one else to pass our lives on to. You see, we kept putting it off and putting it off, and then one day it was too late." Walter finished his dip, but left half of the frites. "Help yourself," he said, pushing the plate to the centre of the table.

Great. Bad enough that I had to worry about Dave; now I should be worrying about my biological clock. I knew Walter meant well; sometimes I got the impression that he regarded me as the daughter he'd never had.

"Thanks for the advice, Dad," I said with a smile, wanting to make sure he didn't feel that he'd overstepped his bounds.

"Time for a coffee? Or another glass of wine?" he asked as Kat cleared the table.

"Hmm, hard choice." I said, recalling my recent hangover.

We went with the wine.

CHAPTER 14

Everyone is nice till the cows
get into the garden.
- Irish Proverb

When I got home, I had a serious look at my calendar and started to panic. The trip to Newfoundland was looming on the horizon, and I wouldn't know how long my research would take for the Senate piece until I'd spent a least two or three days in Ottawa.

So that was what I did. I caught an early train, bunked at my parent's house, and spent three days doing research. I made considerable headway, and by the end was much more confident and in control about the Senate article. I even lined up some interviews with current senators, one from each political spectrum. I would come back to Ottawa after my St. John's trip for those.

There were no further reported developments in the drug squad investigation. Dave was on edge every time I saw him, though he'd never acknowledge it. Talk about an elephant in the room! What was it with men that they had to keep everything to themselves?

Out of the blue, Malcolm invited me to lunch. I liked it when executives invited me out for lunch; I got to eat in restaurants that I wouldn't normally patronize unless I'd recently won a lottery. We met at *Eleven*, an upscale, trendy place located in the shadows of the crumbling Gardiner Expressway.

I could always tell what kind of place a restaurant was by the cost of the hamburger. Upscale restaurants used this as their way of letting you know that if you wanted something cheap and cheerful, you were in the wrong place. The highest I'd seen was $32. Eleven's price was a modest $25.

Being with Malcolm was a bit nerve-wracking, because he always gave the impression of a man who counted every second of the day and used it for business. To that point, he had an irritating habit of placing his Blackberry beside his napkin. It was always on, and during conversations he would keep one eye on you and the other on the Blackberry. And he made no secret of it.

Malcolm waved off the menu, ordered a martini, with a twist, of course, and I ordered a white wine spritzer. One needed to keep one's wits about one when lunching with Malcolm.

"Have you made any plans for the next few months?' he asked without any preamble. Malcolm was not one for small talk. The mere fact that he'd asked me out for lunch was surprising.

"Actually, no. Right now, I'm on the lunch circuit and I'm writing a feature article on the Canadian Senate. I might go back to Ottawa; I have more contacts there. Maybe get back into freelance journalism. I don't think I'm cut out for television. I like working with words rather than being in front of a camera."

"I wouldn't sell yourself short," he said, waving his hand in the air dismissively. "You did quite well, and I think that television suits you. Maybe your show will be revived. Or maybe you could sell the concept to a cable network."

"No, thanks. I'm really more comfortable working on a keyboard."

"But you wouldn't rule it out?"

"Of course not," I replied quickly. Dad's words rang in my ears. "I'm open to anything, really."

Our drinks arrived quickly. The waiter was obviously aware of the value of Malcolm's time.

"How are you spending your days?" he asked, seemingly from out of the blue. Now he was beginning to sound like Dad.

"In Ireland and in the Senate." I replied. I said this as he was raising the martini to his lips.

He paused, cocked his head slightly, and then took a sip. "In Ireland." he repeated, putting down his glass

I told him about my sudden interest in Ireland, starting with Aurora's call and then my father's revelation about my great-grandfather's untimely death. One thing about Malcolm - he was a good listener. Despite his obsession with time, he never hurried you along, or asked dumb questions, or sidetracked the conversation because he was bored. When I finished, he drained his martini and said, "Let's order. I'm having the salmon."

I quickly scanned the menu, knowing time to be of the essence. When all else failed, order a spinach salad. Malcolm raised his hand, and our server materialized in front of us. He ordered another martini and, without asking, a refill for me.

"I'm glad you told me that," he said. "It dovetails quite nicely with some projects I have in mind." He didn't elaborate, nor did I push him.

54

For the rest of the lunch, we, or should I say Malcolm, talked about the future of the broadcasting industry in Canada. This was of great interest to him, and he articulated the problems quite well. It sounded as though he was rehearsing a speech, and for all I knew he was. At the end of it, he picked up his Blackberry, and without missing a beat, typed furiously on the tiny keyboard. Malcolm was the only man I knew who could type as fast on a Blackberry as I could on a keyboard. He didn't apologize for the interruption, but in his defense, it was brief.

The hour went by quickly, and as if on cue, our server materialized with the bill. It was in a nice little black envelope that said 'The Damage' on the front. Nice touch. And probably a realistic assessment.

Malcolm agreed to keep in touch. I got the impression that he was sincerely interested in keeping me on his roster. Maybe I wasn't as bad at television as I'd thought I was. After all, who was I to disagree with Malcolm?

On the way home, I phoned Dave to touch base about the logistics for tomorrow's trip to St. John's. According to him, he was all packed and ready to go, and he'd be over in time for me to cook him dinner.

I said I'd be happy to order pizza. Or he could pick it up.

I was very accommodating that way.

CHAPTER 15

You cannot put an old head on the young.
                                        - Irish Proverb

Our flight to St. John's was mid-morning, but we still had to get up at an ungodly hour in order to check in and get through security. I had lots of unused air miles, so I upgraded us to business class, which gave us access to the airline lounge where we had breakfast and read the papers. Was there really any other way to fly? Who, me... spoiled?

Dave's conference was due to start late Friday afternoon and finish Sunday night. Our plan was to rent a car at the airport, drive to his hotel, attend the evening social, and then I would drive to Trinity in the morning. Our return flight was booked for Tuesday morning, which gave us a free day on Monday.

The flight to St. John's was smooth until we were over the ocean, and then we encountered turbulence. For a while, it felt as though we were on a roller coaster. A young child seated behind us squealed with delight every time the plane dipped. The adults, including me, weren't quite as thrilled with the ride. After what seemed like forever, the pilot came on and told us that we had passed through the rough zone, and that from now on it would be smooth flying all the way to St. John's. I looked out of the window, hoping to see icebergs, but I only saw fog. Normally flying didn't bother me, except when we were in fog or in clouds. As irrational as it sounded, my worry was that if I couldn't see where we were going, how could the pilot? I once mentioned that to Dave, and he rolled his eyes.

We landed safely, picked up the rental car, and drove to St. John's in the same fog. I let Dave drive; I disliked fog on the road as much as I disliked it on an airplane.

Dave's hotel was close to Signal Hill, almost at the bottom of it, in fact. While he was registering, I had an hour to kill, so I walked up to the top. According to a little historical plaque placed there, the first transatlantic wireless signal was received at Signal Hill in 1901, well over a hundred years ago. Now, with my little smart phone, I could call anywhere in the world. Or take a picture of the harbour and upload it to social media for the whole world to see.

The fog hadn't lifted at all. Both the harbour and the city below were shrouded in mist. Despite that, Signal Hill was still impressive. I could hear the sound of the waves breaking on the rocks below. I inhaled the sea air, smelling of salt and fish. There was nothing between me and England other than a vast expanse of ocean.

The evening dinner was pleasant. Many of the conference delegates had brought their spouses along, and the noise level in the room suggested that everyone knew each other. Not so for Dave and I; we didn't know anyone. Two men recognized me and introduced themselves. Both said how much they enjoyed my books, but made no mention of the television show. I guessed lawyers didn't watch very much television. They were too busy making money, I supposed. Hopefully that would be Dave soon.

The fog was still very thick the next morning, which was unsettling. I opted to take the Trans-Canada Highway rather than the scenic route. At least it was a divided highway, and if I was going to run off the road, it would be into a ditch instead of an oncoming car. I made good time and reached the Bonavista peninsula by early afternoon. I was getting excited about seeing Aunt Fionola again.

As I turned off the main highway onto the secondary road, the fog began to lift, and by the time I got to Trinity, the coast was clear, as they say.

Trinity was a village with a rich maritime history. The well-sheltered harbour had been home to many tall ships in the 1800's. Like any other town in Newfoundland, there was always the boast of something being the 'oldest' in the province. Historical plaques abounded in Trinity, and usually started off with 'Here stands the oldest ... ' and continued on from there. It truly was like stepping back into history.

Aunt Fionola's house was the most picturesque and thus the most photographed and painted house in the town, if not the region. In fact, when I stopped in Trinity just to stretch my legs, I walked past a framing store and there, in the window, was an oil painting of her house.

The house wasn't actually in the village; it sat alone in a grassy field at the end of a spit of land that protected the harbour from the ocean. It was a simple design: two stories, with two gables on the second floor, front and rear. It had beige clapboard siding and was clearly a centre floor plan. There were no trees around it to shelter it from the wind, and why the house had never blown away was a mystery to me.

Unfortunately, my aunt's house wasn't the easiest to find, and I didn't think I could actually spot the right cut-off on my own. I stopped in the village and had no trouble getting directions; there wasn't anyone there who didn't know Fionola. When I finally drove up to her driveway, if it could be called that, it was just as I remembered it: a bare dirt track, lined with several telephone poles.

Two cars were parked in front of the house. One was an old green Chevy from an era when cars were still living rooms on wheels, while the other was a fairly new silver Honda.

The front door of the house opened as soon as my car came to a stop, and Cousin Paula rushed out to greet me. In the open doorway stood Aunt Fionola, looking decidedly older than the last time I'd seen her. She was supporting herself on a cane.

I'd forgotten how lively and animated Paula was. Middle age became her. Her cheeks had a red complexion, her curly auburn hair spilled down to her shoulders, and she clearly kept in shape. Within seconds, I was reminded of Rory. They both had the same gift of gab. And I could have sworn that they even had the same accent. I hadn't remembered Paula's Irish accent from our night together on George Street, but then I didn't remember much of that night so long ago.

Aunt Fionola gave me a gentle hug; I didn't think her frail body could withstand anything else. As I looked at her, I noticed the pronounced family resemblance between Fionola and my dad. Her chin and eyes were exactly the same as his. People have always commented that I look just like my dad, but I always figured they said that just to be nice. Now, I wondered how much I also looked like Fionola Reardon.

I took off my coat in the hallway, and Paula hung it on a hook. As I was removing my Irish scarf, Paula looked at it with interest.

"Where did you get this?" she asked, inspecting the pattern very closely.

"In Toronto, at an Irish shop," I said proudly.

"There's a lady in Tilting who makes almost exactly the same scarf. It's an unusual pattern," Paula said.

"Her name isn't Mary Tully by any chance, is it?"

"No, it's not."

Fionola ushered us into what she called the sitting room. It was a large room, furnished with old-fashioned upholstered chairs, each one accompanied by a little side table. The walls were covered with faded family pictures that contrasted nicely with the framed needlepoints . Ah yes, I remembered now. Fionola was well-known for her needlepoints.

"Can I get you some tea?" she asked.

"I'll get it, Mum, you just stay put," Paula said, rising from her chair. She turned and patted me on the arm. "Oh, I'm so glad you could make it. When you told me you were coming, I just knew I had to come see you. I'm staying overnight and heading back tomorrow afternoon. We'll have lots of time to visit."

She bustled out of the room.

"Now then, Aurora, tell me all about your life. And how is that brother of mine, and what's this I hear about him being in Spain hiking? Isn't he too old for that sort of thing?" Fionola asked.

"He doesn't think so. They're hardly home, you know. Not long ago they were in Asia, and then they went to Australia. They just got home from this two-week hike on a trail called the Camino Real in Spain. It's like a religious pilgrimage."

"John, on a pilgrimage? That doesn't sound like him. I thought he stopped going to church."

"Well, I don't think they were doing it for religious reasons."

"Two weeks, you said? Seems like a long time if you're just doing it for the fun of it. But that's John all over. And I understand that you've become a very successful writer. I'm afraid I don't read as much as I used to. I have cataracts and need to have them removed, but I just haven't gotten around to it. I'm glad your parents are well and enjoying life."

"As a matter of fact, I just had dinner with them a few days ago, and both send their love."

Fionola was about to reply when Paula returned with a tray of biscuits and a teapot and cups.

"Can I give you a hand with that?" I offered.

"No, no. I can manage this. Mum insisted I use the fine china, but I said 'For heaven's sake, she's family'. Now then, how do you take your tea, Aurora?"

Conversation was lively for the next hour or so. Paula did most of the talking, but once in a while Aunt Fionola would hold forth, usually about family memories. I loved hearing the lilt in her voice. It was such a distinctive Newfoundlander accent.

Paula, on the other hand, sounded as though she'd just gotten off the boat from Ireland. I asked her why she had such a strong accent.

"Come to Tilting sometime," she said. "You'd swear that you're in Ireland. You see, Fogo is so isolated that very little changes. It's like the outside world hasn't touched us for two hundred years. To be sure, the young people are becoming more worldly because of the internet, but the old traditions still prevail. Sadly, though, when most of them leave for university, very few come back. The ones that stay behind, like my three boys, carry on the island tradition."

"Fishing?" I asked.

"That it is. It's a hard life, but a good one."

"You don't get many tourists up there?" I asked.

"Very few, very few. In a way, we've never encouraged it. The tourist season is too short. But it is one of the four corners of the Flat Earth Society, so they should be coming in droves," she said with a hearty laugh.

"Shouldn't you be checking the roast?" Fionola asked her daughter.

Paula looked at her watch. "It might be ready soon. Excuse me for a couple of minutes. Hope you're hungry." She picked up the empty teapot and bustled out of the room.

"Now then, dear, I understand you're interested in the family history," Fionola said, adjusting the blanket over her knees. "Has your dad ever told you about the shooting?"

"Yes, he did. We talked about it when I had dinner with them. But he really didn't say too much about it. He said you knew more than he did."

"Well, that might be true. Mam never wanted to talk about it, and neither did Da for fear of upsetting her."

"When did it happen?"

"In 1921. In Castleconnell. It's been so long since I've thought about it that I've forgotten most of the details. The only way I found out about it is that I came across some newspaper clippings my mother kept. When I asked her about them, she ranted and raved about the injustice of the British. Da calmed her down, but suggested I not bring up the subject again."

"So what happened?"

"It had to do with the Black and Tans raiding my grandfather's hotel. They were a nasty lot, those Black and Tans. Nothing but a bunch of cutthroats, from what Mam said. My memory isn't as sharp as it used to be, so I'm not exactly sure about the details, other than they shot my grandfather in cold blood for being an IRA sympathizer."

"I have heard of the Black and Tans. They were pretty bad, weren't they?" Aha, my research into Irish history was paying off.

"Yes, they were. British soldiers who were supposed to keep the peace, but who were nothing more than thugs."

Paula poked her head in the door. "I think we're about ready."

CHAPTER 16

A cabin with plenty of food is
better than a hungry castle
- Irish Proverb

Too bad Dave wasn't there to enjoy the cooking; he might have found some new inspiration. At first I thought that we might have Jiggs dinner, the traditional Newfoundland dish of corned beef, cabbage, and vegetables, but it turned out to be the classic Irish Boiled dinner. I smelled the smoked pork emanating from the kitchen even before Paula brought it in. When she served it, my mouth began to water.

The conversation centered around some of my career and adventures, and around life in Trinity and, of course, life in Tilting. Paula was originally from St. John's, but you'd swear that she was born and bred on Fogo Island. She met Joseph McKerr at university. His family had been in Tilting for hundreds of years. They married shortly after graduation and lived in St. John's for a year. Then Joe's father died and Joe, being the eldest son, moved back to Tilting to run the family fishing operation. They'd been there ever since. She had three boys: Trevor, Bradley, and Kevin. All three of them had followed the family tradition of fishing. From what Paula told me, they were operating quite a successful business, which was not easy to do in a remote place like Tilting.

The subject of my great-grandfather didn't come up again until the dinner dishes had been cleared away and we were having coffee.

"I heard you talking about the shooting in Castleconnell," Paula said. "That was a terrible thing. Just terrible. Thank God none of that violence came with the Irish settlers to Tilting."

"What about the rest of Newfoundland?" I asked. "Lots of Irish here, aren't there?"

"That there are," said Paula "but the Protestants and Catholics get along well. Even in Tilting, we have both. Once in a while, there is an intermarriage. Years ago, the priest would rarely allow that, and the few times he did, it was only on the condition that the parents agreed to raise the children in the Catholic faith."

"The priests had a lot of power, didn't they?"

"They had all the power back then. But not any more. And it's just as well."

We then got off the topic of religion and talked about various family members. In time, Aunt Fionola excused herself and went to bed. Paula and I briefly entertained the notion of driving into Trinity and going to a pub. But neither of us wanted to drink and drive, so we decided to stay home. "I guess that means we're grown up," Paula laughed.

We built a fire in the fireplace, opened a bottle of wine, and just talked. Which wasn't hard for Paula.

The following morning, Paula and I walked into Trinity. It was a cool, damp morning, with a stiff offshore breeze. The sun had a hard time breaking through the clouds, but it eventually did. Mary Tully's scarf helped keep me warm. The harbour was quiet, and Paula described to me what it would have been like at the height of Trinity's history as a seaport. When the fishing died in Newfoundland, Trinity, like many other communities, went into a steep decline. Now most of its money came from eco-tours and whale-watching.

When we returned to the house, Aunt Fionola had brought down a box from attic. I'd expected a large cardboard filing box, but much to my surprise it was only a shoebox. I opened it and a musty smell invaded the room. There were several bundles of letters and newspaper clippings inside, held together by elastic bands. When I touched one of the bundles, the elastic fell apart.

"Here's the pile of papers dealing with our great-grandfather," said Paula, taking the elastic off some old newspaper clippings. "Be careful with them, they fall apart easily. Let me put them in order for you."

She handed me the first clipping. Although it had yellowed greatly, it was still quite readable. It was from The Irish Independent, dated April 22, 1921. The article had the headline of *'Military Inquiry Opens'*. Below the heading was a sub-heading, *'Grave Allegations And Denial By Many Witnesses'*. The inquiry concerned a shooting on the 17th of April at the Shannon View Hotel in Castleconnell.

From all accounts, a unit of the British Army Auxiliaries, also known as the Black and Tans, descended on the hotel on the advice of an informant that there were IRA men in the hotel bar. Dressed as civilians, the intention of the Tans was to mingle among the patrons to find the IRA members. But the orders were either misunderstood or ignored, and the Tans burst into the hotel with guns drawn. Unbeknownst to them, there were two Royal Irish Constables, Sgt. Hughes and Constable

Pringle, drinking at the bar, also dressed as civilians. The Constables, armed with revolvers, thought that the invaders were IRA members and drew their guns. A shoot-out ensued, and the Tans ran out of the hotel. A nearby backup force heard the shooting and rushed to the hotel, raking it with a Lewis gun and killing the two RIC constables. When the shooting stopped, two men came rushing out of the back door of the hotel and were told to put their hands up. A third man came out, and was also told to put his hands up and face the wall. He was the innkeeper, Richard Mahoney. A chambermaid, watching from a kitchen window, reported that Mr. Mahoney was then executed while he stood against the wall. He was shot in the back of the head several times. She cried out, "My God, you're after shooting an innocent man!", to which a Black and Tan Officer replied brutally and callously in front of Mahoney's wife, who was now also present, "It's good enough for him, harbouring rebels."

An older couple who were guests at the hotel witnessed the shooting in the bar. The husband, a notable British surgeon, wrote to his brother, Lord Paramor, who raised the matter in the House of Lords. Now it had become a political football.

There were other clippings relating to the military inquiry, including one from The New York Times on the 27th of April that described Lord Paramor reading the letter in the House of Lords from his brother relating the events at the Shannon View Hotel.

Paula was reading one of the other clippings when she looked at her watch.

"Oh, dear. I've lost track of time. I have to go soon; it's quite a drive back to Fogo. I can't miss the ferry, to be sure."

"Not before you have a bite to eat," said Aunt Fionola.

"Make me a sandwich to go, Mum. I'll eat it in the car. I get paranoid about missing the ferry." She put the clipping back in the box. "It's such a sad story," she said. "He wasn't an IRA supporter. He was running a hotel and welcomed business from anyone. The mere fact that the RIC felt comfortable drinking there should have been an indication that he had no political leanings. Yet the British executed him for no other reason than an unfounded suspicion that he was guilty. No wonder the Irish hated the British so much. Now then, I'd better get my act in gear." She stood up and left the room to gather her belongings.

I continued to look at the clippings. Most of them dealt with the inquiry and its result. Not surprisingly, the British military absolved itself of any blame. According to the findings, the maid who saw the execution was *overcome with emotion and her testimony could not be relied upon'.* A young cadet had been presented to the commission who refuted everything the maid had seen. And the comments of Lord Paramor's brother were *'attributed to be doubtful given his age and the emotional state he would have been under that night'.* In the end, the tribunal ruled that it was an unfortunate misunderstanding. The military, of course, issued an apology to the widow of Mr. Mahoney.

While I was going through the clippings, Aunt Fionola stayed in the background, not really offering much in the way of comment. I wondered what was going through her mind.

As if reading my thoughts, she said quietly, "Aurora, my dear, if those are of any interest to you, why don't you take them home with you and go through them at your leisure? They've been sitting in the attic gathering dust and mildew for many years. You can bring them back when you're finished. That way, I'll know that you'll be back one day."

"Are you sure?" I asked hesitantly.

"Of course. If you don't, I'll only take them back to the attic where they'll stay. I never look at them, to be honest. It was a dark day in our family, and there's no point in dwelling on it." There was an unmistakable sadness in her voice.

"I can imagine how devastating it must have been. Your mother was only seventeen at the time. Did the family stay on at the hotel?"

"No. The boys had already left home to work in Cork and Dublin. Grandma Brigid and my mam, Colette, went to live with a sister on a farm outside of Limerick. Brigid carried her deep hatred for the British to the grave. My mum carried the same hatred, but thank the Lord, she kept it to herself." With that, she left the room to make Paula's sandwich.

Paula walked back into the room a few moments later, a coat over her arm. "I can't believe how good it was to see you, Aurora. And look, we didn't even get drunk this time. I hope we don't have to go as long between visits, though. Please keep in touch. Maybe come and visit Fogo. It's a beautiful place in the summer. And even right now, but it is kind of desolate in the winter, to be honest. That's why we take long vacations in Florida," she said, punctuating her sentence with that wonderful laugh of hers.

Fionola brought the sandwich for Paula, wrapped in wax paper. We both walked her to the car, where there were more hugs and promises to keep in touch.

As I watched the car recede down the lane, disappearing in the tall grass, Aunt Fionola was already back in the house. I found her in the kitchen, cleaning the counter. She stopped wiping, put the cloth down, and put her hands on my shoulders. "My mother once told me that I should put Ireland far behind me. She never got over what happened to her father - it must have been horrible. So I just want to tell you that you're welcome to take the box of clippings. But don't get involved with history. Look forward, not back. No good comes of reliving the past. The Irish have been doing it for too long. All right, dear?"

I really didn't know what to say, but I nodded my head slowly and she gave me a hug.

"I hope you'll be staying for lunch. I've invited some friends over to meet you. It's not often we get celebrities here."

CHAPTER 17

Every patient is a doctor after his cure.
- Irish proverb

After leaving my aunt's place, I drove back to St. John's. Without the fog, it seemed to take only half the time. I hooked up with Dave at the hotel. His conference had wound up, and we had a quiet dinner at a recommended restaurant where I told him all about the sad goings-on with my great-grandfather. Then we went off to George Street and listened to some local bands. This time I practiced moderation when drinking.

The next day we played tourists. We went to Cape Spear, bought a postcard from the postmistress in Petty Harbour, and then did a trip around the Avalon Peninsula. A tourist guide book described it as being very similar to Ireland, and from the look of the green rolling hills, one could certainly see why. At one point, we stopped to buy a soft drink at a small grocery store along the way. There was a young girl behind the cash register. I had a question about directions, and she gave me the answer. Her accent was so thick that she had to repeat it several times before I could understand her. She must have thought I was a bit slow on the uptake.

I brought the box of letters with me on the plane. I really didn't want any chance of them getting lost. Once the seat belt sign was off, I retrieved the box from underneath the seat. Again, the mustiness of the paper was noticeable. I could hear a man sitting behind me ask his wife what the smell was.

Most of the letters were addressed to Fiona's mother, Collette. They were from her brothers, friends, and former neighbours. All of them described the economic hardship that existed in Ireland in the 1930's. Inside one of the letters was a photograph, yellowed with age, of a stern-looking man. On the back was the notation 'Richard Mahoney, 1920'. I showed it to Dave and asked if he saw any family resemblance to me. He looked at it closely.

"No," he said, and then asked to look at it again. "On second thought, he has the same pissed-off expression that you get when you don't get your way." That Dave, he was such a kidder.

We again encountered turbulence, so I put the letters away. Besides, even I was getting put off by their musty odor.

Back in the city, I phoned my publisher, Kim Gordon, to float an idea by her. She's always a good sounding board and I really valued her opinions. I asked her what she thought of me doing a book about Ireland. I wasn't sure exactly what angle I would use; maybe Richard Mahoney's murder would be the starting point.

"There are too many books about Ireland, in case you haven't noticed," she responded. "Not to mention all the Irish writers, both old and new. Right now Maeve Binchey alone has saturated the market. Not to mention Marian Keyes, John Brady or Roddy Doyle. Find something else. Ireland won't make us any money."

I was surprised and disappointed at her reaction. I really felt that there was story to be told about the Troubles, possibly through the prism of my family's tragedy, and decided to ignore her advice. I had the time to delve into a possible book on the issue, other than the Senate article, I didn't have any other projects on the go. And I could use the money that a book would bring in.I could only live on my charm for so long to pay the bills.

Dad's comment about my employment status kept popping into my head. That was the trouble with being a freelancer .... you were always unemployed.

Although, come to think of it, that was the best part.

CHAPTER 18

A goose never voted for an early Christmas.
-Irish Proverb

The box of letters from Aunt Fionola had been staring at me from the middle of the dining room table since I'd gotten back from the trip. The musty odour had largely disappeared, but I just hadn't had the urge to go through them. It was all so depressing. So I concentrated on my Senate research. All I needed now was to do the interviews, and I'd be on the home stretch.

Finally, though, guilt overwhelmed me and I decided to tackle the box again. Normally I loved doing research, but this felt like prying.

I took the elastics off the bundles, but kept them separated just in case there was any order to them. Actually, what I was really looking for, naively, was a family tree, neatly done, at which point I could stop my research.

Patrick Mahoney, my great-grandfather, had four children. Three boys - Denis, Liam and Sean, and one girl, Colette. At the time Mahoney was shot, Colette was 17. Some years later, she married Herbert Weeks, and Aunt Fionola was born in 1932. They emigrated to Canada in 1933, and my father John was born in 1942.

I knew nothing about Herbert Weeks, other than what Dad had told me. None of the letters in the box were addressed to him, just to Colette.

An official-looking document caught my eye. It was a transcript from Hansard, the official record of the House of Parliament. Although the paper was yellow and faded, I could still read it very clearly. In it, the Lord Chancellor spoke about the shooting at Castleconnell. His statement recounted in detail the events of that night and the findings of the subsequent military inquiry. One statement in particular made me take notice: *'All the evidence shows that, notwithstanding the very great excitement which naturally prevailed, the cadets were under complete control and ceased fire the moment they were ordered to do so.'* I was sure that any Irishman would have laughed himself silly at that remark. The so called 'cadets,' also known as the Black and Tans, were considered, from the reading I'd done, to be nothing more than thugs. They were the dregs of the British Army, often recruited from prison.

They were given a free hand to keep the peace in whatever way they saw fit.

The Lord Chancellor's statement also stated that *'through the kitchen window, the housemaid saw Mr. Mahoney walking across the yard to the wall with his hands up, and soon afterwards she heard shots and saw Mahoney lying dead'.* Later on in the report, he further stated that, *'whilst the evidence of the housemaid was given in good faith, she was mistaken in what she saw'.* The Surgeon's account of the shooting was categorized as nothing more than *'a man of peace suddenly and unexpectedly introduced into a terrible scene of war .... his observance and judgement are by no means to be implicitly relied upon'.* What eloquence and what bullshit, all at the same time. I could feel myself getting hot under the collar, although I was keenly aware that there was reality and then there was politics. They were neither bedmates nor lovers. Indeed, at times they were so far apart that the real facts didn't bear much relation to the political posturing that surrounded them.

The rest of the report completely absolved the British Auxiliary Division of any blame. The encounter occurred through each party mistaking the others for armed civilians.

It wasn't hard to imagine the outrage and anger the Irish must have felt against the British. Not just for this act, but for many like it. In this case, it devastated the family and all they ever got in return was a lame apology. Not only did the British provoke the shooting, they executed a man in cold blood and then completely fabricated the truth to make it look justifiable. This happened, if I recalled correctly from my reading of Irish history, at a time when there was a movement toward the creation of an Irish Free State. I was sure it was events like this that had put a nail in the coffin of British rule.

I put the transcript down and started reading one of the batches of letters. All of the letters were from Colette Mahoney's oldest brother, Denis. The first letter was dated in the summer of 1934, a year after his sister moved to Canada. Denis was married, had four children, and leased a small plot of land for farming. He and his family lived in a two-room thatched farmhouse that was in a sad state of disrepair. He hoped that life was better for Colette than it was in Limerick County. The RIC and the Black and Tans were still fighting the IRA, but he and his family seemed isolated from the conflict. He mentioned that their youngest brother, Sean, was actively involved with the IRA and was determined to find out which soldier had shot his father and avenge his death. The middle brother, Liam, had moved to Cork County and hadn't been heard from in some time. The letter was signed, 'Your brother, Denis.' A smile crossed my face. When my brother sent me an e-mail, he would sign it merely as B. The e-mails would take a nano-second to reach me, unlike the letters from Denis to Colette, which must have taken weeks to arrive. I tried to imagine the route such a letter would take. From their farmhouse, it would have had to be taken to the nearest village, presumably by walking or by bicycle. Then to the nearest town, then to Dublin, then on a ship across the ocean to, perhaps, Montreal or Quebec City, and then on to Toronto where Colette and Herbert lived. I looked at the address. Amelia Street, in Cabbagetown.

The ringing of my cell phone brought me back to the present day. It was Dave to say that he was sick and tired of studying and wanted to take me out for an early dinner. He suggested an Irish pub on The Danforth called Allen's. I agreed, but only on the condition that there was no fighting, singing, or gunplay.

He said he couldn't guarantee it, but would do his best.

CHAPTER 19

An open mouth often catches a closed fist.
-Irish Proverb

Allen's was too noisy for my liking, but the food was good. I wanted to hear more about Dave's involvement with the drug squad, but he didn't feel comfortable talking about it in public. Not when you practically had to shout to be heard.

I told him about the letters and the Hansard transcript. Then I floated the idea about writing a book about Ireland by him.

"Is there any money in it?" Dave asked, finishing off his Kilkenny beer. Had he been talking to Kim Gordon, I wondered?

"That's not why you write a book. You write it because you want to tell a story."

"What's the story?"

"Well, the shooting at the hotel, of course, would be part of it. But there has to be more. I'd like to find an angle that makes it relevant to the reader of today."

"Like what?"

"That's the part that I haven't figured out yet. I told you what Kim, my publisher said, didn't I? She told me there were already too many books about Ireland." I laughed, and Dave laughed along with me. Mine was a nervous laugh - his was genuine.

"I'm sure there's an Irishman somewhere who would tell you that you can never have too many books about Ireland," Dave said, signaling to the waiter for the bill.

When we were outside, I suggested we go for a walk and get an Italian ice cream.

"We're in Greektown," Dave reminded me.

"All the more reason," I said.

We ambled leisurely past the Greek restaurants filled to capacity. Even the patios were filled, despite the cool air. The sidewalk felt like an obstacle course with strollers, dogs, young children, and kids on skateboards, all competing for the same space.

A man bumped into Dave, rather forcefully I thought. Being a good Canadian, Dave turned around to apologize.

"Well, if it isn't Dave Fullerton. Fancy meeting you here," the man said. He turned to me and extended his hand. "My name is Harry Schulz. You must be Aurora."

We shook hands and moved to the edge of the sidewalk. Schulz was older than Dave by at least ten years. His face was wrinkled, probably because he was a smoker, and there was a pronounced scar on his cheek. Instead of an ex-cop, he looked more like an ex-thug.

Dave hadn't said a word.

"I've been trying to get a hold of you, Dave. Didn't you get any of my messages?"

"As a matter of fact, I did. I've been kind of busy. You know how it is," Dave replied, tersely.

"Yeah, I know. Hear you're going over to the other side. Going to become a lawyer. You'll be good. Listen, can you make a bit of time to have a coffee? Something I need to talk to you about," Harry said, faking a smile.

"Sure thing. I'll call you." Dave took my hand and turned away from Harry, who quickly grabbed his arm.

"I'm serious, Dave. We need to talk."

"So you said," Dave said, pulling his arm away. "I'll call you. Now if you'll excuse me, I have to find this lady an Italian ice cream."

I was glad that Dave had not forgotten what was really important.

"Now you listen to me, Dave .... " Harry barked, his face red with anger. He was obviously a man used to giving orders.

Dave turned his back on him and both of us walked away from Harry, who just stood there glaring. He made no attempt to come after us.

We kept up a brisk pace until we got to Chester Street.

"Let's catch the subway," Dave said.

I wanted to point out that he'd promised me an ice cream cone, but now didn't seem to be the right time.

"What was all that about? How did he know my name? And was that really a chance encounter?" I asked, as we were waiting on the subway platform.

"I doubt it. Harry doesn't leave things to chance."

"You mean he followed us?"

"I'm sure he did. And I'm sure he's been doing a bit of homework. That's why he knows your name. It was his way of trying to intimidate me."

"About what?"

"He thinks I know stuff."

"Like what?"

"Can't talk to you. Remember? You're the enemy."

I made a smart-ass comment that was drowned out by the approaching subway.

It was a short ride back to Bay Street, only five subway stops. Dave remained standing all the way, in spite of the fact that most of the seats were empty. I could see his mind going a mile a minute. Meanwhile, it gave me time to think about the comment he'd made about me being the enemy. I knew that he'd said it in a joking sort of way, but if he really even half-thought that, then our relationship was in trouble.

"Staying over?" I asked, once we were back to my place.

"Sure," he replied, but I detected a lack of enthusiasm.

"Afraid of sleeping with the enemy?" I said, walking into the kitchen to get a glass of water.

He didn't reply, so I poured my water and came back to the living room where he was thumbing through a magazine. His left foot was pumping up and down, a sure sign that he was agitated.

"Look, Dave," I said finally. "Let's cut to the chase. If you really think I'm the enemy, then we have a serious problem. If we can't be honest with each other, what are we doing together?"

He seemed taken aback with my question. Slowly he put down the magazine and started to say something, but then thought better of it.

After being silent for what seemed like a long time, he stood up and came over to where I was standing. He put his hands on my shoulders and looked me straight in the eyes.

"You're not the enemy. You never have been, and you never will be, okay? If I don't tell you something, it's for a reason. Trust me. I have no hesitation in confiding in you."

"Then tell me what's going on," I said.

He took his hands off my shoulders and walked past me into the kitchen to get himself a glass of water.

"Here's the thing," he said, cradling the glass in his hands as he turned back to face me, "I'm not really sure if I know myself. The beers with Francona and Miller were a part of it. Now Harry is pressuring me, and I'm sure it's connected to the same bust that Miller and Francona zeroed in on. I'm assuming they think that I saw something that could somehow implicate them. But as far as my memory goes, it was all above board. Maybe I should get a hold of my notes."

"Who's got them?"

"They're in the archives."

"Can you get access to them?"

"Technically, yes. I'm still on the force. But if I go in now and the bust is one of the cases under investigation, it's going to look suspicious. I can only stall Schulz for so long, though. There are rumours that the police are going to lay charges against the drug squad, and I'm sure Schulz is shit-scared. He's trying to get his ducks lined up in a row before anything comes down."

"So what are you going to do?"

"I'm not sure. Probably go to bed."

"Are you in any danger?"

"No. That's why I'm going to bed."

Wow, I wished I could solve all my problems like that. And he wasn't kidding. By the time I'd finished tidying up and had listened to a couple of voice messages, he was already in bed, sound asleep.

I wanted to wake him and ask if he really was in any danger. Harry Schulz gave me the creeps. The tight grip of his handshake and the way he'd said my name had both felt just a little threatening. Not to mention his appearance. If Dave hadn't told me who he was, I would have pegged him as the boss of a crime syndicate.

But thank God I had my sleeping superman to protect me.

Now why didn't I feel reassured by that?

CHAPTER 20

It is often that a person's mouth broke his nose.
                                                    -Irish Proverb

Two days later, the shit hit the fan, sort of. Dave phoned me bright and early and asked if I still got The Toronto Star. I told him I only had the online version.

"Go online," he said.

I powered up my laptop and clicked on The Star's icon.

'DRUG INVESTIGATION KEPT SECRET', the headline said. In the background, I could hear Dave taking a sip of his coffee.

"Notice that they're not mentioning any names. They're probably holding that information for another day, or have received legal advice not to publish names yet," he said. "What they do have is pretty accurate. Sounds like it's coming from the inside."

"Give me a second, you're ahead of me."

I read the article carefully. The story was long on generalities and short on specifics. Basically, it focused on an internal probe of the drug squad by the new police chief. The probe had been completed, but its results had not been made public. Meanwhile, several criminal lawyers had been quietly getting together as a group to try and bring the results of the probe out into the open. They claimed that the drug squad was corrupt, that members of the drug squad were freely helping themselves to cash and drugs from seizures that they'd made, and that they had abused the rights of the lawyers' clients and fabricated charges against them.

"I talked to some of my friends on the force yesterday. Basically, they confirmed that the police chief has conducted a secret investigation into the drug squad and that everybody expects he'll make the results public soon," Dave said.

Did I detect a note of resignation in his voice?

"Meaning what?" I asked.

"Meaning that they might launch an official investigation, or, if they have enough evidence, lay charges."

"What kind of charges?"

"Obstruction of justice, theft, assault .... you name it."

"Will you be implicated or charged?" It occurred to me that maybe Dave and I moving in together might not be such a good idea. Then I quickly dismissed the thought.

"Don't know. It could be seen as guilt by association."

"But they wouldn't lay charges unless there is solid evidence, would they?"

"You wouldn't think so, but then again, it might be a way to get the media off their back."

"Whose back?"

"The police commission's. Or the police chief's. Once charges are laid, they can always use that as a shield to avoid having to answer questions from the media."

My journalistic instincts for a story were kicking in. But then again, I wasn't sure I wanted to get too closely involved. What if, in fact, Dave was implicated in some way? Would I have to rely solely on 'pillow talk' for information? More importantly, could I trust him to be honest with me without prejudicing his case?

We chatted a bit more, and then Dave said he had other calls to make and hung up.

I searched the other Toronto newspapers to find out if they were carrying the story. Not yet. Presumably they were playing catch-up, but I knew if there was any substance to the story, it wouldn't take long. There was nothing on Twitter either.

I had a quiet breakfast watching CNN, CBC News, and the BBC. My Dave was not mentioned on any of the newscasts. Not that I really expected him to be.

My ears did perk up when the BBC announcer talked about Ireland and its slow road to economic recovery. Would the Celtic Tiger ever be healthy enough to roar again? One of the more interesting background facts we'd dug up for the segment we'd done on my show was that Ireland had actively encouraged more participation in the economy by women during the economic surge. Maybe that was how Mary Tully had gotten her start selling the scarves she knit.

"The rate of growth in mortgage arrears is slowing," the announcer said in a somber tone, as only BBC announcers can. Now there was a sentence for you. Maybe if he'd said it with an Irish lilt, it would have made more sense.

I hadn't made any plans for the morning and decided to do some research on the Troubles.

Although there was a specific time period that the term 'The Troubles' refers to, I quickly came to the conclusion that Ireland has always had troubles. Blame it on St. Patrick, he'd brought Christianity to Ireland. After that, it was all downhill. Whether it was the Vikings, the Normans, or the English, the poor Irish were always being invaded, subjugated, and exploited. Every so often the Irish revolted, but it usually didn't last long before an English king hired the likes of Cromwell to put down the revolt. In Cromwell's case, he promptly confiscated the best lands owned by the Catholics and gave them to Protestant supporters, mostly Scots or English. At one point, the Catholics weren't allowed to own land or vote, to own a weapon or be educated, or to practice being a lawyer, doctor, trader, or professional. On top of that, the Catholic religion was largely forbidden. It sounded a version of apartheid before its time. And all this before the potato famine had ravaged the country.

I stopped my reading to get a glass of water and stretch my legs. Truthfully, I wasn't as pumped up about my Irish roots anymore. Dave's situation had put a damper on things as well. It would be interesting to find out if Rory and I were related, but then what? Was my sudden preoccupation just a diversion from what I really should be doing? Namely looking for another source of steady income? But then, come to think of it, I'd always been a bit of a nomad, preferring freelancing to a salaried position.

Mary Tully's scarf was hanging from one of the chairs in the dining room. I fingered the wool, admired the design, and put it around my neck. It felt warm and cozy, and for a brief second I felt guilty about even thinking that I would abandon the search for my Irish roots. Who knew? Maybe Mary Tully and I were related.

I had a quick shower and was brushing my teeth when the phone rang.

Thinking it was Dave, I answered.

"Huwo," I said, not having rinsed out my mouth out yet.

"Aurora? Is that you?"

I recognized the voice. It was Malcolm Overton. I did a quick rinse, and spat out the water. "Sorry, Malcolm. Just brushing my teeth."

"I didn't mean to interrupt your late-morning routine," he said. Did I detect a trace of sarcasm there?

"No problem. You know how it is when you're unemployed. Wait, maybe you don't know what it's like." Malcolm was as used to my sense of humour as I was with his.

He ignored my comment. "The reason for my call is that I wondered if you wanted to be on a panel for a television special we're doing. The subject of the show is a comparison of the Canadian political scene with other countries similar to ours. Australia, Ireland, and Britain, to name a few. It won't pay well, but the exposure will be good."

"Malcolm, I'd rather have poor exposure but good pay."

"Okay, I assume that you're interested. I'll have my assistant send you the details. Carry on with breakfast."

He hung up before I had a chance for a retort. I knew the ins and outs of our political scene, but the others would take a little research. Given my recent foray into all things Irish, it sounded like fun. When I read his e-mail a few minutes later, he was right; it didn't pay well. And when he said Ireland, he should have said Northern Ireland. Just a slight difference. They wanted me to explore the question of whether there was any similarity between Canada with respect to Quebec and its separatists and the situation in Northern Ireland with its Unionists. I confirmed my participation, had a shower, and went off to meet Wendy for lunch. I decided not to raise the subject of the Irish with her. I didn't even wear my Irish scarf.

Three hours later, I arrived back at the condo. There were days when Wendy and I could talk endlessly. And laugh …. God, did we laugh. I always came away from lunch with her feeling good about myself, good about her, and good about just everything else in the world. Except maybe Harry Schulz. I caught myself looking over my shoulder several times to see if he was lurking on the sidewalk.

None of the e-mails in my inbox were of any interest, so I had the option of researching Senate reform or the political issue in Northern Ireland. I chose the latter.

Canadians don't know how lucky they are when it comes to political parties. Basically, we have three or four, unless you live in Quebec where you might have as many as five or six. Northern Ireland, by my count, had at least thirty-two parties, one of which was called the Official Monster Raving Loony Party. Some parties were organized on an all-Ireland basis, while others were on an all-United Kingdom basis. Just like those who see Quebec as a part of Canada, or those who seek a separate country. The terms Democratic, Progressive, Unionist, and Republican seemed to be used interchangeably and lose their meaning quickly. Some parties had retained their Irish names, like Sinn Fein or Fianna Fail, which to an outsider meant absolutely zilch.

What I'd learned from my study of political structures in various countries was that by and large the more successful political parties overlapped each other in ideology and political aim, be it in Canada, the U.S., or in the U.K. Granted, each had a distinct platform, but once in power, they did whatever they had to in order to get re-elected.

In Ireland, the big difference was the political party named Sinn Fein. The name meant "Ourselves Alone", and the party believed in independence for all of Ireland. They were active in both Northern Ireland and the Republic of Ireland, and had always been linked inexorably with the IRA. In the North, Sinn Fein had always been opposed by the Unionists, who believed in maintaining British rule and who were well aware that the Catholics in the south vastly outnumbered the Protestants in the north. In the south, the Republicans opposed the Unionists because they really didn't want to sleep in the same bed as the Catholics. It was enough to give you a headache.

I closed my browser and sent Dave a text message, asking him to rescue me from the political situation in Ireland. Then I sent an e-mail to Rory. I hadn't heard from her since she'd left Toronto and wanted to update her on my research, scant as it was. In my defense, though, while I may not have done much in unearthing our family's roots, I had found out who my great-grandfather was and how he'd met his tragic death. That was news in itself. I also asked her for an opinion on the current election in Ireland, and who she thought was the better choice.

Before I finished the e-mail, Dave replied to my text. He said that I was on my own fighting the Troubles. According to him, he had enough troubles of his own. I replied back, *Sorry, I'm not taking no for an answer. Seven o'clock fine?*

Within seconds, he replied, *Make it 7:30.* I've got a meeting before then, so I may be a bit late.

For once I was at the restaurant on time, but Dave was not there to witness it. I sat on the barstool for nearly half an hour chatting with Angelo. My phone was on the bar counter. I looked at it anxiously, waiting for a message from him. Finally, I'd just picked it up to send him a text when, much to my relief, he walked in. The anger on his face was unmistakable. When Dave was mad, he might as well have been wearing a sandwich board, his expression was so evident to anyone who saw him.

"You okay?" I asked as he sat down beside me.

"Yeah, I guess," he replied, signaling to Angelo for a beer.

CHAPTER 22

It's no use going to a goat's house looking for wool.

-Irish Proverb

I waited for him to calm down. Between sips of beer, he stared straight ahead at the mirror at the back of the bar. After what seemed like an hour, he shifted his glance and made eye contact with me in the mirror. That seemed to break whatever spell he was under. He turned and looked directly at me.

"Sorry. I finally agreed to meet Schulz for a coffee."

"How did it go?"

Dave glanced around him to make sure no one was within earshot. "Like I figured. It was about one of the drug busts that we were on, the same one Miller and Francona wanted to talk about. It all makes sense now." He shook his head in disgust. "Normally it would have been the four of us getting together. But Harry deliberately didn't come so that I'd be more upfront with the guys without him there. When Miller and Francona couldn't get anything out of me, Harry followed up on his own to put pressure on me. Now I'm really pissed off." The way he was gripping his beer bottle, I thought he was going to crush the glass. He took a long pull of the beer and set it down on the counter.

"When I was on Squad 7, we had a tip-off about a wanted drug dealer hiding out in an apartment building. It was a four-story walk-up. Four of us went there .... Miller, Francona, Schulz, and me. We had a warrant, we knocked on the door, and when it opened, Schulz and the other guys rushed in. I stayed in the hall as a lookout. There was a suspicion that there were other dealers in adjoining rooms, and I was the rearguard in case any of them came out. It was a routine bust, and the dealer was taken down. Then Schulz came out and asked me to race across town and get a search warrant for the apartment next door, Unit 409. The dealer, hoping to make a deal, had said that there was a meth lab there. So I left, got the warrant, and headed back. I was gone about an hour. On the way back, Schulz radioed and asked me to pick up two members of another drug squad along the way - Bill Greeves and another guy whose name I can't remember. We hooked up, and the two of them came back to the scene of the bust with me."

Dave took another pull on his beer.

"I gave Schulz the search warrant, and he told me and Greeves to go into the apartment next door. Schulz and Miller were going to take the drug dealer to the precinct, and Francona was staying behind. I remember thinking at the time that it was odd that Schulz had asked us to go into Apartment 409. As I said, normally I was the rearguard. I didn't take part in the raids themselves. Anyway, there was no answer when we knocked, so we forced our way in and, sure enough, it was a lab. Not only were there hard drugs, but there was also a lot of cash lying around. The apartment was unoccupied, and we secured the premises in short order. Just as we finished, Schulz appeared in the doorway. I came out to talk to him and I noticed Miller escorting the dealer downstairs. We told him what we'd had found, and he radioed the precinct for some uniformed officers to help out. Schulz never set foot in the apartment himself, and I remember at the time thinking that was odd.

"The drugs and money were confiscated, but ownership of the lab was never determined. We thought it was the dealer, but couldn't prove it. On the surface, it was all rather easy and uneventful. Two years later, the dealer came to trial. He was represented by a legal-aid lawyer .... I can't remember his name. The dealer had been charged with assault, resisting arrest, possession, and trafficking, and naturally he entered a not-guilty plea. I wasn't present at the trial because I was involved in a delicate undercover operation at the time. I only learned about the details of what went on from the newspaper accounts. As part of his defense, the dealer's lawyer maintained that the drug squad had helped themselves to some of the drugs and money after roughing the dealer up pretty badly. Well, the jury didn't believe any of it and found him guilty on all counts. Despite that, the accusation against the cops lingered. The Star made a big deal about it at the time, as they always do."

Dave paused as he took a big swig of his beer. "I didn't see or hear anything going on inside the apartment, but I was surprised by how bad the dealer looked when they brought him out. I hadn't had the impression that he'd offered any resistance when they'd arrested him, so I asked Schulz about it and he just shrugged it off. It never came up again until I read the reports in the paper. When I got off the undercover assignment, I ran into Schulz at headquarters. I asked him about the trial, and he said that the dealer was a liar and a scumbag. In fact, I could tell he was surprised at my question. After that, he never really trusted me again and always kept me at arm's length. That's when I decided that maybe it wasn't the best place to be on my career path."

"So what did he want tonight?"

"He wanted to know if anyone from the police chief's office had been in touch with me during the internal probe on the squad."

"What did you tell him?"

"I told him the answer was no, but that even if they had, I wouldn't necessarily tell him. He told me that we had to stick together and protect each other., and I told him that I would follow my own conscience, not his. But he wouldn't let up. Finally, in frustration, I said to him that if he didn't stop badgering me, I'd call the police."

"You are the police," I reminded him, trying to introduce a bit of levity into the conversation.

He looked at me as if I had just arrived from Mars.

"Whatever," he mumbled under his breath. So much for my levity. "Anyway, that's why I was late. Sorry. Let's eat."

After that, Dave clammed up. We had a quiet dinner. I tried to make conversation about any number of things, but he was too preoccupied and just nodded out of courtesy. After dinner, he went back to his place and I went to mine.

As I went to bed alone that night, I hoped that this wasn't the beginning of Troubles for Dave.

Or for me.

CHAPTER 23

Questioning is the door of knowledge.
-Irish proverb

Rory replied back to my e-mail the following day.

Dear Aurora, what a delightful surprise to hear from you and what sad news you discovered. I vaguely know about the Castleconnell shooting, but I'm not exactly sure why. Ireland has so much bloody history, as you have just discovered. I think every family has been touched by it, one way or another. I've been buried in archives on a project for the last three weeks, and I've just scratched the surface. I may never be able to come up for air again. Lol. Sometimes I wish I had picked an easier career. You asked about the election in Ireland. I'm aware of it, but to be honest, I'm of little help. I don't trust politicians at the best of times, and so I don't pay any attention to them. I usually ask Catherine, my sister, who I should vote for. Pathetic, isn't it? If you find out any more about your family, let me know. Rory.

That afternoon I received a telephone call from Malcolm. He told me that a group called "The Friendship League of Ireland" was holding a fundraising event in Toronto in a couple of days. Malcolm had two tickets for it and wondered, since I was interested these days in all things Irish, if I would like to go. He had double-booked himself and was unable to attend.

"I didn't know you were Irish," I said to Malcolm.

"I'm not," he replied, but didn't elaborate.

"I'd love to. I can wear my Mary Tully scarf." Malcolm didn't bite on that, or didn't care. Sometimes it was hard to make small talk with him. His attention span averaged about three seconds.

"I'll courier the tickets to you this afternoon. You'll be at a table with lots of interesting people. Have fun."

By three o'clock, the tickets were delivered to my condo. Malcolm was so efficient.

I googled the event and, much to my surprise, found that the money was being raised for Sinn Fein, one of the larger and probably most controversial of the Irish political parties. They had always been considered the political arm of the IRA, even though the leaders of Sinn Fein tried very hard to distance themselves from it.

I found it curious that an Irish political party would be raising money here in Canada, but then I remembered reading a statistic of how many millions of Irish descendants live in Canada and the U.S. It was an impressive number. And chances were those descendants on this side of the ocean just might be better off financially than the folks back home, especially these days now that the economic bubble had burst in Ireland. Not that the economy was exactly all that rosy for Canada's neighbours to the south.

I wondered just how lucrative such a fundraising effort was, and my question was answered quickly when I learned that the price of admission was $175 per person. It included a free dinner, but not free drinks. A wise move on the part of the organizers. I guessed that with the way the Irish could drink, there would be little left over from the proceeds if there was a free bar.

No sooner had I finished checking out the details of the dinner than I received an e-mail from Paula McKerr saying that her mother had had a bad fall, but that she was all right. Fortunately, it had happened while there was someone else in her house; otherwise it might have had disastrous consequences. Paula asked how the Irish research was coming along, and had I come across the name Flanagan yet? I wasn't exactly sure what she meant by that, but it did remind me that I hadn't really made a dent in the letters that Aunt Fionola had given me.

I turned off my laptop, not wishing to spend the rest of the day caught up in an e-mail whirlpool. Some days it was hard to get anything productive done when all I'd wind up doing was writing e-mails, which would prompt replies, which I'd then reply to.

Out of habit, I turned on the all-news channel on the television. The weather forecast was decent. Sunny with a high of 16 Celsius. Stocks were on an upward swing. Traffic was in chaos on the 401 due to yet another tractor-trailer turnover, and the BREAKING NEWS ALERT was that Toronto's police chief had scheduled a press conference for 4 p.m. Word was that it had to do with the drug squad investigation.

I quickly sent a text to Dave and asked if he knew anything about it.

He replied that no, he didn't.

I looked at my watch. Half an hour to the press conference. I kept the news channel on while I stacked two days' worth of dishes into the dishwasher and threw a load of laundry into my mini-washing machine. I could never figure out where all the dirty dishes come from; I rarely ate in.

At 4 p.m., the press conference started, and it was carried live on the all-news channel. The police chief announced that he had instigated an internal investigation of certain members on Drug Squad 7. The results of that investigation had prompted him to ask the RCMP to launch an independent investigation of the squad. In the meantime, three squad members had been suspended with pay until the RCMP's probe was complete. He named the officers being suspended, and I immediately recognized them: Schulz, Miller, and Francona. Thankfully, there was no Dave Fullerton on the list. I gave a big sigh of relief and wondered if Dave felt the same. I dialed his number, and he answered on the first ring.

"Are you watching the press conference?" I asked.

"Yes. It's not over. Call me back," he said, and hung up.

The police chief didn't really say much more other than to express his regret that it had to come to this, but that the citizens needed to be reassured that the police force was above reproach. And he said that if there was any wrongdoing, charges would be laid. The words 'uh-oh' echoed in my mind.

I called Dave and got a busy signal. I tried repeatedly for the next half hour, until I finally gave up and did some vacuuming to get my mind on something else. When I finished, I saw the missed-call message on my cellphone.

This time when I called Dave, he answered. "Sorry I didn't get right back to you.
A couple of buddies called about the press conference. Looks like the fun is just starting."

"I was glad to hear your name wasn't mentioned," I said.

"So was I, but remember, I'm on leave, so technically they can't suspend me. If I applied to come back, they'd have to take me back and then suspend me."

"Are you under suspicion?"

"I don't know. But I was on that squad, and if the rumours I've heard are right, then of course I would be. I was in on that drug bust."

"But you didn't participate in anything illegal."

"No, I didn't, and I know that. I'm sure, though, that I'm going to have to convince them, if they ask me."

"Who?"

"The RCMP. They'll come knocking .... you can bet your boots on it. I've got another call," he said. "Talk to you later."

I put down the phone, turned off the television, and went online to see what the Twitter world had to say. Nothing much, it turned out.

Drug dealers weren't tweeting their approval of the chief's announcement.

After I made myself a coffee, I went back to the box of letters, if for no other reason than to take my mind of Dave's situation.

Paula's comment about someone named Flanagan had made me curious. I wondered briefly why she just didn't tell me outright who this Flanagan was?

I read two or three more letters from Collette's brother, Liam, and they all had the same tone. Poverty and hardship were the main themes of their life, but despite that they survived, had another child every year, and generally seemed relatively content. The IRA and the continual fight against the British and the Protestants was mentioned again and again. I folded the letters back into the envelopes and decided to tackle another batch.

The handwriting was more flowery this time, and I assumed, correctly as it turned out, that it was penned by a woman. Her name was Bernadette Broaders, and it wasn't clear if she was a relative, neighbour, or maybe a school friend. Whoever she was, she and Colette were good friends. Her letters were filled mostly with gossip about mutual friends or acquaintances. She wrote longingly about their childhood and 'the years of innocence', and the fond hope that she and her husband could soon emigrate to the new world.

The ringing telephone made for a welcome diversion.

"Sorry, I couldn't talk long before," Dave said. "The phone's been crazy since the news conference. Everyone wants to talk about it, and I'm exhausted."

"Did your friend Schulz call you?"

"No, he didn't."

"Does this mean you'll have to continue looking over your shoulder?"

"I don't think I'll have any more problems with Schulz. Now that he's been suspended, he'll keep a low profile, assuming that he listens to his lawyer."

"That's a relief. Before I forget, would you like to accompany me to a fundraising event tomorrow night? My ex-boss asked if I wanted to use his tickets and I thought it might be interesting. It's an Irish club raising money for Sinn Fein."

"Sinn Fein? You serious? Why are they holding fundraisers here?"

"I don't know. I'm sure we'll find out."

There was a long pause. "Okay, I guess. In the meantime, I've got to get back and hit the books. Too many distractions today. What time tomorrow?"

"It starts at seven, at the Convention Centre."
"Okay, meet you at the main entrance at 6:45."
"Deal! I'll be wearing my Irish scarf."
"Anything else?" Dave said, before hanging up.
Men! One track minds.

CHAPTER 24

He'd offer you an egg if you promised
not to break the shell.
-Irish saying

I stood outside the main entrance of the Convention Centre waiting for Dave, watching the steady stream of people heading for the main doors. At first I thought they were all going to the Irish dinner, until I overheard someone ask where the PriceWaterhouse reunion was. The young woman was then directed to Level B2. From then on until Dave came, I tried to guess which event people were attending. Dave finally appeared and, judging by his clothes, he was attending the accountants' function.

We descended into the cavernous building and eventually found a large convention hall brightly festooned with Irish flags, shamrocks, and other Irish-themed artifacts. The only thing missing were the leprechauns.

"Think this is the right place?" I quipped to Dave as we entered.

Bars were set up throughout the room, and Dave steered us to the closest one and ordered two pints of Guinness. Conversation in the room was at the higher end of the decibel range. I figured that everyone would be speaking with an Irish accent, but such was not the case. We could have been in the accountants' meeting, for all I knew.

The lights flickered, and everyone headed to their assigned table.

Ours was close to the front, right by the speakers' podium. We were the last to arrive and introduced ourselves to those already seated. I recognized several men, all politicians, including the former Solicitor General of Canada. At least four of our tablemates recognized me, either from the television show or from my writing. I was always grateful to know that there were people who liked what I did, but it also meant that I had to behave.

A rather gregarious man seated next to me held my hand for the longest time during the introductions and waxed eloquently about my book on the government scandal several years ago. I thought he was never going to let go. He was all set to engage me in more one-sided conversation when a speaker stepped up to the podium.

"Ladies and gentlemen. My name is Eamon McPhail, director of the Irish League, and it is my pleasure to welcome you tonight. We appreciate your support, and I know you will enjoy listening to our special guest this evening, Gerry Adams. Before Gerry takes the stage, though, we are going to enjoy some Irish food, and drink and song. On stage with us, we have The Emerald Isles, who are ready to play. So sit back and relax."

The dinner, served by an army of wait staff, was not something to write home about, and I had to remind myself that this was a convention centre. Cooking for five hundred people at one sitting had to have its challenges. There was little conversation at the table; everyone was busy eating and listening to the music.

Near the end of the meal, the host came back, thanked the band, and thanked us again for coming. "And now, without further ado, I would like to introduce to you a man who needs no introduction - Gerry Adams, the President of Sinn Fein."

Adams walked on stage looking very much like the man I'd seen in the newspaper articles. I judged him to be in his late fifties, although his salt-and-pepper facial hair could be deceiving. His hair was closely cropped, his glasses sat on the end of his nose, and in my opinion, he looked tough and mean. Almost to the point of menacing. Maybe he hadn't liked the meal either. Most certainly he did not look like the average politician I was used to.

"Good evening, ladies and gentlemen. Thank you for coming, and thank you for your support. Irish-Canadians and Sinn Fein share a common ground. Through this financial support, we are able to drive forward our main party goal of securing a United Ireland," he said in a forceful tone.

The room broke out into a thunderous applause. Adams paused for a moment and then continued. He spoke of Irish history and the Catholic experience of British colonization, widespread discrimination, and forced diaspora. "So when we are told that violence is awful and causes suffering, we obviously know it to be true. But we also know it to be a product of persecution and injustice, and that without it, we change nothing." His face had reddened, and his body language was clearly confrontational. For him, violence was justified if it meant that unification was achieved.

"If the British government, if the Unionist majority, had agreed to treat us equally, there would have been no support for armed resistance." He stepped away from the podium and sat down. This time, the applause was not as loud as before. I looked around the room. Most people had remained seated; only a small few were giving him a standing ovation.

The band returned to the stage for an encore and without prompting launched into 'The Patriot's Game'. I'd heard the song many times and had to confess that I'd never really paid attention to the words before. I knew it was about young men going off to fight John Bull's tyranny. But I really hadn't known what that meant other than in abstract way. After listening to Adams promoting violent insurrection, and justifying it, the song was suddenly cast in a new light.

When the band finished, our host thanked us again and everyone started drifting out. I was stunned by what I'd heard. Growing up in a political family, I'd sat through many political speeches. But none had promoted violence like this. Maybe Adams was related to Arafat and all the others who believed that the killing of civilians was justified in war. I wanted to shout out in my best Irish accent, "Holy Mother of God, do you think we were born yesterday?"

On the way out, I asked Dave what he thought of the speaker.

"He shouldn't be allowed to own a gun, or be near a microphone," he said flatly.

CHAPTER 25

You must take the little potato with the big potato.
                                                    - Irish proverb

Malcolm called me first thing the next morning.

"So what did you think?" he asked, without any preamble.

"Your money could have been put to better use."

"I know. He's dangerous. That's why the Americans banned him from speaking. Anyway, do you know of Michael O'Neil?"

"Not really."

"He's from Northern Ireland, and he's running for the presidency of the Irish Republic. He's also with Sinn Fein, and like Adams has an IRA past. We're going to do a half-hour special profiling O'Neil and others who have had violent pasts and who in later life became peacekeepers. Are you interested in doing the O'Neil segment? It might mean a trip to Ireland."

I'd never liked sounding too eager. I'd always felt that it put me at a disadvantage.

"When do I leave?" I heard myself say.

"Give me a few days to set something up. I'll call you."

That's what I liked about being unemployed. You had the flexibility of time to grab new challenges as they came along.

The thought of going to Ireland appealed to me. I could meet Rory on her home turf, and who knew, maybe even meet Mary Tully. And with some prodding and a bit more research, I might meet some distant relatives.

After my initial excitement died down, I thought that perhaps I should at least finish going through Aunt Fionola's shoebox.

I picked up another bundle of mail, and discovered that the letters were from Colette's brother Liam. He mostly talked about hardship and local politics, but one particular section in one of the letters caught my eye. 'Sean visited a month ago and confided that he had discovered the identity of the Black and Tan who killed our father. He has been obsessed with this for many years, as you know, and vowed revenge if the opportunity ever presented itself. I cannot tell you who it is. I swore on our father's grave that I wouldn't reveal his identity. Sean wants to deal with the man on his own terms.' The rest of the letter talked about the family, his children, his wife, and the other uncles and cousins.

That was the second letter in the bunch. The third letter, dated six months later, was much the same. The fourth letter, dated three weeks after that, was short and to the point. 'Father's murderer has been brought to justice.' The envelope contained several newspaper clippings. The first was about a man named Fergus Flanagan who was found beaten to death in a Belfast alley. It said that the death had all the signs of an IRA execution. The second clipping said that the IRA had taken credit for killing Flanagan in revenge for the murder seventeen years earlier of Richard Mahoney at the Shannon View Hotel in Castleconnell. There were several other letters in the bundle, but no further mention was made of Sean.

I put the letters back in the box and dug around in my purse for Paula's telephone number.

"Hello, the McKerr residence," said a female voice with a distinct Irish accent.

"May I speak with Paula, please?" I asked.

"That you may. Give her a minute, will you?" the woman said, placing the receiver on a hard surface. In the background, there was loud conversation among several women, all seemingly talking at once. I could hear the clip-clop of shoes and the telephone being picked up.

"Hello." It was easy to recognize Paula's voice.

"Hi, Paula, it's Aurora. Sounds like I've caught you at a bad time."

"Aurora. How wonderful to hear from you." She turned the telephone away from her mouth and said to her friends, "It's my cousin Aurora in Toronto. She's the author I was telling you about."

"Want me to call you back later?" I asked.

"No, it's just the girls from the book club. They can carry on without me for a while. I didn't read the book anyway. Hold on and I'll grab the phone in the other room." There was a silence, then some background noise, and then the click of the phone being picked up. "Now then, Aurora, to what do I owe this pleasure? Are you calling about my mother?"

"Well no, but how is she? Has she recovered from her fall?"

"As much as can be expected. It will take her some time to get back to normal, but she seems to be okay. I have someone coming in on a daily basis to check on her."

"That's good to hear. I was actually calling because I just read the letter about Flanagan. Why didn't you tell me about that when we were in Trinity?"

92

"I didn't want to upset Mother. She may not show it on the surface, but she gets very angry about all the killings that have taken place. You see, she thinks that her uncle Sean was either directly responsible for the killing of Flanagan, or that he arranged it. As much as Liam said that it wasn't Sean, she believes it was. And she can't stand the thought of her uncle being a murderer. She feels that it puts him in the same class as the man who murdered her grandfather."

"Why did she give me the letters, then? Surely she knew I would find out."

"I've been thinking about that myself. I looked through the letters by accident years ago. When Mum found out, she was very cross with me. She said that she didn't want talk of murder and violence in her house, and she refused to ever talk to me about it again. Until you came. It is curious. Maybe she finally feels that others in the family have a right to know. Maybe she no longer believes that her uncle killed Flanagan. You might have to ask her to get the answer."

"But if it upsets her so much, I'd be very reluctant to bring it up. There's not much to be gained by it, is there?"

"No, probably not."

"What ever happened to Sean?"

"I'm not sure if anyone really knows."

"Is there anything else in the box that I'm going to be shocked at?" I asked, hoping there wouldn't be.

"No, you know it all now. It all seems so distant, doesn't it? It's like reading a history book instead of a batch of family letters - you feel so detached from it all."

I quickly told her that I might be going to Ireland shortly and why. I heard her cover the receiver with her hand and yell, "Be right there."

"I'll let you get back to your book club. And I'll let you know how the trip went. I don't know how much time I'll have when I'm there, but if I get a chance I'll make a side trip to Castleconnell and Limerick. Is there a family plot?"

"That I don't know .... maybe Mum will know."

"I'll save it for another time. Take care. Out of curiosity, what's the book of the month?" I asked.

"'Ulysses', by James Joyce."

"Did anyone actually read it?"

"Not a one," she said with a hearty laugh. "Have a good trip. Stay away from the IRA."

"I will. I think our family's had enough of them."

"To be sure," she said, "to be sure."

After my conversation with Paula, I was tempted to write to Dad and ask him what he knew about all of this and why had it been kept such a secret, but decided that it could wait. As Paula said, it was all history now. Nothing was going to change what had happened.

I looked at my cellphone and noticed that a text had come in while I'd been talking to Paula.

Am at RCMP being interviewed. May be here for some time. Will call when through. Have you got lots of money for bail in case I need it?

Was he kidding me or what? I knew he had a good sense of humour, but was now the time? I replied quickly, *If it's any more than fifty bucks, you're out of luck.*

I returned the shoebox to my bedroom closet. I'd had enough of the past, and reflected that maybe Aunt Fionola was right that we should look ahead and not back. But then I heard my inner voice say, *'No, she's not right. You can't look ahead if you don't understand who you are and where you've come from. We wear the past like an invisible cloak whether we want to or not.'* I sat down on the bed, feeling a bit worn out by the rather depressing events in my family history. Not to mention the speech by Adams. It didn't exactly fall into the uplifting-of-the-spirit category, unless you were an avowed killer.

When I left the bedroom, I thought about Dave. Even though his text about bail was in jest, I began to wonder just how much I could raise if I had to.

I hoped I wouldn't have to find out.

CHAPTER 26

Both your friends and your enemy
think you will never die.
- Irish proverb

Dave didn't call until just after ten that night. He was in a taxi on his way to my place.

When he arrived, he looked very tired, and his eyes had lost their sparkle. In all the time I'd known him, he'd never looked like that. Not even when he'd arrested me.

Without saying a word, he took his coat and shoes off and sat down on my living room couch, exhaling loudly. I honestly didn't know if I should get him a pillow and a blanket or a stiff drink.

"Would you like a stiff drink?" I asked.

He looked at me uncomprehendingly. Perhaps because I really didn't do stiff drinks. I changed my approach. "Beer?"

He nodded.

I poured the beer for him, and he took it without making eye contact. He took a long sip, leaned back on the couch, and said, "I needed that. It's been a rough day."

"Do you want to tell me about it? Or you can wait till the morning. It's up to you. At least I didn't have to bail you out."

He swung his legs up on the couch and lay back and closed his eyes. "Remember that drug bust I told you about? The one where I was on the outside and Schwartz and others were on the inside? That seems to be one of the cases they're really focusing on."

"Who's 'they'?" I asked.

"Oh, sorry, the RCMP. They're in charge of the investigation."

"So how did it go?"

"We spent the whole time talking about the drug bust. They asked me to detail what happened, step by step. After the first time I went through it, they gave me my notebook and asked me to look at it to see if there was anything I might have forgotten."

"And had you?"

"A couple of minor details, but by and large my story was consistent with what I had filed in my notes. Then we went through it all again. It

95

was as if they were trying to trip me up. Mind you, I can't blame them. It's probably what I'd do if I was in their shoes."

"So did you get any sense whether you're a suspect? Are you under suspicion?"

"I'd be crazy to think I wasn't. Of course I am. But I don't know exactly what the allegations are other than what I've heard secondhand. I never was inside 407, the first unit we raided, so I can hardly be accused of stealing anything. And in 409, I went in there with two other guys."

"Have you talked to them yet?"

"No. One of them resigned from the force, and I don't know what happened to the other one."

"So what now?"

"I'm going to get a sub. I'm hungry. Want to come with me?" he asked, as he sat up, ran his fingers through his hair, and drained the last of his beer.

I looked at my watch; it was getting close to midnight.

"Sure," I said, without hesitation. If that was what the man needed, fine by me.

We left the condo and walked west along Bloor. It was a crisp night, with not a cloud in the sky. A full moon hung over Varsity Stadium. The sidewalk was surprisingly busy considering the lateness of the evening. At first, Dave was walking quickly, but within a block he had slowed down, and after that he walked at a more leisurely pace. He said nothing, but that didn't bother me. I knew what it was like to need time to get your thoughts in order.

I wanted to tell Dave about Fergus Flanagan and Sean Mahoney, but I thought that he'd had enough drama for one day. They weren't going anywhere, unless I moved the shoebox.

We found a Mr. Sub just on the other side of Spadina. Dave ordered a classic, and momentarily I had an urge to join him. But in the end, I just ordered a diet coke. He practically inhaled the sub, making small talk about nothing and everything. When he finished, he wiped his lips with his napkin, leaned over the table, and gave me a kiss.

"Thanks," he said, not explaining what he was thanking me for. It must have been for my witty conversational talents.

We took a different route home. Since neither of us had a steady job, we didn't have to worry about getting up early. We walked along the quiet residential streets just north of Bloor. It was an area of large and stately brick homes, many of which had been converted to business use or student housing. Most houses were in darkness.

Dave stopped at a beautiful three-story brick Victorian house on St. George Street. It had a 'For Sale' sign on it.

"I love this area," he said. "One day I'd like to own a house like this."

"Before or after you get out of jail?" I said, squeezing his arm.

He laughed and gave me a playful punch.

"After," he said. "And you can live with me."

"Is that a proposal?"

"No, I just need someone else to help pay the mortgage."

This time, I gave him a playful punch and said, "I'll be living in Ireland. Pay your own mortgage."

CHAPTER 27

May misfortune follow you all your life
and never catch up.
                                        - Irish proverb

As I lay in bed the next morning, watching Dave's chest slowly rise and fall as he slept, I started to mull over an idea in my head. Gerry Adams had clearly said in his speech that violence was justified when there was tyranny and persecution. I wondered, though, how much of the killing in Ireland was motivated by reasons other than patriotism. Richard Mahoney was killed by the British for being a suspected IRA member. Flanagan was killed by the IRA out of revenge. Both sides had taken the law into their own hands, and in the process perpetuated the seemingly endless cycle of killing, retribution, and more killing. I wondered just how much of Gerry Adams' talk was rhetoric, fabricated to suit his political agenda.

According to my research, close to four thousand people had died during the Troubles. Given what had happened in other countries during outbreaks of sectarian violence, I was actually surprised that the number of dead in Ireland wasn't higher. Religious warfare was hard to suppress. Neither side wanted to lose for fear of being dominated or persecuted by the other. The big irony in Ireland's case was that a lot of the violence was aimed at the British, who would have happily washed their hands of the Irish if they could have.

I really didn't want to wake Dave. He deserved to sleep in as long as he could. I eased myself out of bed in the dark, and went to my study and powered on the laptop. While it was doing that, I went out and put on a pot of coffee. When it finished brewing, I checked the newspaper headlines. None of them mentioned Dave Fullerton. I sighed with relief, sipping on my mug of caffeine.

With coffee in hand, I returned to my laptop and logged into my e-mail. Here was a pet peeve of mine .... people who send needless e-mails. Particularly charity e-mails, jokes, links to yet another viral YouTube video, and all other forms of 'legitimized' spam. When I'd see these e-mails, I always wanted to reply, "Get a life, would you!" My frustration as my inbox filled with these things would get so great that it made me feel a little unhinged at times.

Calming myself down, I sent off a quick e-mail to Rory.

Hello, Rory. Hope you have found your way out of the cave, or at least have come up for air once in a while. I came across something of interest. It concerns a man named Fergus Flanagan, who was found dead in an alley in Belfast in 1938. This man supposedly was the Black and Tan who executed my great-grandfather, Richard Mahoney. I googled the name, but couldn't find anything. Any suggestions? My reason for asking is that I'm interested in pursuing the murder as an angle for a book. It's all your fault, by the way; you got me interested in my Irish roots. Good news. I may actually be coming to Dublin in the near future. I'll make sure I have enough time to pay you a visit in Galway. I will let you know when my travel plans firm up. If you can't find anything on Flanagan, don't worry. I realize that after all this time, it's a stab in the dark.

As I finished typing the e-mail, a pair of hands gently touched my shoulders. I looked up and Dave was standing there in his underwear, a sleepy smile on his face.

"Coffee?" I asked.

"No thanks. Come back to bed. It's too early to be up."

I took the subtle hint, closed the laptop, and followed him back to bed. If nothing else, Dave was still filled with testosterone.

And I glad about that!

We rolled out of bed an hour later and brewed another pot of coffee. Dave called his lawyer and headed out shortly after breakfast. My goal was to work out in the gym and then spend time researching Michael O'Neil, the Irish politician Malcolm wanted me to interview. By the time Dave left, he seemed himself again, convinced that it would all work out all right. I really didn't know if he was trying to convince me or himself. Regardless, he left my place in a good frame of mind.

I put on my lululemon work-out clothes and headed to the condo gym, ready to kick butt. But when I got there, a sign on the door said 'Closed due to flooding'. I went back upstairs, added a couple of layers, and headed out for a run.

If I persevered through some busy streets, I could easily make my way to the Rosedale Valley Ravine, which was what I did. It was a cool day for a run, and partly cloudy. All of the leaves were turning, and the trails were ablaze with colour. For an hour, I completely blanked the drug squad, Ireland, and the Senate out of my mind. Instead I thought about children. My niece and nephew in particular. Walter's comments kept coming back to me, following me all through the ravine.

When I returned back to the condo and had a shower, I started to do research on O'Neil, but my heart wasn't in it. Instead, I went shopping. That was my favourite stress reliever. Nothing like browsing through Winners to take your mind of your troubles. I bought two tops, one pair of jeans, new sneakers, and holiday gift wrapping that had been heavily discounted. Now I just needed to buy some gifts so that I could actually use the wrapping paper. I had a bad habit of buying things that I'd think I need and then never using them. There was probably a name for that.

Back home, I checked my e-mail, and there was a message from Dad saying that they were back from the cruise, but had decided to spend an extra week with friends. His tone was apologetic, and I wondered if he was getting homesick. Since they'd retired, it seemed as though they hadn't stopped travelling. They'd sailed almost around the world until Mom had said that she was homesick and wanted to see her grandchildren. So they sold the boat in Tahiti, flew home, and spent a couple of weeks with my brother Barrie and his family.

Within a month, Mom was cured of her homesickness and off they went to spend a week in Iceland. Heaven knew why .... it was so expensive at the time. And since then, they seemed to spend at least half their time in some exotic location or other.

I wrote Dad back and asked why he'd never told me about Fergus Flanagan and Sean Mahoney. As I wrote the e-mail, I somehow knew exactly what he would reply in return.

CHAPTER 29

Better be sparing at first than at last.
- Irish proverb

A week quickly flew by. Sometimes in my life, it was a case of either feast or famine. The panel that Malcolm had asked me to participate in took much more time to prepare for than he'd originally let on. When I counted up the time I'd spent and the amount I was paid, it was less than minimum wage. I surprised myself with the amount of knowledge I'd gained about Ireland's political system, although in the end I didn't really need it. The moderator of the panel wanted me to analyze the good and bad in the Canadian system instead. However, I did listen with interest to one of the other panelist's analysis of Ireland. Her point was that the political system in the Republic was sound, but that it was still a divided country and that until that was resolved, it would always be the elephant in the room. I guessed that Canada fell into that category too, since Quebec seemed to morph into the elephant in the room every time there was a federal election.

As soon as my work on the panel was finished, I headed off to London, Ontario, where I was one of several guest lecturers in a creative-writing workshop at the University of Western Ontario. It meant an overnight stay, courtesy of the university, in a downtown hotel.

One of the other lecturers was a writer, Lise Desroches. I was familiar with her work, but we had never met. She was bubbly, in her late thirties, and stood no more than five feet tall. Her defining characteristic was her smile. When this woman smiled, it was all you noticed. Her smile radiated outward, engulfing the room and putting a glow on her face that was mesmerizing.

Desroches wrote fictional history novels, none of which I had ever read. I confessed that to her during a break in the workshop. She smiled and then broke out in a big laugh. "That's okay," she said. "I've never read any of yours, either." After that, we became fast friends.

We went out for dinner at a pretentious bistro that was recommended by the Prof who hired us. Neither of us was excited by the menu, but we decided to stay anyway. The Prof couldn't join us due to scheduling conflicts. He probably didn't like the menu either.

"I can't tell you how nice it is to have an adult evening out," said Lise, once we'd ordered drinks and scanned the menu for the tenth time. I settled on a chicken wrap, and Lise ordered curry. "Most of my evenings are spent being a peacekeeper. I have three boys, aged seven, six and four. After two boys, I was desperate for a girl, so I agreed with Mark that we could have one more. He actually wanted four or five. If he wanted that many, I told him, he'd need to find another woman. Know why? He spends a lot of time travelling, so I'm left at home with three overly active boys. Literally, he travels two weeks out of the month. And when he comes home, he brings them presents, is a big hero, lets them get away with murder, and then hops on a plane again. Anyway, I didn't get the girl. And I've given up. I had my tubes tied."

"Who's looking after them tonight?" I asked.

"My father, God bless him. He does it very rarely, and I always notice that it seems to take him a week to recover. My mother died before the kids were born, and he's the only close family member I have. I really wish I had started a family sooner. Look at me - I'm 37, and I have a four-year-old. Do you have any children?"

"No .... I'm not even married. When do you ever get a chance to write?"

"Lately, not often. Mark babysits two nights a week when he's not travelling, and I go off to a local coffee shop. And that's about the extent of it. Ever thought of having kids? I mean, you don't have to be married to have kids, you know. I have a very good friend who adopted a Chinese baby, and she's single and doesn't plan to ever get married."

I probably paused too long before answering the question. Partly because of my thoughts on the run the other day. Was Lise a mind reader?

Lise noticed my hesitation, if not discomfort. "Sorry, I didn't mean to pry. As long as you're happy, that's all that counts. Just remember, though, you're not getting younger. And you need someone to look after you in your old age," she said, with that trademark smile of hers. Had she been talking to Walter, I wondered?

She changed the subject at that point, but I couldn't get it out of my head. Was I happy? The only answer I got was the flip side of the coin: I wasn't unhappy. I liked my career, I liked what I'd done so far, and I liked the relationship I was in with Dave. Would I want to have children with him if he popped the question? Probably, but I'd never consciously thought about it.

Lise asked what I was currently working on, and I told her about my seeming obsession with Ireland.

"I wrote a story about the Black Donnellys once," she said. "That's as close I got to Ireland. It was a tragic story, but I found it so fascinating. Do you know of it?'

I confessed that I knew who they were, but that was about it. I'd had the impression that it was another case of the Irish fighting the Irish.

Lise then gave me a quick outline of the events that had led up to the gruesome murder of five members of the Donnelly family in 1880 in Lucan, Ontario, a small community located not that far from where we were staying. The Donnellys had emigrated from Ireland two decades earlier. They'd had a number of brushes with the law, including charges of arson and assault, and had become involved in a local feud involving different factions of Irish settlers. After a series of conflicts with neighbours, they were killed one night by a vigilante mob. Despite an eyewitness to what had happened and two trials, no one was ever convicted of the murders. The surviving family had a tombstone erected with the name of each of those who died that night engraved on the stone, along with the word 'MURDERED' under each name. For decades afterwards, the tombstone attracted curiosity seekers and was routinely vandalized. It was also a reminder of Lucan's morbid past, and eventually the tombstone was removed and hidden from public view. As Lise was telling me this, I reflected that the town had collectively had the same mentality as Dad and Aunt Fionola about the murder of Richard Mahoney. Keep it hidden and maybe it will go away.

Lise offered to take me to Lucan after our lecture in the morning, but I declined. I wanted to get back to the city in case Dave needed my moral support. He'd been very quiet lately, especially since his last interview with the RCMP. Something was troubling him, but he hadn't shared it yet. I was praying that he would know how to deal with it.

And keep out of jail.

CHAPTER 30

There was never a scabby sheep in a flock
that didn't like to have a comrade.
- Irish saying

I sent Dave a text after the morning session ended and told him that I'd be back in time for him to buy me dinner. As it turned out, I made it back to the city by early afternoon, and to my surprise, there was no text from Dave. Normally, he'd reply quickly. My next text read, So, am I going hungry? By 5:30, I started to get worried. Not about dinner, but about Dave. With everything going on, I was starting to worry excessively whenever Dave was late or incommunicado.

Finally, at 6:15, my cell phone rang.

"Sorry, I've been tied up. Welcome back," he said.

"Not much of a welcome home party," I responded.

"You've only been gone a day. Meet you at Angelo's at 7:30. I'll buy you a glass of wine."

"That's all? No dinner?"

"Not sure if I can afford it. I might need to set up a legal fund."

"In that case, I'll buy. I think I made just enough today to cover the cost. See you there."

Although we were only going to Angelo's, which was practically an extension of my dining room, I changed into some of the new clothes I'd recently bought. When I saw myself in the mirror, I decided that they actually went quite nicely with the Mary Tully scarf.

Angelo's wasn't crowded, and Dave was already at the bar. As usual, Angelo was putting away glasses from the dishwasher. When he saw me, he came out and gave me a hug. Then he held me at arm's length and said, "Welcome home." I saw Dave and Angelo exchange smirks.

"Nice touch," I said to Dave, after he gave me a kiss on the cheek.

The glass of wine was already poured, and I clinked it against his beer glass. "Here's to tomorrow."

"Tomorrow?"

"When I was a kid, I loved the movie 'Annie', especially the part where she sings that song. She was always full of hope that the next day was going to the best ever."

"In that case, here's to tomorrow," Dave said.

We talked about my workshop, my newest friend Lise, and The Black Donnellys.

"You can't escape this Irish thing, can you? They're everywhere, it seems," Dave said, although I wasn't sure whether he was being sarcastic or not.

"Where are your relatives from?" I asked.

"They're Ukrainian and Polish on one side, as far as I know, and English on the other. Oh, and with some Lebanese thrown in for good luck. Somewhere we have a family tree, and I can't pronounce half the last names on it."

"Have you heard from your father lately?" I asked.

"Yeah, I talked to him the other day. He's okay, or at least he tells me he is. I may go and see him soon. I'm feeling guilty."

"Why don't you invite him to come for Christmas? It's only a couple of months away."

Dave's mother left his dad about three years ago for another man. It destroyed him, according to Dave, and he still wasn't over it. Chances were he never would. Dave had a big argument with his mom over it, and relations between them had been badly strained ever since.

"I'll think about it," Dave said. "It might actually be a good idea."

Quick thinker, my Dave.

We finished our drinks, and Angelo seated us at our usual table.

Giorgio was our server. He was one of the brightest men I knew. He spoke a variety of languages, had a degree in psychology, and could remember the most minute details of conversations that he'd overheard.

"Would you like the papardelle again this evening?" he asked me.

"As a matter of fact, I think I would, Giorgio." Then, as an afterthought and as if to prove my point, I asked him, "Do you know of The Black Donnellys?"

"The Irish family that was murdered by vigilantes?" he replied, without so much as batting an eyelash.

"That's the one," I said, trying not to look surprised.

"I saw the play," he replied in an even tone.

"There was a play?"

"Yes, at the Tarragon."

Like I said, he was one of the brightest men I knew. Sorry, Dave.

He took Dave's order, and after he left, I wondered out loud as to who needed Google with Giorgio around?

Dave smiled politely, humouring me.

"So, tell me about your day," I said, taking the hint.

He took a deep breath. I took that to mean that we were in for a long evening.

"Here's the thing," Dave said quietly. "I've been doing a lot of thinking about the drug bust. Because Schulz had been hounding me, I figured that there must be a reason. Same with the other two guys. They were all pumping me for information."

Giorgio arrived to pour us each another glass of wine and then left without a word. He was such a good server that he instinctively knew when to interrupt and when to become invisible.

"I had a long chat with a friend of mine today," Dave resumed once Giorgio was gone. "He's a well-respected lawyer. I think I might have mentioned him before, his name is Peter Brennan. He's a really good guy. Does a lot of police work. Peter and I go way back, and he owes me some favours. So we spent most of the day together, going over my situation. If I ever had to get a lawyer, I would only want him defending me."

Silently I felt reassured. At least my man had a good lawyer. So why wasn't I dancing for joy?

Dave continued, "I laid out the whole thing for Brennan to see if he could spot any holes and weaknesses in my case. And let me tell you, if there were any, he'd spot them. He was cross-examining me the way he would if we were in a real courtroom. In the end, he couldn't see where they'd have any legitimate reason to charge me with anything."

"Well, that's comforting." I said, letting out a sigh.

"Yeah, but that doesn't mean it's over. What worries me is that there's something else. Something I can't quite put my finger on, and until I figure out what it is, I can't rest."

"Let's hope you remember." I said, reaching over to hold his hand. "I know you will."

That was as far as my public display of affection went. What I really wanted to do was get up and give him a big hug, just to let him know that I was standing behind him, all the way.

Last night's conversation with Lise came to mind. The part about children. I wondered if I should bring up the topic. Not that I'd made up my mind, but I wouldn't have minded talking about it. Sometimes I needed to articulate things for them to become real, and Dave was someone I wanted to explore it with.

My family-planning discussion was rudely interrupted before it even got started by the arrival of the papardelle. Dave was digging into his cannelloni, and I decided that the time wasn't right for this kind of conversation. Dave had enough on his plate, not to mention the fact that we were both unemployed.

Besides, the thought of having kids scared me. I didn't know why. I came from a happy family, I made a good aunt or so my brother had told me, and I adored my niece and nephew. Maybe it was the responsibility that I was afraid of. Or maybe I'd just never met a man I wanted to have children with. Martin, my almost-husband, had made it clear that he never wanted kids. They cramped his style. At the time, it hadn't seemed to be an issue; in fact, the idea of not being tied down by children had appealed to me. Lately, though, I kept seeing Marisa Tomei stomping her feet in 'My Cousin Vinny' as she railed about her biological clock ticking. So between Lise, Walter and Marisa, I was beginning to feel the pressure.

As usual, Dave came back to my place for the night. We had a nightcap before heading to bed, and the topic was on the tip of my tongue. Yet I couldn't bring myself to raise it. The timing didn't seem to be right again.

I went to sleep wondering when exactly would the right time be?

CHAPTER 31

Do not mistake a goat's beard for a fine stallion tail.
- Irish proverb

Later in the week, I heard back from Rory.

Dear Aurora, I am finally able to see daylight again, and the Irish sky is as blue as ever. I'm happy to report that the Flanagan family wasn't that hard to track down. In fact, it was a welcome diversion. Belfast has excellent municipal records, as does the local paper. I found an article in The Belfast Daily about the death of Fergus Flanagan that was published two weeks after his death. He came from a well-to-do family in Belfast, but must have been somewhat of a black sheep. He joined the British military at a young age, but was imprisoned for unspecified crimes, and then was recruited as a Black and Tan (as so many were). He served for four years until he was dishonourably discharged for excessive violence. He returned home, got married and had children, and worked in the Belfast shipyards. There he was known to boast of his deeds as a Black and Tan. One night he had a confrontation with a suspected IRA member, and a fight broke out. Flanagan was taken to hospital, but released within a short time. The other man, whose identity is unknown, suffered severe stab wounds. A week later, Flanagan was found dead in an alley. He had been brutally beaten. The IRA claimed responsibility and said that it was an act of retribution for the execution of Richard Mahoney in Castleconnell by Fergus Flanagan many years earlier. As of the time of the article, no arrests had been made. I did a little more digging and found that Flanagan's children, a daughter and two sons, still lived in Belfast. Curiously enough, I also came across an article from 1970 that reported the drowning of a young man also named Fergus Flanagan, but I'm not sure if he is of the same family. I hope this is the kind of information you're looking for. Are you still coming to Ireland? Give me lots of notice, and I will come and meet you wherever. Cheers, Rory

P.S. While walking along the waterfront the other day, I saw this plaque on the side of a wall. I thought of you and your great-grandfather, so I took a picture of it that I am attaching. The Black and Tans were a terrible lot.

The attached image showed a plaque on the side of a building that was inscribed in both Irish and English: IN MEMORY OF MICHAEL WALSH WHO WAS MURDERED BY THE BLACK AND TANS ON THE 19TH OF OCTOBER 1920. R.I.P.

Underneath it, Rory had typed in one last comment. *Busy lot, those bastards!*

I pondered the e-mail. Was Sean Weeks the other man mentioned in the newspaper article as the one who had been injured in the fight? And why was nothing more ever heard from him by his family? Was it Sean who had murdered Flanagan? And had Sean himself suffered the same fate as Flanagan? It had been nearly ninety years since my great-grandfather had been executed by the British, and seventy-three years since the IRA had avenged his death. I was left wondering how much had changed since then. The shooting had stopped in Ireland. The IRA had turned in their weapons, so they said. And their former commanders had become peaceful politicians, so they said. Yet it was still a divided country. And there was still a big gap between the Protestants and the Catholics, and the Unionists and the Republicans.

I decided to follow up on her e-mail right away.

Dear Rory -- Many thanks for your e-mail. Hope it didn't put you to too much trouble. Fascinating reading about Fergus Flanagan being involved in a fight a week before his death. The fight might have been with my great-uncle, Sean Mahoney, who had vowed to find the Black and Tan who had killed his father. No one in the family seems to know what happened to Sean, other than that he joined the IRA in his quest for revenge. I hope he didn't meet the same fate as Flanagan. Tell me something - in your current election, one of the candidates running for the Presidency of the Republic is a former IRA commander. How is that viewed? Would the general population be comfortable with someone like that in power? And if he won, would you support his 'republican' platform? We didn't talk politics when you were in Toronto, and I hope you don't mind my asking such a question. I'm sure your views are as relevant as anything I've read here. I haven't heard yet when I'm coming, I think it's scheduled for next week.

CHAPTER 32

A wild goose never reared a tame gosling.
                                        - Irish proverb

Malcolm arranged a meeting for me with Rob Cohn, the producer of the documentary. The working title was "Hawks to Doves", and it would document the lives of five men who'd started out as terrorists and ended up as peacekeepers. O'Neil was one of the five. I looked at the list of names of the other men.

"Hmm. There are no women on this list," I said, to no one in particular.

Cohn gave me a curious look. "Can you think of one?"

"No, I guess we don't go around killing innocent people."

Cohn just shrugged. I think he had more important things on his mind than to get into a debate on it. To be sure, history had its share of dragon ladies, but they were in the minority. Besides, we women were much more subtle. We would get the men to do all the dirty work. Point for us.

"O'Neil is very sensitive about his IRA past, especially right now with the election going on," Cohn said, cleaning his glasses and then holding them back up to the light. "He knows the nature of the documentary and, surprisingly, he still consented to the interview. But I suspect he'll want to focus more on the future than his past. Probe as much as you can about his goals and ambitions if he wins. The interview is scheduled to take place in Dublin, but there is a strong possibility that it may be in Belfast instead. I've contacted a freelance producer in Belfast who is setting it all up for you. She used to be a journalist as well .... might still be, for all I know. She's well-respected and can open a lot of doors for you. Her name is Meredith McCaughan."

"Not that I don't want to go, Rob, but why don't you use her? I mean, wouldn't it make sense to use someone locally?"

"It might. But our viewers will know you; they don't know Meredith. Besides, O'Neil will play up to you more. His party needs the financial support they get from this side of the ocean. He'll figure the publicity for him and for the party will be good." He took his glasses off again and started to wipe them with a tissue. The cleanliness of his glasses was of

110

obvious concern. When he was finally satisfied, he put them on and looked at me as if I had just materialized out of nowhere. "Here's a list of issues for you to probe with him," he said, handing me a sheet of paper.

I looked through the list. It was all standard stuff.

"When do I leave?" I asked.

"The interview has been arranged for November 1st, which is a week before the election. You should probably allow a day for travelling there and a day to get set up with Meredith. Working backwards, that means you should leave in about five days."

"Would you mind if I leave a couple of days early? I wouldn't mind taking a little side-trip. I have distant relatives there. Naturally, I'll be happy to pay for any personal expenses."

"No problem. Call the travel department and make whatever arrangements you need. Here is McCaughan's contact information. You can make your own arrangements with her." He handed me a slip of paper, and I looked at the name. Good thing he'd pronounced Meredith's last name for me; I wouldn't have the slightest clue.

After making arrangements with the travel department, I sent an e-mail to Rory detailing my travel plans. I'd be arriving Dublin Saturday morning, and would have two free days until the interview, which was currently scheduled for Tuesday morning. In the back of my mind, I hoped to have enough time to visit Castleconnell and see the Shannon View Hotel. I also sent an e-mail to Meredith, introducing myself and giving her my arrival date. On the home front, I think Dave was happy to see me go. With everything going on in his world, he felt that he was falling behind in his studies. The bar exam was looming large in his mind, and I think he was becoming tired of being a student. Who could blame him? When you're 42, you want to get on with your life, I imagine.

We had a good-bye dinner at Angelo's and talked about many things. And, as I had before, I wondered if it was a good time to talk about children. In fact, it did seem like a good time, if there ever was one, and yet something held me back. Maybe I was afraid of the answer.

What if he said 'yes'?

CHAPTER 33

It's no use carrying an umbrella
if your shoes are leaking.
- Irish proverb

The flight to Dublin was not relaxing. The airline chosen for me by the travel department was a tour operator that jetted snow birds to Florida and tourists to Europe. They were not known for luxury. The seats were close together, and the food was nothing to write home about. I felt like a sardine in a can. I brought along a book on the history of Ireland, and my iPhone had several new music albums that I'd downloaded but not listened to. Before the plane took off, I quickly checked my e-mails and was disappointed that I still had not heard back from Rory. Meredith had already replied several days ago, and we'd arranged to meet for dinner on Monday night.

Fortunately the airline had one redeeming feature, and that was free wine, if and when you could get the steward's attention. After a couple of glasses of red wine, I took some melatonin and opened the history book. The combination of all three of those was enough to lull me into a decent sleep.

I'd learned long ago that if you want to enjoy flying, don't have luggage to check. Aside from the fact that you have to stand in long lines to check it in, you then have to wait interminably to retrieve it.

As I waited my turn to go through Customs at the Dublin airport, I couldn't help but think of my trip to New York after my identity had been stolen. At the time, I was gripped with fear that I'd be arrested again at the border. Now, as I stood in line at Irish Customs, the same thoughts went through my mind. *What if they still have the wrong information in their system? What if I'm turned back?* Or, worse still, *What if I'm arrested again?* I'd read of people who spent years getting their identity back.

"Top of the morning to you," said the ruddy-faced Custom's agent. He put my passport through a scanner, and I held my breath. "How long will you be staying with us?"

"Four days," I answered, in what I thought was a confident voice.

"Welcome home," he said with a smile, handing my passport back. I almost asked how he knew I was of Irish origin, but I quickly figured it must have been Mary Tully's scarf that gave me away.

In the arrivals area, I looked around carefully, just on the off-chance that Rory had decided to meet me. I even loitered a bit, but there was no sign of her. I finally went out to find the taxi stand.

Before this trip, I'd purchased a European roaming plan for my iPhone. I'd grown attached to my phone, and being without it made me antsy. There was a name for this obsession, but I didn't care. As I stood in the taxi line, I checked my e-mail, but still nothing from Rory.

I'd travelled enough not to have high expectations when it came to finding a comfortable taxi to ride in. This time I was pleasantly surprised. The taxi was a large spacious black cab, like the ones in London. The driver, whose name was Paul Brogan, was as Irish as they came. When he heard that it was my first time in Ireland, he took it upon himself to point out all the landmarks as we drove into the city. There was only one problem. His accent was so thick that I probably only understood half of what he said.

I hadn't realized that they drove on the left side of the road in Ireland. I thought that England was the only European hold-out in that department. I was glad I hadn't rented a car. I didn't think I could have both navigated the narrow streets and concentrated on keeping on the left side of the road at the same time.

Sometimes I'd heard people say that they didn't like big cities and all that came with them: traffic, noise, pollution, and big buildings. Yet I loved the cities as much as the country. I hadn't been to a city yet that I didn't find vibrant and challenging. Even Toronto was starting to feel like that to me. And so it was with Dublin.

My first impression, looking out of the taxi window, was that of traffic chaos, with double-decker buses hurtling in every direction on mostly narrow streets. The sidewalks were crowded with pedestrians, and there was noise everywhere, the big city noise of cars honking. But beyond that, it certainly had no shortage of charm and vitality. As we drove down O'Connell Street, I couldn't help but think I was in the belly of the Celtic Tiger. And from all appearances, the tiger was very much alive.

Originally, the travel department had booked me into the Dublin Hilton so that I would get the corporate rate. I'd objected and asked for something more local than an international chain, and in an exasperated voice, the woman I dealt with relented and booked me into hotel called The Fitzwilliam. It was located across the street from St. Stephen's Green, which the taxi driver proclaimed to be the most beautiful park in Dublin. I told him that I could use a walk and that as soon as I checked in, I would go for a stroll.

The name of the hotel clerk who checked me in was Niamh Callan, an overly cheery young woman with a delightful smile. I asked how to pronounce her name and she said "Neeve", delighted that I took the trouble to ask. Her name tag said she was from Galway. Along with my room keys, she handed me a tourist map on which she drew circles around the most popular tourist attractions. Then she wished me a pleasant stay, as if I was the most important person in the world.

Often when you check into a hotel in the morning, the rooms aren't ready yet. Luck was with me, though, and by 9:30 a.m., I was settled into my room. It was bright, with a bed big enough for three and a television the size of a small theatre. Best of all, though, was the view of St. Stephen's Green. It really was a sea of green.

Despite the fact that my body clock said it was the middle of the night, I was anxious to go out and explore Dublin. There was another city guide on my night table, and I flipped through it. Then, after a quick shower and a change of clothes, I was ready to tackle the city. It was a chilly, grey day, and I made sure to dress warmly.

Before leaving, I dug Rory's contact information out of my purse and called the number she had given me. After several rings, a computerized voice said, "The voice mail box you have reached is full." I idly wondered why the computer didn't have an Irish accent.

I grabbed my purse and sunglasses, wrapped my Irish scarf around my neck, and with city walking guide in hand, I eagerly set out.

As I walked away from the hotel, I began to wonder if I shouldn't take a bus tour instead. Quickly turning to ask the doorman where I might find one, I walked squarely into an older man, scattering my maps on the sidewalk. He, on the other hand, was unmoved, such was his build.

I hastily retrieved my papers, all the while apologizing. The man was in his late fifties, with thick red hair billowing out from beneath his cap. His face had very ruddy complexion, the kind you see on men who spend a lot of time sailing. He was tall and had a pointed nose that jutted out from his face. In fact, it didn't make you want to stand very close to him for fear of being punctured. He wore a tweed jacket with a long scarf loosely draped over his shoulder, and he carried a cane. I apologized profusely, as Canadians are wont to do.

"Judging from your accent, you must be Canadian," he said with a smile. "I lived in Ottawa for several years, working at the Irish Embassy. My name is Patrick Moore. This your first time in Dublin?" he asked, with an accent that was even stronger than that of the cab driver. It took a great deal of concentration to understand what he was saying.

114

I shook his outstretched hand. "Nice to meet you, Mr. Moore. I'm Aurora Weeks, and yes, I am Canadian. I'm originally from Ottawa, but I now live in Toronto. And judging by your accent, I take it that you're Irish." And then, like a good Canadian, I apologized again.

"No harm done, I assure you. I take it you are going sightseeing," he said, pointing at my tourist map.

"Yes, I just arrived. I thought I'd walk around the city a bit."

"Well, I just dropped my wife off on Grafton Street to do some shopping, and I am going for a walk. I'm not much of a shopper, and Mary prefers it if I'm not with her. If you'd like, you can walk with me and I'll be more than happy to point out some things of interest. And please, call me Patrick."

"I'd like that. I'd like that a lot." I put away my tourist map and put myself into the hands of Mr. Patrick Moore.

"Let's start off with Stephen's Green, shall we?" he said, and turned on his heels and off we went, his nose pointing the way.

CHAPTER 34

The Irish forgive their great men
when they are safely buried.
                    - Irish saying

"I'm a bit of a history buff on Dublin, I'm afraid," Patrick said as we walked along. His pace was brisk; I was glad I had my trainers on. "Mary says I go on too much, and I try not to get carried away, but this city is so rich in history that it's hard to stop. Do you know Dublin was originally settled by the Vikings? And, at various times, was invaded by the Normans, the English, the Danes, and Lady Gaga?" I think he threw the last name in just to make sure I was listening.

We crossed the street and walked through an ornate arch into the Park, which according to Patrick was laid out in 1663. We stopped at a statue reclining on a large rock. I didn't need to be told it was Oscar Wilde. Patrick gave me a quick outline of Wilde's life in Dublin as we walked along the treed pathways. I told Patrick that Oscar Wilde was one of my favourite writers to quote.

"What's your favourite quote then?" he asked, not slowing down.

"'The truth is rarely pure and never simple,'" I replied.

"Mine is 'Always forgive your enemies. It annoys them so much.'"

We exited the park and crossed the road to Kildare Street. Patrick pointed out the famous Georgian houses and their doors of different colours. Within a short distance, we came to a number of old buildings, the most notable of which was Leinster House, the seat of Parliament. Then we crossed another major street and passed through one of the entrances of the famed Trinity College. Patrick pointed out the various buildings and told me when they were constructed and who the architect was. Although the College was now in the heart of the city, when the land was donated to establish the college, it had been out in the country.

We stopped in front of a statue beside the bell tower. "This is George Salmon," he explained. "He was an important man in his time, the Dean of the School for some years. What is of interest is that he was opposed to women being accepted as students in the school. Eventually, he was overruled, and much to his chagrin, he had to sign the by-law granting women to right to study here. And now the female students outnumber the males. Poor George. I'm sure he's turning over in his grave."

"I'm surprised that his statue has such a prominent place on campus," I mused.

"No secret there. He donated a large amount of money to the College with the proviso that his statue be in a conspicuous place," replied Patrick, as he turned on his heels and walked towards one of the exits. We came out across from the Bank of Ireland. "This," he said proudly, arms outstretched to encompass all the buildings, "was the first purpose-built parliament in Europe." And, as if the emphasize the point, he added, proudly: "In all of Europe." Then his voice dropped an octave. "Didn't last long, I'm afraid. The English imposed direct rule in 1801, and that was the end of that." I gathered from the tone of his voice that this was still a sore point, some two hundred years later. The sidewalk was narrow and crowded, but Patrick plowed on, with me struggling to keep up. The way Patrick parted the crowds was like the parting of the Dead Sea.

"Now we will be going over O'Connell Bridge," he said as we waited for a traffic light to change. "It is the only bridge in Europe that's as wide as it is long," he added with a touch of amusement. The light changed in our favour and off we went, walking across the bridge. Patrick stopped in the middle of it so that I could see the River Liffey, while he pointed out the various bridges and important buildings.

O'Connell Street was a wide boulevard as grand as any found in Paris or Berlin. Patrick stopped at a large monument of Daniel O'Connell, the Irish politician who had campaigned in the first half of the 1800's for Catholic Emancipation, as we entered the street, and he pointed out the glove on one hand. "Wore that glove all his life," he said, but the roar of a passing bus drowned out the rest of the explanation. We proceeded to the famed The General Post Office, scene of the Easter Uprising.

"Here, on Easter Monday, 1916, Republican forces stormed the building and issued the Proclamation of the Irish Republic," Patrick said with his deep baritone voice. "After a week of shelling by British forces, the building lay in ruins and the rebels were captured. Thirteen of them were executed, including the leaders. Ultimately the building was restored, and it became a working post office." I noticed that several people had stopped to listen to him. Perhaps they thought he was a tour guide. "And over there," he said, pointing to the middle of the intersection, "stood the Nelson monument. It was blown up by the IRA on the fiftieth anniversary of the uprising." He let the words sink in for a moment, and then he said "And now we have The Spire in its place. It

117

rises 395 feet and can be seen from any vantage point in the city. And does it have a function? No. Bloody waste of money if you ask me." A lady beside me gasped, and Patrick gave her a hard look. Our little group of two had grown to about five or six.

Patrick checked his watch. "Still up for a bit more of a walk?" he asked, although I knew it was a rhetorical question.

We turned down Henry Street, one of several pedestrian streets in the city. There was nothing of architectural interest to slow Patrick down, and before long we came back out to the banks of the Liffey at the Ha-penny Pedestrian Bridge. Patrick explained how it used to cost a ha-penny to cross the bridge. Now, of course, it was free and well-used. The ornate wrought-iron railing that lined it on both sides was festooned with locks of all kind left behind by lovers as an expression of their eternal love.

At the other side of the river, we crossed into the Temple Bar quarter. We walked up narrow, cobblestone streets lined with pubs and a variety of small boutiques. The streets were almost deserted at this early hour, but, according to Patrick, at night it was wall-to- wall people. As we walked along, Patrick gave me a history of the area. Once derelict and ready to be torn down, the boom of the Celtic Tiger had given the area new life and it was now one of the most vibrant parts of the city. If this was Toronto, I reflected, the area would be overrun with condos.

We exited on Dame Street, where the sidewalks were narrow and crowded. Within a short time, Patrick led me up a side street, past O'Neil's pub, and finally stopping at a large statue of Molly Malone just across from Trinity College. Tourists were gathered around, having their pictures taken beside the statue of the tragic fishmonger, who had been immortalized in the famous song "Cockles and Mussels". One older man, an obvious tourist, put one hand on Molly's breasts and asked his wife to take a picture. She refused. Patrick harrumphed at the vulgarity, and we set off again. "Not long now," he said, as we entered Grafton Street, the main pedestrian-only shopping street. "If you fancy a bit of shopping, this is the place," he said, waving his hand down the street. "And that is the end of the tour for today. Mary is meeting me in a restaurant just along the way. Will you join us for lunch?"

"Oh, but I don't want to impose," I said, guessing that Mr. Patrick Moore wasn't the kind of man to take no for an answer.

"Nonsense," he replied. "Come with me."

We strolled down the middle of the street at a more leisurely pace, and he stopped in front of Bewley's Oriental Cafe.

Patrick checked his watch. "Right on time," he said, more to himself than me. Then he opened the front door and beckoned me to enter. The maitre d' greeted him by name, and took our coats, and Patrick led me to a table near the rear that was occupied by a woman probably the same age as Patrick. She looked up as we approached, and he leaned over and kissed her on the cheek.

"Mary, meet Aurora, our Canadian guest. She comes from Ottawa."

Mary stood up and shook my hand. "Nice to meet you. Let me guess, Patrick's been giving you a guided tour of Dublin," she said with a smile. "I hope you didn't find him too overbearing."

"Quite the contrary, Mary. It was very educational. And a good work-out as well," I said as we sat down. It felt good to sit and just relax for a while. I didn't know how long we'd walked together, probably the better part of two hours, but I wished I'd had my step counter on. Oh, the calories I must have burned.

"That's a lovely scarf you have," Mary said, reaching out to feel it. "Did you buy it here?"

"No, I bought it at an Irish shop in Toronto. It was made by Mary Tully in County Mayo, so I'm told."

"Well, it's really lovely. I love hand-knitted goods."

Patrick picked up a menu and opened it. He reminded me of a minister, about to give a sermon. "Mary and I usually just order a variety of appetizers. They're very good here. Shall I just add in some extra for you?" he asked, although I could tell it was another rhetorical question.

A server appeared, and Patrick ordered a Guinness. Mary was sipping tea, and I was tempted to order a glass of wine until I realized that according to my body clock, it was still early morning, and so I ordered a club soda instead.

"Now then, Aurora, what brings you to Dublin? How very rude of me not even to have asked you that question before," Patrick said, polishing his glasses with a serviette.

"I'm a journalist, and I'm on assignment to do an interview. I came a few days early so that I could spend a bit of time seeing the rest of the country while I'm here. I have Irish roots, but have never really explored them."

"Who are you interviewing?" Patrick asked with some interest.

"Michael O'Neil, the politician," I said. "I assume you know him?"

Patrick and Mary exchanged glances.

"Oh, indeed we do," Patrick replied. "Are you familiar with Irish politics?"

Mary leaned close to him, touched his arm with her hand, and said in a stern yet gentle voice, "Now Patrick, don't get carried away." She turned and looked at me. "He loves politics and I warn you, you might be here a few hours."

"I think I understand the basic structure. I come from a political family, so politics runs in my blood."

"Wait a minute," Patrick said, looking at me alertly. "Are you related to John Waverly Weeks?"

"I'm his daughter. How do you know him?"

"Remember I mentioned that I worked at the Irish Embassy? I dealt with your father when I was arranging a trade mission trip for some Canadian politicians. I remember him quite well. What a pleasure it is to meet you, and what a small world. Is he still in politics?"

"No, he's retired, as is my mother, and they spend most of his time travelling, or so it seems."

"I retired too, not long ago as a matter of fact. Thirty-five years of political service was enough. Right, Mary?"

Mary nodded and then said to me, "He's been driving me crazy at home, but I'm glad for his sake. The stress was too great. He's not a young man any more. But since his retirement, I swear he looks younger every year."

"I'm sure it's the brisk walking," I said, with a laugh.

"What's your interest in O'Neil?" Patrick asked.

"It's for a documentary about men who have exchanged guns for olive branches."

"Well, you've certainly picked a good subject. Although if O'Neil handed me an olive branch, I'd handle it very gently. Are you doing Gerry Adams as well?"

"No, we're not. I did hear Adams speak in Toronto not long ago. My boyfriend came with me, and at the end of the speech, I asked him what he thought of Adams. He said that he shouldn't be let near a microphone or own a gun."

Both Patrick and Mary burst out laughing.

"How very true," Patrick agreed. "He is not a man to be trusted. He only has one agenda, and that's to unite Ireland and kick the British out, using whatever means necessary. And if you know anything about Irish politics, that is not the easiest thing to do."

Our appetizers arrived, and we dug in. Patrick spent the next twenty minutes giving me a rundown of the political scene, much in the same way he gave me the walking tour. Finally, Mary tapped him on his arm, and asked "I think you should give Aurora time to breathe, for heaven's sake." She turned to me. "You said you had Irish roots. Where were your ancestors from?"

"Kilkenny," I said, and then I told them the story of my great-grandfather. When I finished, Patrick nodded gravely and said, "I can see the Black and Tans doing that. They were ruthless bastards. There are many stories like that. The British were never kind to the Irish, to put it mildly."

Mary looked at her watch and said to Patrick, "We must be off. We promised to pick up Simon from his soccer game."

Patrick signaled for the bill, which arrived promptly. I offered to pay for my share, but they wouldn't hear of it. He pulled a card out of his wallet and handed it to me. "If you ever need another walking tour of Dublin or want to talk politics, don't hesitate to call me," he said with a smile. "And when you see your father, give him my regards. He many not remember me, though."

"My father never forgets anyone," I said. "That's what made him a great politician."

We made our way outside. Mary gave me hug and told me how glad she was that Patrick had invited me to lunch with them, and that she hoped that he hadn't been too "over the top", as she put it. "Take good care of that scarf," she said with a smile.

Patrick, being a consummate politician himself, clasped both of my hands in his and wished me well with O'Neil. Then the two of them set off down Grafton Street. Patrick walked at least three paces ahead of Mary, who made no effort at all to keep up with him. Marital harmony at its finest, I thought.

I sat down on a nearby bench to collect my thoughts. Rory was uppermost in my mind. The fact that she hadn't left a message and was unreachable bothered me. I called my hotel to see if there were any messages for me, but struck out. Then I called her home number again. Much to my relief, it was answered on the second ring by a man.

"May I speak with Aurora?" I asked hopefully.

"I'm afraid not. Who's calling please?"

"My name is Aurora .... " I was about to explain when the man cut in.

"From Canada? Rory has told me about you. She said you were coming to visit. I'm Neil, her brother."

"Will she be home soon?"

"I take it you haven't heard?"

"Heard what?"

"She's in the hospital. In a coma."

CHAPTER 35

When the sky falls, we'll all catch larks.
                                        -Irish proverb

"In a coma? What happened?" I asked anxiously.

"She fell down a long set of stairs at the reference library. One of the staff discovered her lying in a pool of blood at the bottom of the stairs, unconscious."

"How long ago did this happen?"

"Thursday of this week."

"What's the prognosis?"

"She suffered a severe concussion. There may be some brain damage, but the doctors don't really know yet. They've done x-rays, but they have to wait till she comes out of the coma to assess how functional she is ."

"Where is she? Can I come and see her?"

"She's in Dublin, at the St. James hospital. I was with her this morning and had to come back to her house in Galway to make sure everything was all right. She has a couple of cats here. A neighbour's been in to see them, but I wanted to make sure they were all right. Rory is very attached to them. I also wanted to get her some clothes for when she wakes up. I'll be there again in the morning. I'm usually there every morning. My sister Catherine will be with her later in the day. She usually comes after work."

"I'll go over there right now."

"Word of warning. The IC unit is pretty strict about visiting. You'll have to convince them that you're close family."

"Thanks. With a name like Aurora Weeks, I can't imagine I'll have any trouble."

"Good luck. See you tomorrow. Oh, by the way, where are you staying, in case I need to reach you?"

I gave him the hotel information and my cell phone number, and he hung up. The bench I was sitting on suddenly felt cold. Or was it the shock of what I'd just heard? After a moment of reflecting how a person's life can change in a heartbeat, I headed away from Grafton Street in search of a taxi.

It was a short taxi ride to St. James Hospital. The driver made little conversation, and I checked my e-mails on the way. Meredith had written to say that the interview was now scheduled for Belfast, on Tuesday morning. She suggested that I come up by bus on Monday, and that she would meet me for dinner.

St. James was a large hospital with several wings. Fortunately, they had an excellent signage system. I stopped at the nursing station of the IC unit, and an older nurse asked me who I wanted to see.

"Aurora Weeks," I said confidently, feeling like I was playing some kind of prank.

She looked at me with a blank face. "Are you family?"

"Yes. I'm her cousin. My name is Aurora Weeks, too"

She looked at me skeptically. "Really? How did that happen, then?'

"Cruel trick by our parents," I said, without elaborating.

"But you're not Irish," she said.

"No, I'm not. I'm Canadian, as a matter of fact. But Aurora and I are very close nonetheless."

The nurse asked me to fill in the daily log. Then she directed me to room I-415. It wasn't hard to find, just down the hall from the nurses' station.

It was a large room with a single bed in the middle and a visitor's chair on each side. Despite all the wires and equipment hooked up to the figure lying in the bed, I recognized Rory immediately. She looked very peaceful, as if she was in a deep slumber, which I suppose she was.

I touched her hand and whispered "Hello, Rory", but there was no response. As I looked closer, I saw bruises on her cheeks and arms. Her complexion was pale, a sharp contrast to when I'd last seen her.

The windowsill and bedside dresser was covered in flowers and cards.

What do you do when you visit someone in a coma? It was something I had never experienced before. I sat there, a bit stunned I suppose, trying to act rationally. That didn't last for long - maybe a minute or so. Then I felt my tear ducts open. I felt so sad and helpless for this young woman who I had barely gotten to know, yet with whom I felt so close.

A nurse came in, checked the charts, adjusted the IV drip, made some entries on a chart, and then set it down. "Everything seems to be normal," she said, not addressing me in particular. "Her heartbeat has risen a bit since yesterday; that's a good sign. She'll come around in no time." The nurse left without further explanation.

I didn't know how long I sat there, staring at Rory, watching her chest rise and fall, listening for any audible sound. Horrible thoughts ran through my mind. What if she never came out of the coma? What if they had to put her on life support? What if she stopped breathing? I looked at my watch and found that it was close to four o'clock. My eyes were half closed, and I felt very drowsy. A different nurse came in and asked if I could take a seat in the lounge. They were going to change the sheets. I nodded and patted Rory's hand. "See you later," I said quietly, and then leaned over to give her a gentle kiss on the cheek. In the lounge, I realized that fatigue was setting in. The lack of sleep on the plane and the invigorating walk with Patrick made for a dangerous combination. It was still only late afternoon, and I was determined to stay up as long as I could and try to quickly get my body on Dublin time. I decided to go back to the hotel, have a bite to eat, and then come back to see Rory in the evening. Visiting hours didn't end until nine.

I looked at my map of Dublin and wondered how long it would take me if I walked. 'Stupid idea', I quickly thought, and instead hailed a taxi outside the hospital.

Back at the hotel, I poured myself a glass of wine from the mini-bar in my room and sat on the chesterfield scrolling through the e-mail on my iPhone. I felt myself nodding off to sleep, and closed my eyes for what I thought was a brief moment. When I opened them again, it was dark outside. I looked around the room, confused. I had barely touched the glass of wine, and there was a gnawing in my stomach. It was just past ten in the evening. I thought about calling Dave, but was afraid I'd fall asleep mid-conversation.

I pulled back the covers of the bed, threw off my clothes, and crawled under the duvet. My first day in Ireland was not how I envisioned it would be.

CHAPTER 36

There's no need to fear the wind
if your haystacks are tied down
                    -Irish proverb

It was still dark when I awoke. The clock on the dresser said 4:15 a.m. Too early for anything, so I lay in bed thinking about Rory, my upcoming interview with O'Neil, my walk with Patrick Moore, and the empty feeling in my stomach. I looked at the clock again, counted six hours back, and realized that it would be a perfect time to call Dave. He answered on the first ring.

"Hey, Aurora. Top of the morning to you." How he could sound so chipper at the end of the day was beyond me.

"Hi, Dave. It's not quite morning yet. In fact, it's pitch black outside."

"Black? I thought everything in Ireland is green."

"Funny!" I said, pulling the covers up around me. I then proceeded to tell him about my first day in Dublin. When I was finished, I asked him if he'd had anymore brainwaves about the drug bust.

"No, I haven't, but yesterday I happened to be driving by the building where we made the bust. There was a vacancy sign in one of the windows, so I jotted down the number. I made an appointment to see the apartment tomorrow morning."

"Are you thinking of moving in?" I asked incredulously.

"No, no. I'm just going to pretend to be interested. I want to see the building and a typical unit just to see if it rings any bells."

"Well, be careful."

"No worries there. The building seems to have been gentrified."

We chatted a bit more, and I said I would call him tomorrow to see how he made out.

Now I was awake.

Room service didn't start until six. I checked the online editions of the Toronto newspapers, especially The Star. No further news on the drug investigation. As Mom would say, no news is good news. The grey light of dawn was creeping through the blinds, so I called room service and ordered a full Irish breakfast and did half an hour of pilates while waiting. The food arrived and it smelled wonderful. Bacon, scrambled eggs, sausages, and toast. I looked at it incredulously - I would never have ordered all of this at home. Fortunately the guilt only lasted a few seconds, and I dug in. While devouring the plateful of food, I watched the local news, much of it devoted to the upcoming election. Michael O'Neil had a good chance of becoming president, according to the commentators. Depending on whose poll you believed, he was either going to win or lose by a narrow margin. I'd long since learned not to place any faith in polls, though. Many people never make up their mind until voting day, and there is no way the pollsters can anticipate what goes through the mind of a voter when push comes to shove.

I was happy to say, for the sake of my waistline, that I didn't finish all of my breakfast. I left half a slice of toast and the fat rind from the bacon. And I was also happy to say that I felt much better, and was ready to visit Rory and do a little more sightseeing in Dublin. I called the front desk, made a reservation at The Fitzwilliam in Belfast, checked the weather in Dublin. Rain. Then I checked the forecast in Belfast. More rain.

By 8:30, I'd left the hotel armed with a map of the city and an umbrella, heading in the general direction of the hospital.

The sidewalks were empty, and traffic was light. It was overcast, with darker clouds approaching from the west. The air had a chill to it that made me glad I was wearing a warm jacket and Mary Tully's scarf.

St. Patrick's Cathedral was about halfway to the hospital, and I decided to go and see it on my way there. After getting lost twice, I finally found it, but by that time I was too anxious to see Rory to linger long, so I didn't go inside. From the outside, the cathedral looked magnificent. I wished Patrick Moore was there with me to give me a quick history lesson.

The rest of the walk to the hospital was a bit touch and go. Very few streets followed a straight line, and in the end I went quite a bit out of the way to find the main avenue leading to St. James.

Rory was in the same position as when I'd left her the day before, sleeping peacefully. A sadness overcame me. How could someone look so peaceful and yet be in such a terrible predicament? I pulled up a chair and spoke to her in a low voice, hoping that she could hear me. I told her what the weather was like outside, how I'd met Patrick and Mary Moore yesterday, and what my plans were for the next few days. As I listened to myself, I thought that already I had acquired the gift of gab.

I heard the clicking of footsteps in the hall and a woman entered the room, taking off her coat and dropping it on a nearby chair.

"Hello, luv," she said, bending over Rory to give her a kiss on the cheek. Then she straightened up and turned to me. "I'm Catherine,

127

Aurora's sister. You must be the Canadian I've heard so much about." I stood up and shook her hand. She was slightly taller than Rory, but still shorter than me. Her auburn hair was pulled tightly back into a pony tail. She had a pale complexion that made her blue eyes stand out that much more. I guessed her to be in her early thirties.

"I checked at the nurses' station, and there's been no change," she said. "She's very stable, but that's all they would tell me. No one really knows how long she will be like this. Could be minutes, could be hours, could be days. Terrible, isn't it?" Catherine wiped her eyes. "But we must be strong, right, luv?" she said, taking her sister's hand and kissing it. "Look at the bruises," she continued. "It must have been a terrible fall. And it's not like she's clumsy. I don't know what must have happened. Maybe she just wasn't paying attention and lost her footing. It's a good thing they found her when they did .... otherwise she might have bled to death. She's very lucky to be alive. God was watching over her, to be sure."

I couldn't help but be touched by the sibling concern. My brother Barrie and I were close as kids, but as we grew up, we went our separate ways. I often wondered about that. Was it wrong that we'd drifted apart? Should we be closer emotionally? We were connected, but only by birthday celebrations and parental ties. I sometimes envied large families and their get-togethers. And then I would think that such things were nothing more than a Hollywood scriptwriter's imagination. Yet the Irish were known for their close family relationships. Maybe I wasn't so Irish after all.

"My sister tells me you're a writer and broadcaster. She was very impressed when she met you in Toronto. Couldn't stop talking about you when she came back.   Rory and I are very close. We talk every day. Usually she does all the talking, though sometimes it's hard to get a word in edgewise," she said laughingly. "She was determined to find out what happened to Fergus Flanagan before you came. That's why she was at the library, you know."

"Fergus Flanagan? He died a long time ago. She knew that," I said, somewhat confused.

"Not him, but the younger man with the same name who died in the bombing. She wondered if he was from the same family, so like the good ancestor sleuth that she is ...." she stopped mid-sentence to pat her sister's hand, " .... she did a little more digging. And then she rang me up, all excited. She'd found something out, but she needed to verify it. Didn't tell me what it was. Said she'd ring me again, and then the accident happened. That's one thing about Rory - she doesn't like loose ends. There has to be an explanation for everything. It drives me crazy sometimes, but I suppose that's what makes her so good at what she does."

"You're right," I said. "She did mention finding a newspaper article about another Fergus Flanagan. It's all rather tragic. Did she tell you why I enquired about him?"

"He's the one who murdered your great-grandfather?"

"Supposedly. I don't think it was ever really proven. I hope Rory didn't spend too much time on her search. I feel guilty about it."

"I think she had a hidden motive, to be honest. You see, if we're related somehow, then Richard Mahoney was also related to us, albeit by marriage only, I should think. And that's what really intrigued her."

Our conversation was interrupted by a man entering the room carrying a small satchel. He quickly introduced himself as Neil, the brother I'd spoken with on the telephone. He took off his overcoat, put the satchel beside the dresser, and inspected his sister closely.

It quickly became apparent that Neil was the extreme opposite of his two sisters. He talked very little, chose his words carefully, and probably would not be a candidate for small-talker of the month.

Shortly afterwards, the head nurse came bustling into the room and informed us that this was not a social event and that we still had a very ill patient. She said that at most only two visitors were allowed in the room.

I volunteered to leave, since I had been there the longest. Catherine thanked me profusely for coming and gave me a long hug. "I just know we're related. I can feel it," she said.

Neil, on the other hand, just shook my hand and said that he was glad to meet me. Maybe the Irish gift of gab only ran in the women's side of the Weeks family.

Both siblings were staying for the remainder of the day, but invited me to come back and I promised that I would.

I left the hospital feeling at loose ends and guilty. Had I set the wheels in motion for the events that led Rory to be at the library?

I took a taxi back to the hotel. Instead of going to my room, I went for a long walk in Stephen's Green. A light rain was falling, and in a way it was welcome. It resembled my mood. Halfway through the park, fog rolled in and much of the parkland disappeared. I thought of Rory lying in her own fog, wondering if she was conscious on any level. 'Stay positive,' I heard my inner voice say. 'This is her body's way of healing.' Mom would have a saying too to fit the situation, but none came to mind. I was too confused, too worried, and too upset to even think straight.

As I walked out of the park, I realized that I was nearly drenched and feeling a chill setting in. That's the last thing I needed - to be sick as well.

Back in my room, I hung up my wet clothes and had a long hot bath. That energized me. I wanted to call Dave, but thought he'd still be asleep, so I sent him a long e-mail and then went off in search of lunch in the hotel restaurant.

By three in the afternoon, I was ready to go back to the hospital. The rain had intensified, and the doorman offered me the use of an umbrella. He also called for a taxi to take me to the hospital.

When I arrived back at Rory's room, Neil had stepped out for a few minutes and Catherine was alone with her sister, reading a book. We chatted about Dublin, Canada, our lives, and, of course, Rory. Catherine was easy to talk to, although sometimes, like her sister, she would just go on and on. What was amazing about it, though, was that she wasn't at all boring or overbearing. She went from one subject to another with a transition that you'd never even notice. And all through this, Rory slept peacefully. At one point Catherine giggled loudly, and we both looked at Rory to make sure we weren't disturbing her. "Maybe that's what she needs," Catherine said, "a good giggle. That'll snap her out of it. Oh, before I forget, I was going through Aurora's agenda to see if I needed to cancel any appointments and such, and I found this piece of paper." She handed it to me. On it were two notations. One was 'Cecil Flanagan, The Fiddler's Head, Belfast', while the other was a girl's name, 'Emeline'.

I looked at the piece of paper with Rory's neat but tiny handwriting.

"The Fiddler's Head is a pub in the east side of Belfast that's owned by the Flanagan family," Catherine explained. "Rory went to see him, as far as I know, but I don't know who Emeline is. Maybe that's what she was so excited about."

"Can I keep this?"

"Of course. I'm sure we'll find out soon enough what it all means."

Neil returned and sat on the other side of the bed. He may have been a man of few words, but his concern for his sister was unmistakable. He sat close to her, holding her hand with a hopeful expression on his face as if he was expecting her to wake up at any minute.

Catherine left briefly to stretch her legs by walking around the corridors. When she returned, I told her what my plans were for the next two days and that I would return on Wednesday before heading home.

130

Catherine promised to contact me in the meantime if there was any change in Rory's condition.

The rain had eased by the time I left the hospital, but not enough that I didn't need the umbrella. On the spur of the moment, I took a taxi to St. Patrick's Cathedral with the intention of walking home the remainder of the way.

The Cathedral was immense and almost overpowering. It was the largest church in the country, something that hadn't escaped the attention of Oliver Cromwell's troops, who'd turned the nave into their stable when they occupied it.

A group of tourists were gathered around Jonathan Swift's tomb, and I circumvented them and slid onto one of the pews. Despite the tourists, the cathedral was quiet, and I closed my eyes, leaning back on the smooth wooden seat.

The grandeur and enormity of the church moved me. There was a peace there that I found comforting despite the many tourists walking around. I wondered if Rory had a patron saint and concluded that it would probably be St. Patrick. And so I asked him to help her. It wasn't a prayer as such. I just asked him to guide her safely out of her blackness, back into the world of the living.

CHAPTER 37

Even a tin knocker will shine on a dirty door.
-Irish proverb

I was still waking up early in the morning, or should I say late at night. Today, I was wide awake at three o'clock in the morning. Hopefully my body would start adjusting soon. I didn't like getting up so early with nothing to do. But it was an ideal time to call Dave.

"So did you rent the apartment?" I asked, when he answered.

"No, too small. But it was a worthwhile exercise."

"How so?"

"The unit that was vacant was on a different floor, but I asked the rental agent if all the units had the same layout and he confirmed that they did. He even gave me a print-out of the layout with measurements included. I didn't stay long. The agent was too pushy, and I had a hard time faking interest. Anyway, I saw what I wanted to see. When I got home, I had a close look at the floor plan. And that's when it hit me. Hold on a sec."

Dave put the phone down. In the background, I heard a bottle being opened.

"Sorry," he said, picking the phone up again. "I got myself a beer and needed two hands to open it. Now, where was I?"

"You were at home, looking at the floor plans."

"Okay, here's what I realized. The common wall between each unit is the hallway, and all of the rooms lead off that with the living room at the end. When Schulz came out of the first unit to tell me to get the search warrant, I got a glimpse into the hallway inside. Not long, but enough to see an open door. And it was on the common wall. The thing is, these apartments don't have adjoining doors like you might find in a hotel room. And yet this one did. That's when I realized that the dealer must have installed the door between the units - probably illegally. And when the drug squad went in, they would have seen the door, opened it, and seen the lab. They couldn't legally enter that apartment without the warrant, so that's why Schulz asked me to get one. But after I was gone, there was nothing to stop them from going in and helping themselves to any of the cash or drugs."

"But you didn't see that?"

"Of course not, but they had the opportunity. That's all I'm saying."

"Now what?"

"I haven't figured that out yet. I don't know if this information is really relevant to the investigation. And if it is, they might want to know why I didn't disclose it before."

"But you know why. You didn't think it was important at the time, otherwise you would have made a note of it, right?"

"Right. Anyway, I'll figure it out. I might talk to Brennan and see what he thinks. What's happening with you today?"

I told him I was heading off the Belfast, and he wished me luck. The way he said it made me actually wonder if I needed it. Belfast was peaceful these days.

Hopefully!

CHAPTER 38

An old broom knows the dirty corners best.
-Irish proverb

The bus ride from Dublin to Belfast was a good news/bad news situation. The good news was that it only took two hours; the bad news was that it rained the whole way. The Irish countryside was obliterated by either rain, or fog, or both. I read The Irish Times from cover to cover, flipped through my Fodor's guide to Ireland, and read some O'Neil research reports that I'd brought with me. Finally, we pulled into Great Victoria Station in downtown Belfast. To my delight, my hotel was a mere block away.

I called Meredith McCaughan as soon as I was settled in my room. We had a brief chat about the logistics for tomorrow. Although she had originally suggested going out for dinner, she now had a family problem and asked if we could get together for a drink instead, at around 4 p.m. We arranged to meet at the coffee shop in the Hotel Europa, which was practically next door.

The mental picture I'd had of Meredith based on her voice did not match the real person. She looked more Scandinavian than Irish, especially with her short blond hair. Her fair skin accentuated the bright red lipstick she wore. But most of all, what you immediately noticed about Meredith was her dazzling smile. With beautiful white teeth like that, I'd be smiling all the time too.

"I'm sorry about tonight," she said, taking off her raincoat and draping it over an empty chair at the small table we'd chosen in the coffee shop. "My little one has a terrible cold. Mum's minding her right now, but she can only stay till six."

"How many children do you have?" I asked as we took our seats.

"Two girls. I wouldn't mind another, hopefully a boy. I think Andrew wants a boy that he can teach soccer to. The wee girls aren't showing any interest. Now then, welcome to Belfast. Is this your first time here?" She signaled for the waiter and ordered a white wine spritzer. I ordered one as well.

"It is, and hopefully the rain will stop so that I can actually see it. Have you always lived here?"

"That I have, and sometimes I wonder why, what with all the violence and troubles. But when I really think about it, I realize that it's my home, as dysfunctional as it may seem."

"Tell me about Belfast."

"When the rain stops, you'll see what appears to be a very thriving city. Lots of new development, new buildings, lots of shops. But that's only one side of it. The other side, or underbelly if you will, is still very much a war zone. We still have walls and barricades. Even though we've had years of peace, it doesn't take much for tempers to boil over. Every year there's something." Meredith paused as the waiter came with our drinks. "But what I fear most is the future for my children. Young people can't get jobs. They're all leaving for places like London, New York, or Dubai. And there's no end in sight."

"What about the Troubles? How did they affect Belfast?"

"Ah, the Troubles." She took a deep breath, carefully choosing her words. "The Troubles destroyed the soul of Belfast. I mean, really, who'd want to live here with our legacy of violence and bloodshed? Yet we do, those of us who believe we can rebuild Belfast. But it's going to be a long, uphill road. We've had a few years of shaky peace, long enough to make Northern Ireland seem normal and give us all a bit of self-confidence. But sometimes it seems as if we're walking on eggshells, and that at any moment one of the shells will break. Then it will start all over again. It's happened before. Antrim for example."

"How does O'Neil fit into all of this?"

Meredith looked at her watch and then picked up her wineglass. "We could be here all night answering that question," she replied with a good-natured laugh. "Don't worry, I'll give you the short answer. Mum would kill me if I was late. O'Neil has reinvented himself as a peacemaker. That's supposed to negate his career as an IRA terrorist. The Brits are happy, the Republicans are happy, and the Unionists are depicted as Sinn Fein's bedmates. To an outsider it must sound absurd," she said, shaking her head.

"Why are the Brits happy?"

"Because they want to believe that Ulster has finally come to its senses. We're not playing with guns anymore, and all the horrible and messy problems that caused so much terror in Britain have now been cleverly contained. The Brits would like nothing more than to be rid of us and give Northern Ireland political legitimacy. And they see O'Neil as a man who can do that."

"What about you? Do you think he can?"

Meredith drained her wineglass and set it down gently. "I have two young children, and I want them to grow up in a country of peace, not bloodshed. O'Neil has helped to bring us that peace, fragile as it may seem at times. But, and this is a big but, it's one thing to be the leader in Northern Ireland; it's another to be the figurehead of the Irish Republic. O'Neil is a product of the North. We need him here in Belfast, and I wouldn't want to see him abandon us now. If he does, our delicate peace may be at risk." She leaned over, picked up her purse from the floor, and extracted her wallet. From one of the pockets, she pulled out a picture of two children and handed it to me. "This is why the peace is so precious to me. I don't ever want them to know violence and bloodshed."

I looked at the picture of the two young girls, both of whom bore an uncanny resemblance to Meredith. Neither of the girls had blond hair, but they had the same eyes. As I looked at the picture, I noticed Meredith wiping away a tear.

"I'm sorry. I get very emotional when I think of my children and politics." She pulled a tissue out of her purse and blew her nose. "Now then, about tomorrow. A word of caution. At the best of times, O'Neil doesn't like to be confronted with his IRA past. Especially now with the election so close. Any time the subject is brought up, he deflects the question and then either shuts down the interview or totally changes the subject. He feels that his military past is a non-issue at this point, so tread very carefully."

"Thank you, I'll keep that in mind."

She pulled a large envelope out of her briefcase and handed it to me. "I printed out some of O'Neil's speeches that we had on file. You might find them interesting background material." She stood up, walked over to the window, and looked out before returning with a smile on her face. "The rain has stopped. You might be able to see something of this fair city after all. I'll see you at the studio at 9:30. O'Neil has a press conference in the same room, and our interview will follow that. Allow yourself fifteen minutes of walking time from here, unless you're taking a taxi, in which case allow yourself thirty minutes." We both laughed, and she added, "Once a mother, always a mother."

She opened her wallet and extracted some Euros. I stopped her and said that it was on me.

"All right then, thank you," she said with a smile. "I feel badly about not being able to spend more time with you. Maybe tomorrow, after the interview."

"I'll look forward to that. Hope your little one gets better quickly."

"She will. They always do."

I walked outside with her. The rain had stopped, but the dampness hung in the air.

"Our city hall is just around the corner," Meredith said, pointing across the street. "It's a grand building, even in the rain."

The thought of doing any sightseeing in such damp weather didn't excite me at all, but I needed some fresh air. Meredith was right, the city hall was a grand building, in all regards. As I was admiring the ornate structure, modeled on St. Paul's in London, it started to rain again. I ducked inside the front entrance, and the view of the great dome nearly took my breath away. I didn't think I had ever seen a city hall with such elaborate artistic and architectural flair. Unfortunately, the building was closing for the evening, and a short time later I found myself walking back to the hotel in the rain.

Back in my room, I checked my e-mail, hoping for some news from Catherine or Neil. Both had promised to write if there was any change in Aurora's condition. To my disappointment, there was nothing from either of them.

As I quickly changed into some more casual clothes, the picture of Meredith's two little girls flashed into my mind. They looked so sweet and innocent, as young children do. It was not hard to understand why Meredith became emotional .... I guessed that I would too, in her situation. For that matter, what mother wouldn't?

With the envelope of O'Neil's speeches in hand, I headed across the road to Robinson's Bistro. I had walked past it earlier and checked out the menu. It looked much better than the hotel restaurant. I decided to try it, and had the most delicious meal of pork and leek sausages with champs and gravy. Okay, so maybe it wasn't the healthiest meal I'd ever had, but I always tried to sample the local cuisine wherever I travelled.

After the rather filling meal, I rolled myself back to the hotel and had an early night. Something told me I would need all my wits with me tomorrow, and a little bit of Irish luck.

CHAPTER 39

To the raven, her own cluck is white
-Irish saying

Meredith was right, it was only a fifteen-minute walk to the BBC, although I left early to make sure I'd arrive on time. There were still black clouds hovering in the sky, but it was a pleasant morning. The streets were filled with cars, and the sidewalks were filled with pedestrians. Belfast had the look and feel of a thriving city.

I entered a large room and saw Meredith talking to a cameraman off to one side. On the other side of the room, the press conference was in full swing. Questions were being shouted by a throng of reporters, and in the middle of the media scrum stood Michael O'Neil. I recognized him immediately and was surprised. I'd expected him to be more imposing in person, but instead he looked like a harassed civil servant.

Meredith quickly came over and greeted me.

"How's your daughter?" I asked, taking off my coat.

"Her temperature has gone down, but she's still at home. Mum is with her all day. Did you have a good night?"

"I spent most of it reading the material you gave me. Thanks for that, by the way."

"You're welcome. They should be wrapping up soon."

"Is the press conference about the election?"

"No, it's about a local issue that O'Neil feels very strongly about. He's a strong advocate of ....." Her voice trailed off as she noticed the cameramen packing up on the other side of the room. The press conference had come to a close, and O'Neil had stepped away and was speaking to a man who held a clipboard in his hand.

"He's talking to Pierce Foley, his chief of staff," Meredith said, nodding in the direction of the two men. "Foley's the one I made the arrangements with. I know him quite well. He can be a bit surly and heavy-handed at times, but he's highly organized and efficient. He doesn't let O'Neil waste a minute of his time."

Meredith pointed to an area of the room that resembled a small living room. There were two soft chairs arranged to face each other, with a round coffee table in between. "I assume that this set-up is fine with you," she said, and called over two cameramen who were waiting off to the side. She introduced them, and we quickly went over my requirements. Standard interview routine.

As we were talking, Foley came over. O'Neil was still on the other side of the room, talking to a woman who was taking notes.

"Good day to you, Pierce," Meredith said as he approached. "Hope the press conference went well. Pierce, this is Aurora Weeks, from Toronto."

Foley looked a bit startled. "Canadian?" He looked momentarily confused. "You're not Irish, then?"

"I mentioned that when I set up the interview, Pierce," Meredith pointed out, sounding put off.

"Oh yes, of course. I'm sorry, I was thinking of someone else," he said, shaking my hand. Then he turned to Meredith. "Is twenty minutes all right with you? I know we said thirty, but something has come up and O'Neil's schedule has tightened. If not, maybe we can continue later in the day."

"I'm sure that should be all right," I said, knowing that once you got a politician talking, they had a tendency to ignore time constraints.

"Good, I'll get O'Neil." He left us, walked across the room, interrupted O'Neil in his conversation, and steered him over to us.

"Don't worry about the time," Meredith said in a low voice as the two men approached.

"Good morning, Meredith," O'Neil said, thrusting out his hand to shake hers. "Always a pleasure to see you. How are your little girls?"

"They're fine, Michael, thanks for asking. Keeping me busy, I'm afraid. Michael, meet Aurora Weeks, from Toronto."

O'Neil had already turned to shake my hand. "Weeks? Are you Irish, by any chance?"

"No, I'm afraid not. My grandfather was, but I'm a second-generation Canadian."

Foley interrupted. "Shall we get started, then?" Meredith was right - not a moment wasted.

We sat down and the cameramen took up their positions.

At the cue from the head cameraman, I led off. "First of all, Mr. O' Neil, let me thank you for taking time out of your busy schedule. I'm sure that this is a hectic time for you." All politicians liked to think that theirs was the only hectic life.

"Thank you," O'Neil said graciously, "for coming all this way and showing an interest in our election. It tells me that this presidential race is an important one, and I'm sure that Irishmen all over the world, especially in Canada and America, are watching it with a great deal of interest."

"Tell me then, what make it so special?" I asked.

With that, O'Neil, like the good politician he was, was off. First, he gave a brief but generalized history of Ireland, North and South, and moved on to the Troubles and now the new peace. His remarks were factual and impersonal, as if he'd watched much of it from the sidelines. He turned the conversation to what he called Ireland's greatest threat - the International Monetary Fund. I noticed that he'd deliberately refrained from criticizing the British Crown in any manner, other than in a historical context. I asked him to elaborate on his views on the IMF.

"Irish people should not have to have second-class citizenship imposed on them by anyone. Not the IMF, not the EU, or anyone else." I could see he was getting wound up. He was starting to sound like Gerry Adams.

"Mr. O'Neil, I wonder if we could talk about Sinn Fein for a moment. You've been intimately involved with Sinn Fein for many years. Tell me how the party has changed over time and what aspirations it has now."

If nothing else, O'Neil was very articulate and skilled in steering the conversation away from any potential pitfalls. Not once did he mention the IRA or his direct role in it, which was well-documented. In fact, he subtly distanced himself from any involvement in the armed struggle. I then pressed him on what qualifications he possessed to be the president of the Irish Republic.

As he was talking, I wondered about Meredith's caution not to bring up the IRA. Yet that was the crux of my interest in him. Our time was winding down, and I had to take the risk.

"Mr. O'Neil, do you think that your paramilitary past is seen as an obstacle to becoming president?"

To my surprise, he didn't flinch. "I've risked my life for the peace process, and everyone knows that. I've seen the issue from both sides, and the Irish people respect that. It's a new world, and I will always be passionate about freedom, justice, peace, and reconciliation. Sinn Fein is the only party that can lead us to a restoration of Ireland's glory and independence."

I could see Foley giving hand signals to O'Neil indicating that time had run out. We had already gone well past Foley's time estimate.

"I wish you the best of luck, Mr. O'Neil. Thank you for your sharing your thoughts."

"You're more than welcome. I know there are a lot of Irish-Canadians who support our cause, and I hope they'll be pleased with the results of the election." He removed the microphone from his lapel and handed it to Meredith.

We stood up, and O'Neil shook hands with Meredith. "Thanks for arranging this, and look after your wee ones," he said to her, and then he turned to me.

"Pleasure to meet you, Miss Weeks. I hope you've enjoyed your visit to Ireland."

"I have, thank you. The Irish are a very gracious people."

"Yes, they certainly are, thank you. Well then, we must be off," O'Neil said, turning to go.

"Mr. O'Neil," I said, touching his arm. "You asked about my Irish heritage. Does the name Richard Mahoney mean anything to you?"

O'Neil cocked his head sideways and slowly repeated the name. "Mahoney? The name doesn't ring a bell. Should I know him?"

"Not really. I was just curious."

O'Neil started to say something, but Foley interrupted and steered him toward the door. Meredith was busy giving instructions to the cameramen who were packing up their gear. Just before O'Neil left the room, he turned around and looked at me, as if he wanted to remember my face. Or tell me something. Our eyes locked briefly, and then he was gone.

I didn't like the expression on O'Neil's face. I'd seen it before, usually on the faces of men who wanted to harm me.

CHAPTER 40

It's difficult to choose between two blind goats
-Irish saying

"That seemed to go well, didn't it?" Meredith asked as we settled into two chairs at a pub steps away from the studio. It was still a bit early for the lunch crowd, so we had our pick of tables. Meredith had chosen one away from the doorway, near the back.

She and the waiter were on a first-name basis. "Is it too early for a spritzer, Jeffery?" she asked.

"No, mum, it's not. Anytime I'm here, it's not too early for a drink." he replied.

"Make it two," I said to Jeffery. He nodded and left. "Yes, it did go well. I wish I could have probed more into O'Neil's earlier life, but I have a feeling he would have been very evasive, as you predicted."

"Regardless, you did manage to ask him about it," Meredith said, picking up a menu. "Well done for leaving it until the end. I was surprised he didn't take umbrage. He usually does, especially if the media asks the question. His standard answer is to say that the only ones who talk about the past are the media."

"Not that he revealed anything, as I recall. His answers always seem to have a double meaning. I wonder if that's a ploy, or just the way he is?"

Jeffery arrived with our drinks. Meredith and he engaged in some lively banter that I found quite amusing. Once he was gone, Meredith whispered to me that Jeffery had a crush on her despite the fact she'd explained to him that she was almost old enough to be his mother. Since then, he'd begun calling her 'mum'. She laughed and showed that dazzling smile of her. "It's always nice to be found desirable, isn't it?"

I nodded, smiling. 'Yes, indeed it is,' I thought to myself, thinking of Dave.

"Now then, who is Richard Mahoney?" Meredith asked, giving me a curious look.

"He was my great-grandfather, who was murdered by the Black and Tans. Years later, the IRA tracked down the soldier who shot him and they murdered him in revenge."

"Why did you ask O'Neil if he knew him?"

"From what I've read about O'Neil, he grew up in an IRA family. His father Eamon was very active both in the IRA and in Sinn Fein. So young Michael would no doubt have heard about all the injustices that the British had perpetrated on the Irish. It's not hard to imagine; I grew up in a political family and know how historical rights and wrongs are dredged up all the time. So when I put the question to O'Neil, I was really curious to see if the incident at Castleconnell had become part of folklore within the IRA. If he'd answered yes, then it would have been a telling sign of how immersed he'd been within the IRA."

"Pity that Foley hustled him out so quickly. That would have been an interesting exchange to watch," Meredith said, signaling to Jeremy.

I quickly looked the menu.

"I'll have a spinach salad," Meredith said to Jeremy.

"Why am I not surprised, mum?"

"Same," I said to Jeremy. When you're in Rome do as the Irish do.

"Let me ask you something, Meredith," I said once Jeremy had left to fill our order. "Why do you think Foley was so surprised when you told him I was Canadian?"

"No idea, but he did seem to have been caught off-guard. Foley is very protective of O'Neil, but why he should have any concern about you being Canadian is beyond me. I don't know what you can read into that, to be honest."

"Neither do I. It just struck me as odd."

"How long are you staying in Belfast?" Meredith asked.

"Actually, I'm catching a bus back to Dublin later this afternoon. I have to visit myself in the hospital."

Meredith gave me a puzzled look. I ordered two more spritzers from Jeremy and then explained, finishing just as our salads arrived.

"Now tell me about your little girls," I said, digging into the spinach.

"They are the most precious little creatures in the world, without a doubt. Do you have any?"

Not yet, I thought, not yet. Dave popped into my mind; I still hadn't found a good time to broach the subject with him.

It was a hurried lunch; Meredith had a meeting that she was already late for. It was early afternoon when we finished, and the buses to Dublin left every twenty minutes. I remembered the piece of paper that Catherine had given me with the name of Flanagan's pub on it. I googled it for the address. If Rory had felt that it was important to talk to Cecil Flanagan, then I guessed that I did, too. Yet there was a nagging feeling in the back of my mind that I should take Dad's advice and let sleeping dogs lie. Or was it Mom who usually said that? No, she would have said, 'Nothing ventured, nothing gained'.

I hailed a taxi, gave the driver the address, and off we went.

The driver was a chatty, pleasant older man named Derek Skinner. He asked if I had been to Belfast before. When I told him that it was my first time, he asked if I wanted to see the murals along the way, since most tourists usually did. It wouldn't be much of a detour, he assured me. I said yes, and within a short time, we were driving along Lower Newtownards Road. The driver pointed out two giant yellow cranes in the distance with the letters H & F painted on them.

"Those cranes launched the Titanic, Miss. We call them Sampson and Goliath. It was built right here, you know." I hadn't known that, actually.

He slowed down and pointed to the left. A mural on the end of a building depicted a large Union Jack. Beside it was a wall on which the words 'Freedom Corner' had been painted in bold red letters. Then came a long stretch of unbroken walls and buildings all painted with colourful murals, many of them with a grim air showing paramilitary men with machine guns and clenched fists. One of them had an ominous message: FOR AS LONG AS ONE HUNDRED OF US REMAIN ALIVE WE SHALL NEVER IN ANY WAY CONSENT TO SUBMIT TO THE IRISH FOR IT'S NOT FOR GLORY HONOUR OR RICHES WE FIGHT BUT FOR FREEDOM ALONE WHICH NO MAN LOSES BUT WITH HIS LIFE. That seemed to sum up one side of the Troubles quite nicely.

The Fiddler's Head was located deep in the heart of what would have been a working-class area. It was at the end of a long row of Victorian houses, mostly empty and in disrepair. Children played soccer on the street, and a small group of young men stood in the doorway of one of the houses, smoking and watching us arrive.

"Would you like me to wait, Miss?" Skinner asked. Clearly he didn't expect me to be there for a social visit.

"If you don't mind, yes. I won't be too long."

The pub was very narrow and long. The bar rail had at least twenty stools, and there was a series of small tables along the other wall. There was a larger seating area at the end of the room.

The pub was almost empty, with just two men seated at the bar, three stools apart from each other. Behind the bar, a bearded older man with a rather large stomach was talking to one of the men.

A young woman who had been cleaning up the tables came over and asked if I wanted to be seated at one of them.

"Is Cecil Flanagan here?" I enquired.

"That's him over there," she said, indicating the bearded man behind the bar with a nod of her head. "Cec. Someone here for you," she yelled, and pointed at me as he turned around.

Cecil hung up a drying towel, said something to the patron, and then came over. "Can I help you, Miss?" he said, gruffly.

"Perhaps .... I'm not sure. My name is Erin Weeks. You might have spoken with my cousin Aurora last week." I decided not to confuse the issue by having the same first name.

"What of it?" he said, folding his arms across his chest.

"Actually, she would have been here on my behalf. Was she asking whether you were related to Fergus Flanagan?"

"Yes, she was. What's your interest?"

"I'm a journalist. I'm writing a book about the Irish Free State in the 20's and 30's. Aurora was doing some research for me."

"I don't follow," he said, impatiently.

"I'm researching the IRA. In the 30's, a man named Fergus Flanagan was murdered by the IRA. I wondered if he was related to you."

"That he was. He was my grandfather. Happened before I was born. Never knew the man."

I thought of the other Fergus Flanagan that Rory had mentioned, the one who'd died in the car bombing. He probably would have been the same age as Cecil.

"Did you by any chance have a brother named Fergus?"

"Look, Miss, young Fergus died forty years ago, may he rest in peace. He was a good lad." Cecil uncrossed his arms and laid his hands on the bar. "Fergus was the first in our family ever to go to college. Then the IRA murdered him, too."

"I'm sorry to hear that, Mr. Flanagan,....."

He cut me off. "The IRA has destroyed our family twice. No good will come of talking about it now. I said that to your cousin when she was here, and I'm saying it to you now. Leave the Flanagan family alone. Good day to you, then."

"I am sorry, Mr. Flanagan. I didn't mean to offend you."

Cecil had already turned and walked to the end of the bar and then down a stairway.

I left the pub quickly, trying to collect my thoughts. Now I realized why Rory was excited - she'd discovered that another member of the Flanagan family had been murdered by the IRA, although I couldn't imagine how the two incidents were related.

My thoughts were interrupted by the driver asking me where I wanted to go. I told him to take me to the bus station.

"If you have time, Miss, you can see the Catholic murals on Falls Road," he suggested. "It's not far from the bus station."

"Absolutely," I said, and off we went.

In my mind, I replayed my conversation with Cecil. I wished I'd handled it differently, but it was too late now. It would have been interesting to ask him about O'Neil, although I could guess what he would have said. I had obviously touched a raw nerve with Cecil.

Ten minutes later, we were cruising along Falls Road.

"We have a saying here in Northern Ireland, Miss," Skinner said, slowing down as we approached the first mural. "Protestants make the money. Catholics make the art."

It was easy to see why. The Catholic murals were indeed very artistic. One in particular stood out, a large portrait of Bobby Sands. He was among ten prisoners who had died of a hunger strike in Maze prison held to protest being treated as common criminals rather than political prisoners. The mural described him as an M.P., a poet, a revolutionary, and an IRA volunteer. One of his more famous quotes surrounded the large drawing of him. EVERYONE, REPUBLICAN OR OTHERWISE, HAS THEIR OWN PARTICULAR ROLE TO PLAY. OUR REVENGE WILL BE THE LAUGHTER OF OUR CHILDREN.

I thought back to Meredith's comments about the fragile peace that existed in Belfast. With the hardened attitudes many people held, it would take generations to overcome the animosity.

I asked Mr. Skinner, my driver, what he thought. He chose his words very carefully.

"That's a loaded question, Miss. I lost my uncle in the Troubles, not far from here. There's an Irish proverb that I wish he would have followed. 'It's better to be a coward for a minute than dead for the rest of your life.'

I didn't ask him to elaborate.

CHAPTER 41

It's a bad hen that won't scratch herself
-Irish Proverb

The bus ride back to Dublin gave me time to think. My original schedule had me booked on a noon flight tomorrow, but truth be told, I didn't really want leave. It felt as though I had too much unfinished business here, not that I really knew what it was. But more than anything, I couldn't leave Rory just yet. I knew I could stay if I wanted to - Rob would receive the interview tape electronically, and I didn't have any other pressing commitments back home. The Senate articles weren't due for another month, and I was sure that Dave wouldn't mind me staying longer. It would give him more time to study.

I closed my eyes and heard the booming voice of Patrick Moore describing the various Dublin buildings and their place in history. It made me realize that I had just scratched the surface. I needed to explore the city within.

Another thought nagged at me. Dublin was home to so many great writers .... Wilde, Shaw, Swift, Becket, O'Casey, Behan, Yeats, and, of course, James Joyce. I wanted to see where they lived, where they walked, and where they studied. As a writer myself, how could I not want to immerse myself in their world?

Lastly, I thought of Aunt Fionola, who had indirectly led me there. I thought of my Dad, and of Colette and Herbert, sailing to an unknown world to escape poverty and violence. I thought of Sean Mahoney. Had he murdered Flanagan? And if he had, had he ever been charged? Now that I had actually tracked down the Flanagans, shouldn't I do the same for my family by closing the loop of that dreadful event at Castleconnell?

By the time the bus reached the outskirts of Dublin, my mind was made up. I'd be a fool to leave just yet. In my head, the story I wanted to write had begun to take shape. Now I needed to do some research, and what better place to do it than in Ireland?

It was early evening when I arrived back in Dublin and checked into The Fitzwilliam. I quickly called the airline and put my ticket on open status. Then I sent an e-mail to Dave telling him of the change in my plans. I also sent an e-mail to Malcolm telling him that I'd decided to stay in Dublin a few more days. When all that was done, I still had time for a quick visit with Rory.

Her condition had not changed. I held her hand and told her about my trip to Belfast, especially my conversation with Cecil. I also told her about my talk with St. Patrick a couple of days ago. "He listened to me, I know he did. You just wait and see. In fact, I've changed my plans, and I'm going to be around for a few more days, just to make sure that he did listen." I gave her a kiss on her forehead, squeezed her hand, and said goodnight.

Back at the hotel, I ordered dinner and turned on the television to watch the local news. Michael O'Neil was front and centre in the presidential campaign. New polls showed that it was a close race, but that he was pulling away from his nearest rivals. I listened to him intently and had to concede that he was a very shrewd politician. He knew how to appeal to the public. My food arrived, and I turned the television to something less challenging. Yet O'Neil's voice and face stayed with me for a long time. So did the look that he'd given me at the doorway after the interview.

I phoned Dave, but my call went to voice mail. This time I was too tired to leave a clever message, so I just said, "Hi, it's me .... I'll call you in the morning."

CHAPTER 42

A nod is as good as a wink to a blind horse
- Irish proverb

Okay, so this was crazy. I was still waking up early in the morning. I tried phoning Dave, but it went straight to voice mail again. I left him a long, sexy message inviting him to come to Dublin for some gratuitous sex. Actually, I did no such thing. I merely said, "Hi, it's me .... sorry I missed you again." I lay in bed wondering if he had resolved his dilemma. Personally, I didn't think he had a dilemma. He saw what he saw, and no more. There was no harm in revealing that to the investigators. Let them deal with it. Okay, problem solved. Anything else that needs solving?

I made up a list of everything I had to do today. I thought that maybe the sheer enormity would overwhelm me, and I would fall back asleep. But in the end, there were only two items on the list. 1. Call Patrick. 2. See Rory. Not exactly a full plate.

Mary Moore answered the phone when I called. She sounded genuinely delighted to hear from me.

"Patrick will be so pleased that you called. He's out for his morning constitutional, but shouldn't be long unless he's giving someone else a tour," she said with a hearty laugh. "Give me your number, and I'll have him ring you as soon as he gets in."

I gave her my number, and twenty minutes he rang back, as they say here.

"I understand from Mary that you rang," he said, sounding out of breath.

"I did. You told me I should call if I wanted you to give me another tour. Well, it just so happens that I would very much like it if you would give me a tour of the IRA."

There was silence at the other end of the line, although I could hear him breathing.

"Did I hear right?" he said finally. "Did you say the IRA?"

"I did. Let me explain. I've extended my stay because I'd like to see if I can track down one of my relatives, Sean Mahoney. Reputedly, he was active in the IRA in the 1930's. You might remember the story I told you of the shooting at Castleconnell. Sean was the son of the innkeeper who was executed by the Black and Tans. Because you have such

149

fantastic historical knowledge, I thought you might be able to offer some advice on how to track Sean down."

After a brief silence, I heard him call out to Marry. "What time are we expected at the Club?"

Mary replied from what sounded like another room. "Half-twelve."

"Aurora, it's just past ten," he said, coming back on the line. "If you can meet me in an hour uptown, I would be more than happy to chat to you about this. If you have a pen, I'll give you the name of a coffee shop and directions how to get there. Are you still at the same hotel?"

He gave me the details, which I hurriedly wrote down. Patrick talked as fast as he walked, and I had a hard time keeping up with him. Without further ado, he rang off. I congratulated myself for getting the hang of the language. Rory would be proud.

An hour later, I found myself outside the coffee shop. It was a quaint place, selling pastry, fresh bread, tarts, and other baked goods. In the back of the store was a small seating area, and there sat Patrick Moore, paper in one hand, tea in the other. I greeted him, and he quickly jumped up and asked if I wanted coffee or tea. I told him that I was tired of coffee and that a tea would be nice.

"Let me get you one," he said as I sat down in the other chair at his small table. "I brought you some reading material. You can browse through it while I get your tea."

I looked at a stack of books. All of them looked old and, by my definition, valuable. I picked up the top book. 'The Politics of Illusion: A History of the IRA'. The next book was simply entitled 'The IRA'. I began to flip through it just as Patrick returned with my tea.

"This is Roibus, one of my favourites. I hope you like it," he said, setting it in front of me. "I take it with a wee bit of sugar," he added, passing me a little bowl as he sat down. "Now then, I brought you some books you may wish to look through. Sorry I couldn't find any others on such short notice. I think you'll find these helpful to set the context for your search."

I tried the tea. It was hot, so far so good. It was somewhat sweet, thanks to the sugar. But it wasn't coffee! No offense, tea lovers, but it just wasn't the same.

"Lovely," I said, hoping that I sounded sincere.

"Good, I thought you'd like it. It's from South Africa. They make good tea; we make good beer." He took a sip of his tea and pointed to the books. "I brought these to give you some background. The IRA is a very complicated subject. Its history is interwoven very closely with the struggle of Ireland to gain independence. Most people outside of Ireland

150

don't really understand why there is so much fighting. They think it's just Catholics and Protestants squaring off against each other. There is that, I grant you, but it's deeper than that. It's about our ethnic heritage, our culture, our history, our language, and our relationship with Britain. Nothing here is simple. You just have to study Irish history to quickly realize that. I'm a keen student, and let me tell you, I have only scratched the surface. When you read these books, you'll see what I mean."

"I'm sure I will," I said, trying not to grimace while drinking my Roibus.

"Now then, if you'll permit, let me give you a simplistic history of the IRA. It will help you to understand the books much better, and you may be able to just skim for the most part."

I nodded my head, and with that Patrick Moore was off. Talk about a history lesson! But it was witty, informative, and to the point. Patrick had missed his calling as a lecturer. Not once did I lose interest or find my mind wandering. I even noticed an older couple sitting nearby who had stopped their conversation and were now listening to Patrick. His little talk must have lasted twenty minutes, and in all that time I swear he didn't stop to take a breath once. He did manage to continue sipping his tea, but only after a dramatic event had occurred in his narrative that needed a few extra moments by the listeners, myself and the older couple at the next table, to comprehend.

When he finished, I wanted to applaud.

"So, do you think I'll be able to track down Sean Mahoney?" I said, holding up his books. "Sounds like I'll be looking for the proverbial needle in the haystack."

"Probably not," he conceded. "There were thousands of men in the IRA, scattered all over the country. Unless Mr. Mahoney rose to a rank of some prominence, chances are there won't be any reference to him in any of these books. But don't let that discourage you. Also, when you've gone through everything here, go to the National Library on Kildare Street. I'm sure you'll find quite a collection of books on the IRA there. Some are accurate, some not, I'm afraid. And speaking of books, you must go to Trinity College and see their library and the Book of Kells."

"I'll do that. Back to the IRA for a moment .... what about now?" I asked. "Is the IRA is still active?"

"In theory, no. They've laid down their weapons, so we're led to believe. But every so often there will be an issue, no matter how slight, no matter how trivial it may seem to the outside world, and suddenly they come out of the woodwork. I would venture to say it'll take another lifetime." Patrick looked sad at that, or regretful .... it was hard to tell which.

He looked at his watch and started gathering up his things. "Right then, I must be off. Mary will be waiting. Let me know if you find anything," he said, pointing to the books. "And don't forget the National Library. Spend lots of time there. I always do."

We shook hands, he wished me luck, and then he was off. The older couple beside me watched him leave. When he was gone, the man leaned over. "I couldn't help but overhear .... is that gentleman a professor? He certainly speaks well, doesn't he?"

"He may as well be a professor for all the knowledge he has about Irish history," I replied, gathering up the books and my coat. "I just wish he wouldn't walk or talk as fast. It seems like he's always going a hundred miles an hour," I said, putting on my jacket.

Outside, I hailed a taxi for the short drive to the hospital. When I arrived in Rory's room, Neil was there in his usual spot, holding her hand in one of his and texting away on his smartphone with the other. Her condition had not changed at all. We chatted briefly, but it was clear that he was not in any mood for small talk.

I pulled up a chair on the other side of the bed and started reading one of the books that Patrick had given me. After I was halfway through, I began to fear that Patrick was right. This might be near impossible. But I didn't give up. I knew that the truth was out there, somewhere. I just had to keep looking.

Two hours passed by very quickly. Neil excused himself, and said he'd be back later on in the evening. I said that there was a good chance I'd still be there. Honestly, it was just as easy to read in Rory's hospital room than it would be back at the hotel. By 7 p.m., I'd finished one book. My head was now filled with so much history that I needed a break. Something along the line of People magazine.

My stomach told me that it also needed food. Just then, Neil returned. Again, we exchanged a bit of small talk, and then I kissed Rory good night and made the little trek back to the hotel. On the way, I stopped at a pub that was advertising fish and chips to go. I picked up an order, went next door to an off-license shop and bought a bottle of wine, and had a nice little picnic back in my room. By the time I was finished, the wee leprechauns had sprinkled sand dust in my eyes and I dragged myself to bed.

CHAPTER 43

You must crack the nut before you eat the kernel.
- Irish proverb

The next morning, it appeared that my body had finally gotten the message and was adjusting to the time zone. As a result, I slept until 6:30. When I got up, I didn't think Dave would appreciate me calling after midnight his time, so I powered up my laptop to send him the latest news, of which there was actually very little. Much to my delight, an e-mail from him awaited me in my inbox.

Hi Aurora – Sorry I missed your call. I didn't hear from you by the time I went to bed, so here's a quick update. I spoke with Brennan, who said I should definitely tell the investigators that I saw the open door. It may not have been important to me, but maybe it is to them. I know he's right, but to be honest, I don't want to have to testify against any of my old colleagues. Cops don't like cops who rat on each other. What do you think? I've got too many friends on the force, and I don't want them to think that I'm selling them out. Hope things are going according to plan on your end. When are you coming home? By the way, I've got a chance to do some fishing with a buddy for a couple of days, so if you aren't able to get a hold of me, that's why.

Hope you're having fun.

Love Dave.

'Love Dave'? What was that, an order? Where were the x's and o's? Obviously he hadn't read my mind yesterday when I solved his problem. I quickly replied:

Dave – This isn't about ratting on your friends or not supporting them. This is about what you saw, end of story. If it incriminates Schulz in some way, that's not your problem. You have an obligation to tell them what you saw, and then let them fill in the blanks. And besides, you're no longer a cop. I called to tell you that I'm staying a few extra days. Now that I'm here, I want to do a little bit more research into my great-uncle and see some more of Dublin. Sounds like the timing fits in with yours, since you're going fishing. Don't forget – catch and release. That's an order.

Love, Aurora xxoo.

153

After sending that e-mail, I finished reading the second book Patrick had given me. But Sean Mahoney's name hadn't shown up anywhere. I did slowly realize that the shoot-out at the Shannon View Hotel was not as much of an isolated incident as I'd originally thought. Violence, insurrection, and rebellion was seemingly the norm in Ireland for the last hundred years. How in the world had Mary Tully survived and lived to be such a ripe old age? How did any of them? No wonder there were probably more Irishmen outside of Ireland than inside.

Finally, I'd had enough of reading and decided to go see the famous Old Library, as it was called, at Trinity College. Some people get a kick out of old churches - I get a kick out of libraries. I love the look and feel of books, the older the better.

But first, I made a quick visit to Rory. I told her about my search for Sean Mahoney, what I'd had for breakfast, and what kind of a day it was outside. I'd brought a copy of The Irish Times with me and read her some of the headlines. O'Neil now had a slim winning margin, according to the latest poll. After half an hour, I kissed her on the forehead and said goodbye.

I took a bus to Trinity College. As I entered the gates and saw the students on campus, I was reminded of my own university days. A part of me suddenly longed to be a student again. It was such a wonderful and carefree period in my life. Of course, I hadn't thought that way at the time; it had been hard work. But now, upon reflection, I realized that it really had been the best time of my life. Maybe I should go back and get a doctorate. Dr. Weeks had a nice ring to it.

The Old Library took my breath away, especially the Long Room. Bookshelves rose nearly forty feet from the floor to the barrel-vaulted ceilings. The room housed hundreds of thousands of old books. Unfortunately, you couldn't touch them, the aisles were roped off. Busts of famous philosophers and writers lined the narrow central hallway. There was a solid line of tourists filing through the room, yet it was strangely quiet. This was a place where you spoke in whispers for fear of offending the books.

After the Long Room, I found the Book of Kells and lined up dutifully with all the other tourists to see it. Over a thousand years old, the book was considered to be the most striking manuscript ever produced in the Anglo-Saxon world and one of the great masterpieces of early Christian art. Rebound into four volumes, one book on display was open to an illumination, another to a page of text. What was also amazing about the book was the fact that it had miraculously survived invasions by Vikings and others over the course of many hundreds of years.

I finally stopped playing wide-eyed tourist and headed off to the National Library, which, to my disappointment, wasn't quite as grand. Regardless, I found a daunting selection of books about the IRA. Picking out five out at random and sitting down at a carrel, I began to skim through them. I was no longer interested in the IRA's history .... I just wanted to find Sean. But if he was there somewhere, which I was sure he was, he was keeping a low profile.

Eventually, all of the names had a very familiar ring. Connelly, de Valera, right up to Adams, Paisley, and O'Neil. It got to the point where it felt as though I was suffering from battle fatigue. One book detailed individual IRA bombings during the height of the Troubles from the 60's to the 90's. Each incident listed the location, the number of injured and dead, and the subsequent reprisal, if any. And arrests, if any. I almost put the book away, thinking that this was the wrong time period for Sean, but I kept flipping to the 70's, and there it was - the bombing in Belfast that killed young Flanagan, along with two others. A typical car bomb, going off on a busy street, killing innocent civilians. No arrests were ever made. As I read this, a sense of frustration came over me and it took me a while to understand why. Everything led me back to the Flanagans, and nothing was leading me back to my family. Without finding Sean, the loop was incomplete.

My watch said it was time to call it a day. Deep down, I felt defeated. I walked to the River Liffey and sat on a bench, watching the ripples on the water from passing boats. Questions were assaulting me from all sides. Why was I there? What was I accomplishing? What was it really that I was looking for? Unless there was an answer to those questions, I might as well go home. Rory, of course, was uppermost in my mind, but I could be there for a long time, sad as that may be, without her coming to. More than anything, I supposed, I wanted to come full circle on the murder of my great-grandfather. His death had resulted in reprisal, and for some perverse reason, I supposed, I wanted to know if that reprisal had come at the hands of my family. That would make for an interesting story, or so I thought. But only if I could find out if Sean was involved. Maybe I should have asked O'Neil directly.

I don't know how long I sat there, oblivious to my surroundings other than watching the ebb and flow of the Liffey. My mind was half made-up to book the return ticket, and yet there was still something nagging at me which wouldn't leave me alone. Finally, I stopped staring at the water and made my way to the hospital.

155

Neither Neil nor Catherine were there. And understandably so; both had jobs, and other obligations. Their absence only reinforced my own frustration. I sat there, holding Rory's hand, feeling in need of someone to talk to. I needed Dave, if for no other reason than to have him be a sounding board. Dave was good at that. He knew when to listen and just let me rant, or vent, or just talk. Wendy was good, too. So was Mom. And so was Dad. What was it all of a sudden? Was I homesick? I listened to Rory's breathing; I had never really been conscious of it before. It had a rhythm all of its own, and in a way it was a very calming sound. I closed my eyes, listening to Rory's breathing, and imagined her slowly gathering strength, mending what needed mending and healing what needed to be healed.

I didn't know how long I sat there with my eyes closed, feeling Rory's pulse. I was in a trance, and as I came out of it, I was conscious of another person in the room. Neil had entered quietly, sitting down in his usual spot and just letting me be in my little altered state.

"Neil, sorry .... I didn't even hear you come in," I said apologetically.

"No worries. I didn't want to disturb your meditation."

We made small talk, hard as it was for Neil, and then I said goodbye to Rory. Oh God, what I would have given for her to open an eye, or say something, or squeeze my hand.

I picked up some more fish and chips on the way home. No need for wine, though, there was still lots left from last night. It was relatively early in the evening, and I planned to stay in. If nothing else, I thought that I would put my thoughts down in an e-mail and send it to Dave. Maybe that would help me sort out my growing paralysis of what to do next.

Much to my surprise, the message light on my telephone was flashing when I arrived in the room. I dialed the message centre. Patrick Moore's baritone voice boomed at me over the phone. "Hello, Aurora. This is Patrick Moore. Mary and I were just watching the news, and I see that O'Neil has emerged as the front runner. It made me think of you, and I wondered how you were making out. I hope you visited the National Library. Grand place, isn't it? In any event, if I can help you out any further, don't hesitate to call me. You have my number. Mary sends her regards."

Just hearing his voice made me feel better. I devoured my fish and chips, went easy on the wine, and then called Patrick. Mary answered the telephone.

"Oh, Aurora, I'm so glad you called. Patrick will be pleased to hear from you. He wondered how you were getting along. Just a minute, I'll fetch him," she said, and then she put the telephone handset down loudly. I could heat receding footsteps in the background, muffled voices, and then another set of footsteps approaching, unmistakably Patrick's.

"Aurora, we were just talking about you," he said, coming on the line. "How are you making out?"

"I spent the day at the library as you suggested, and I've read the books you gave me, but I hate to say I'm no further ahead. Thank you for the recommendation, though. Oh, and I went to the Old Library at Trinity as well, and loved it. The Book of Kells was magnificent."

"That it is, to be sure. I'm sorry you didn't find Sean Mahoney."

"So am I. I think it's a lost cause."

"Doesn't surprise me, but I wouldn't give up just yet. Did you come across the name Tomas Kensella at all?"

"Kensella? To be honest, I've come across so many names that they're all starting to blur. Was he in the IRA?"

"Yes, he was originally, but then he worked for Sinn Fein for a long time. I met Tomas many years ago when I was doing some research, and I keep in touch with him from time to time. He's an interesting man to talk to, although I'm afraid he might be losing some of his mental faculties. He's 92, and physically still going strong. I took the liberty of calling him today at the nursing home, just outside of Dublin. I told him we might come round and see him. Are you up for that?"

"I most certainly am. It's either that or go home."

"Fine, then. I'll pick you up at half-eleven tomorrow at your hotel. It's about a half-hour drive."

"Thank you, Patrick. Are you sure?"

"Absolutely. I was due for a visit with Tomas anyway."

"I'll bring along the books you lent me."

I never did send the e-mail to Dave about my predicament. Patrick's call gave me a glimmer of hope. So did the rest of the red wine.

But it did take some serious thinking to figure out if 'half-eleven' was 10:30 or 11:30.

CHAPTER 44

Show the fatted calf, but not the thing that fattened him.
- Irish saying

I waited at the hotel entrance at 10:30. Just to make sure, I asked the doorman if half-ten was the same as 10:30.

Within minutes, Patrick pulled up in a pumpkin-coloured Land Rover. When he stepped out, I thought he was dressed to go hunting; all that was missing was a shotgun in his hand, and dogs milling around in front of him.

He shook my hand, opened the door to the pumpkin coach, and off we went into the Irish mist. Actually it was into lots of stop-and-go traffic. And as expected, Patrick kept up a running commentary on the historical, architectural, or otherwise significant landmarks we passed. When we reached the edge of the city, he switched topics.

"Just so you know, my sympathies don't run with the Irish Republican Army at all. I've never agreed with their ambitions, their tactics, or their philosophy. They're nothing more than but a bunch of terrorists, as far as I'm concerned."

"Oddly enough, I've come to the same conclusion. So how did you meet Mr. Kensella?"

"It's from my days in the civil service." He paused, and I didn't press the point. "Like I said yesterday, Kensella is in his nineties. His mental faculties are still good as far as I know, but I haven't talked to him in quite some time. A bit of background for you - Kensella was a rebel in his youth who hated the British. Perfect recruit for the Provisional Irish Army. Then he got shot and went to jail. When he got out, he worked with Sinn Fein. Looked after money, rosters, and administrative details. Rose to some level of prominence, but was never one of the decision-makers. He does fancy himself to be a bit of a historian, which is why I suppose he and I get on so well. You do have take what he says with a grain of salt, though. Let's hope he speaks English today .... he does have a habit of lapsing into Irish. I can understand it to some extent."

The Land Rover slowed down. We were well into the country, with rolling hills everywhere, fenced off into little parcels. He pulled into a driveway that led to a two- story, sprawling brick building. A large sign on the lawn proclaimed it to be The Emerald Isle Retirement Home.

"The top floor is for those residents who need supervision. The bottom is for the ones that can still manage on their own. There's a lovely garden in the back. It's a bit chilly, but I think we might be able to sit outside. Kensella likes that."

At the reception desk, Patrick introduced himself.

"Ah, you're here to visit Mr. Kensella," said the young woman on duty. "He's out in the garden, waiting for you. You know the way, don't you?"

Patrick nodded and led me out a side door.

We stepped onto a patio that had a variety of wrought-iron tables and chairs. At the edge of the patio was a well-maintained garden with inlaid brick walkways bordered by boxwood hedges. Many of the flowers had died already, but there were still lots of roses in bloom.

There was only one person on the patio. He was seated at a small table, a blanket spread out on his lap, staring out into the garden.

"There he is," said Patrick. "Tomas, you old rascal, how are you keeping?" he said in his booming voice.

Tomas looked up, momentarily surprised. Then a large grin spread across his face. "Never been better. And you?"

"I'm as fit as fiddle, thank you. Tomas, meet Aurora Weeks, a Canadian friend of mine."

Tomas brought his hands out from under the blanket and offered one to me.

"Ta athas orm buaileadh leat," he said, extending his hand to me.

Patrick leaned over and translated. "He said 'Nice to meet you'".

Tomas' wrinkled face had a pallid colour, and when he reached out his hand, it looked so fragile that I was afraid to shake it for fear of breaking his bones. Much to my surprise, his grip was quite firm. I gave him a big smile. I was desperate to reply in Irish, but none of the phrases that I'd memorized in my guide books rolled off my tongue.

Patrick pulled out a chair for me, and I sat down.

"I'll get us some tea, shall I?" he said. Without waiting for an answer, he disappeared inside the building.

"An bhfuil Gaeilge agat?" Tomas said to me.

He saw my puzzled expression and repeated the question in English. "You're Canadian? Just visiting then, are you? You're not one my nieces, are you? I have several in Canada. One is in a place called Regina. I think that's it."

159

"No, I'm not one of your nieces. I know Regina, it's on the Prairies. Have you ever been to Canada, Mr. Kensella?"

"Not that I recall. I've been to many places, but never overseas. One of these days, I should do that," he said with a chuckle.

Patrick returned with a large tray containing a teapot, teacups, a small jug of milk, and a bowl of sugar. There were also several shortbread cookies set out on a plate. "Shall I pour?" he asked, and filled the three teacups. He reached into an inside pocket of his jacket and pulled out a silver flask. He poured some whiskey into Tomas's cup, and offered me some as well, which I declined.

"There you go, Tomas," he said, handing Tomas his tea, "that'll keep you warm. Did Aurora tell you that she's a journalist doing some research on the IRA? That's why I brought her to see you."

"That's very kind of you Patrick," Tomas said, accepting the cup and taking a sip of the tea. "Very kind. Did you say she was my niece?"

"No, Tomas, she's not your niece. She's researching some family history. One of her relatives was in the IRA, in the 30's."

"I remember the 30's. They were tough times, tough indeed. I served with the RIC for many years."

"Tomas, the RIC was disbanded in 1922. You were three years old. I think you must be thinking of something else. Perhaps the Gardai?"

Tomas looked Patrick sternly. Then his face mellowed. "I was just letting on. It was the Gardai. But not for long. Then I joined the IRA. But it was a different organization then. I was with the Provisionals."

"When did you join Sinn Fein?" Patrick asked.

"Not long after I got out of jail. It was safer, and they paid me a decent wage. I liked the work, to be honest. I felt that I was making more of a difference than the lads blowing up the British. Or trying to."

Patrick poured more tea for Tomas, who had quickly emptied his cup, as well as another shot of whiskey.

"Tell me something, Tomas .... did you ever hear of a man named Sean Mahoney?" Patrick asked.

Tomas looked at him blankly.

"He was my great-uncle," I explained, "and supposedly he was in the IRA for a long time. In the 1930's, I believe."

Tomas looked at me with great interest, as if I had suddenly just appeared. Then he looked at his hands, picked up his teacup, and handed it to Patrick. Taking out the hip flask, Patrick poured another shot into the cup.

"Mahoney? Sean Mahoney? Can't say I've ever heard of him," Tomas said, looking at Patrick and then back to me as if we could help him.

"Are you sure?" asked Patrick, taking the words out of my mouth.

"Aye. But my memory's not as good as it once was," he said, sipping his tea, and turned his gaze back to the garden.

After a long moment of silence, he said something in Irish to Patrick, who nodded and replied, also in Irish.

"What about Fergus Flanagan? Have you ever heard of him?" I asked.

Again Tomas looked at me with a puzzled expression, but there was no hint of recognition on his face

I elaborated. "In April of 1921, there was a shooting in Castleconnell, at the Shannon View Hotel. Flanagan was a Black and Tan who executed the innkeeper for being an IRA sympathizer. In 1938, the IRA murdered him in retaliation."

"Fergus Flanagan, you say?" Tomas replied.

I nodded, and Tomas took another sip of tea.

"Did you say 1938?" Tomas asked with a frown. I was beginning to fear that my question was another dead end.

"Yes, he was killed in Belfast. The IRA took claim for the killing," I replied.

"No, no," Tomas said emphatically. "It was Belfast, 1970. Three people were killed, and one of them was a young man named Fergus Flanagan. I remember it very well. It should never have happened."

Tomas paused, sipping more of his tea. I wanted to tell him that there were two Flanagans, but I didn't want to confuse him.

"So why did it happen?" I asked.

"O'Neil was behind it," Tomas said matter-of-factly.

"Which O'Neil?" Patrick interjected.

"Michael O'Neil, of course," Tomas replied, as if it was obvious. "He was a young hothead. He set the bomb, but it was supposed to be transported to Armagh. O'Neil said he stopped to pick up some supplies, and the bomb went off accidentally. Some time later we found out that one of the victims, Fergus Flanagan, was engaged to O'Neil's sister, Emeline. Flanagan was a Protestant, and Emeline's father was a staunch Catholic. He was dead set against the marriage. Eamon O'Neil also knew the Flanagan family history, and he was going to be damned if his daughter was going to marry into that family."

It took me a nano-second to make the connection with the name that Rory had written on that piece of paper. Had she made the connection too? Was that why she had been so excited when she'd talked to Catherine?

"So are you saying that the bombing was a deliberate attempt to murder Flanagan?" I asked Tomas.

"Aye, that's my way of thinking. Nothing could ever be proven, of course, and Michael denied that that was the case."

Patrick looked at him sternly, his brows furrowed. "That's a bit of a horse's hoof, I think, Tomas."

Tomas looked offended. "I'm not just acting the gom," he said in an agitated voice. "I may be old, and sometimes I don't remember everything I should, but some things you can never forget."

"I'm sorry, Tomas. I shouldn't have doubted you," Patrick replied, reaching out and laying a hand on Tomas' arm.

"I never trusted Michael. Never," Tomas said emphatically. "He's nothing but a cute hoor."

"Wasn't the bombing investigated? Were any charges laid?" I asked.

Tomas laughed. "The police never found out who planted the bomb. They wouldn't have made the connection to Emeline. To them, it was a random act."

"Why did Sinn Fein or the IRA let him get away with it?"

"Oh, it caused a lot of heated discussion in Sinn Fein, believe me. They wanted to throw him out, but Eamon O'Neil was very influential, and in the end it was all swept under the rug. Sinn Fein didn't want to draw attention to themselves in that light. Besides, the IRA was happy. More bombings followed shortly after, like the one at Ballymacarrett."

"How many people know about this, Tomas?" asked Patrick. There was a faint hint of disdain in his voice.

He shrugged his shoulders. "Not many now, I should think."

'Except the Flanagans,' I thought.

"How do you feel about him running for president?" I asked

Tomas looked uncomfortable. "I've never trusted O'Neil. Not when he was with the IRA, and not when he became a politician. He's a bit of a sleeven."

I didn't know what that meant, but from the tone of his voice, it wasn't complimentary.

"Tomas, you said that Eamon O'Neil knew the Flanagan family history. What did you mean by that?" I asked.

Tomas looked a bit uncomfortable. He said something in Irish to Patrick, who nodded and gave him another shot of whiskey.

"Eamon was very active in the IRA," Tomas said finally. "One of our lads told us about finding this Flanagan fellow and what he had done when he was with the Black and Tans."

"What was the lad's name, Tomas? Do you remember?" Patrick asked.

Tomas was silent, staring out at the roses. "I think it was Colm. Yes, I'm sure it was. He was in the Irish Army, I remember that very well. He told us where to find this Flanagan. Then the fool joined the British Army."

"Joined the British Army? Why would an IRA member do that?" I asked.

"He wanted to fight the Germans. The Irish wouldn't let him because they were staying out of the war." Tomas replied.

Patrick turned to me and explained, "Ireland maintained neutrality in the Second World War. About 5,000 Irish soldiers turned in their uniform and joined the British Army to fight the Germans."

"Tomas, do you remember Colm's last name?" I asked.

"Of course, I do," Tomas said, giving me an aggrieved look. "Colm Mahoney."

"Not Sean?" The words tumbled out of my mouth.

"No, not Sean," Tomas replied emphatically.

"Did Colm Mahoney murder Flanagan?" Patrick asked.

Poor Tomas. With both Patrick and me lobbing questions at him, he must have felt as though he was on a firing line.

"No. I told you, he was in the army," Tomas replied, with a hint of frustration. "We took care of Flanagan ourselves. Couple of lads came up from Cork. One of them nearly died in a fight with Flanagan, but we brought him back. That's why Eamon knew all about Flanagan."

"One more question, Tomas. Do you know what happened to this Colm Mahoney?" I asked, touching his arm.

"Aye. He died on the beach at Normandy. I remember seeing his name in the paper. Many of the boys died there," Tomas replied in a soft and wistful tone. He turned and said something in Irish to Patrick, who nodded.

"Tomas is tired and wants to have a lie-down before lunch," Patrick said to me.

We both stood up. Tomas remained sitting.

"Well, Tomas, it was good as always to chat with you," Patrick said, adjusting the blanket over Tomas' lap. "I'll send someone out to help you to your room."

"Aye, please do. And it was good to see you too, Patrick. And your niece. I hope you both come again."

"We will, Tomas. Take care." Patrick leaned down to touch his arm in a parting gesture. With their difference in height, poor Tomas looked dwarfed. It made me feel sorry for him. He looked frail and lonely.

"Tomas, it was a pleasure to meet you," I said, picking up his hands. They felt warm, but brittle.

"Saol fada chugat," Tomas said. Patrick looked at me and was about to translate.

"Slan," I replied, hoping that I pronounced it correctly.

Tomas smiled. He had a serene expression on his face, which made it all that much harder to associate him with any kind of violence.

CHAPTER 45

A windy day is not a day for thatching.
-Irish proverb

"I'm sorry you didn't find Sean," Patrick said as he backed the Land Rover out of the parking spot. He was extraordinarily quiet. "But I was impressed with your Irish."

"That's the extent of my Irish vocabulary." I replied with a laugh. "Oh wait, I also know 'Slainte mhaith', but I couldn't work it into the conversation."

Patrick chuckled.

"What did you think of Tomas?" he asked curiously.

"I don't think there's anything wrong with his memory, do you?"

"No. He may not remember what he had for breakfast, but I think there's nothing wrong with his recollections. Many old people are like that. Including myself."

"That's what I thought. Yet do you think he could have mistaken Colm Mahoney's name? I mean, the coincidence is just too much."

"I agree with you about that. But I can find out. If what Tomas says is true about Colm joining the British Army, it will be easy enough to find out," Patrick said.

"Really?"

"Oh, yes. You see, when the men who had enlisted with the British came home, they were treated as outcasts and brutally punished by the government. They were stripped of all pay and pension rights, and their names were put on a list that banned them from being hired by any government agency for seven years."

"Why? It sounds so cruel and oppressive."

"That it was, but at the time many Irish wanted the Germans to win for the simple reason that they were fighting the British. Not a pretty chapter in our history. I will be able to find out from the military records who this Colm Mahoney was."

"That would be great, thank you. We may not have found Sean yet, but at least I know the Emeline connection now. Rory had been doing some research on Flanagan for me before she fell down the stairs. She had made a little notation on a slip of paper, and all it said was 'Emeline'.

Somehow she must have found out about the young Ferguson and Emeline O'Neill. What a story! I'd love to talk to her."

Patrick pulled the Land Rover off the road onto the shoulder, and turned to look at me with a very serious expression on his face. "Aurora, don't even think of trying to find Emeline. No good will come of it. It's one thing to have Tomas telling you stories. Most people would say he's not a full shilling at the best of times. But I know that he's telling the truth. He may be old, but he's not a fool. And his mind is not impaired. But if you're thinking that you can somehow expose Michael O'Neil for the murderer that he is, forget it. There are powerful forces behind him, and they've all closed ranks. Sinn Fein would like nothing more than for him to win the election .... for them at this point, it's about the future and what they can achieve with him in office. They won't appreciate you meddling in his past life. So you best leave them alone."

I was stunned by his outburst and remained silent. He engaged the gearshift and pulled back on the highway. For what seemed like an eternity, he drove without saying anything. Finally he spoke. He didn't look at me, but kept his eyes on the road ahead. "You know that I was in the Irish Civil Service. I was privy to a lot of sensitive information, and you'll have to trust me that I know what I'm talking about when I warn you off this. Had I known what Tomas was going to say, I would never have brought you to see him."

The silence in the Land Rover was overwhelming. I knew Patrick was right. Powerful men have powerful allies. I'd learned that lesson several times already and had no real urge to repeat my mistakes. I also knew that eventually some of those men would get hoisted on their own petard. They'd get careless; they believed in their own invincibility. And they would do anything and everything to protect their status quo.

I took a deep breath and exhaled slowly. "Patrick, with all due respect, you're a politician. I'm a journalist. If I didn't keep you honest, I'd be out of a job, wouldn't I? And you would have a free rein to do whatever you wanted. Because after all, who would stop you? Not your advisors; they're merely protecting their own asses. The people who elected you think you're doing a wonderful job because they only hear your side of the story. And so you'll keep doing whatever you want to because you have no opposition. You're unchallenged. You're unaccountable. And one day you'll turn into a dictator, and people will say, 'Gee how did that happen?'"

I was shocked at my own outburst, and I immediately felt sorry. I never would have used that tone with my father. Why had I used it with Patrick, the most generous man I'd met in a long time?

166

Patrick remained silent during my verbal explosion. I knew he had children of his own, and I wondered how he would have reacted to an outburst like mine from one of his daughters. Regardless, I knew that even if my own father had ever made a comment like the one Patrick had, I would have said the same thing.

We were on the outskirts of Dublin. Patrick exited the M1, and a short time later, we pulled into the parking lot of a pub.

"Let's have a bite to eat, shall we?" he said, turning off the ignition.

I hoped this wasn't going to turn into a father/daughter talk. Whenever Dad wanted to have one of those, I could always tell. He would become overly solicitous - the calm before the storm, so to speak. Then wham, in an even tone, he would lay out his view on whatever subject needed to be talked about (boyfriend, school grades, jobs, attention to money, etc). His sermons were always delivered in a calm, rational, off-handed way. So much so that it would take me quite some time to understand that what he was saying was important, and that it would behoove me to pay attention. Or, if nothing else, to at least humour him.

Patrick was clearly well-known at the pub, and we were quickly shown to what must have been his usual table. A young woman materialized from out of nowhere. "The usual, Mr. Moore?" she asked.

"Yes, thank you, Jennifer," Patrick replied as he turned to me. "Would you like some beer or wine?"

"White wine spritzer would be great," I said, still uneasy at what was to come. Jennifer smiled and left to fill our order. We both opened the menus she'd left us, if for no other reason than to delay the inevitable conversation.

I quickly decided what to have - a Tuscan chicken wrap. How very Irish, I mused to myself. Patrick didn't even really look at the menu; I was sure he had it memorized. Jennifer came with our drinks and took my order. Then she turned to Patrick and said, "The usual?" Patrick nodded, and off she went. Easy as that.

"I'm sorry for my flare-up in the car," he said, finally. "Fair play to you. Someone has to keep the politicians in check. Mind you, our parliamentary system takes pretty good care of that. For every successful politician, there's another one wanting to prove him wrong. Or to dig up some dirt. I'm sure it's the same in Canada, and, for that matter, all over the world. The media is our conscience, I understand that - as long as it does its job properly and doesn't go off half-cocked."

I wasn't sure if that was a jibe aimed at me or not.

"So, what's your take on what Tomas said?" I asked, glad to hear Patrick's conciliatory tone.

"As I said, Tomas is old and most people would be skeptical of anything he said. Even if he's right about O'Neil, it would take a long time to actually put a case together. And let me tell you, it would not rest on Tomas' story. No one would believe it, except maybe Cecil Flanagan. And trust me, Sinn Fein would dismiss any such allegation as an out-and-out fabrication by an old man who is no longer in his right mind. Tomas had his own detractors in Sinn Fein, and they would neutralize him very quickly."

"Emeline might believe it," I interjected.

"I'm sure she would. And probably did at the time. But she wouldn't have any more proof than you do. Besides, Michael's still her brother, and powerful at that. He destroyed her life once; do you think she'd want more of the same?"

I pondered this turn of events as our food arrived. Patrick's curry surprised me in a pleasant way. I didn't associate curry with Ireland, although I knew it was very popular in England. The smell made me wish I'd ordered the same thing. I wondered if it was as spicy as Dave's.

"What's your plan now?" Patrick asked.

"To be honest, I'm not sure. I really wanted to find Sean Mahoney, and I seem to have hit a roadblock there. I'd like to stay until Rory comes out of her coma, but it could be a long time before that happens. In a way, I'd like to find Emeline and hear her side of things, but not for the reasons you've alluded to. I don't particularly like O'Neil, but what do I really know? Sure, I've been studying Irish history, and I can tell you why things are the way they are. But the bottom line is that I am still not Irish. I'm on the outside looking in. There's a world of difference between those positions." My phone pinged while I was talking. I glanced at it discreetly. It was a text message from Catherine Weeks. *Aurora is conscious.*

I dropped my fork and picked up my phone as Patrick looked at me with alarm. "She's conscious. Aurora is conscious." I said, typing a quick reply. *Good news. Will be there soon.*

"I'll drop you off at the hospital, if you'd like," Patrick offered.

"That would be fantastic. You know, you've been so kind to me. I don't know how to thank you. Really. And I am sorry for my little tirade earlier. I know you meant well."

Patrick didn't say anything. He didn't need to. His face had a fatherly smile that said everything. He signaled for the bill, refused to let me pay for any of it, and we quickly departed.

168

Within a short time, we pulled up to the hospital. "Please let me know how she is when you get a chance," Patrick said. "I will make some enquiries about this Colm Mahoney."

I assured him that I would and quickly went in the front door.

I signed in at the nurses' station and rushed to Rory's room. Catherine was seated at one side of the bed, and a doctor was standing at the other. As soon as I came in, Rory moved her head in my direction. She gave me a weak smile. The doctor stood aside, and I reached out to hold her hand.

"Has she said anything yet?" I asked.

"She's been trying to. But nothing so far," Catherine said, looking at me briefly and then refocusing her attention on her sister. "Take your time, luv. Take your time."

Rory looked directly at me and we made eye contact. I could see her bottom lip quiver. Her mouth opened, but it was several seconds before a sound came out.

"I was pushed," she said, and closed her eyes again.

CHAPTER 46

The longest road out is the shortest road home.
                                                    - Irish saying

We were so dumbfounded by what she'd said that the three of us just stared at her to see if she would say anything more. Speaking those three words must have taken a lot out of her. Her eyes were closed, and her breathing was shallow.

"You mean, deliberately?" asked Catherine. "Who would do such a thing?"

"I think you better save the questions till later, Catherine," the doctor said, leaning close to Rory's face.

"Aurora, I'm your doctor. If you can hear me, can you wiggle your fingers for me?" the doctor asked in a gentle voice.

We watched with eager anticipation as she weakly wiggled the fingers on both hands.

"Good," said the doctor. "Now, can you wiggle your toes for me?"

The doctor pulled back the sheet at the foot of the bed, and again we watched closely. There was nothing. No movement at all. Horrible thoughts flashed through my mind: the thought that she might be paralyzed, that she'd wind up trapped in a wheelchair. I got this from my mother; she was a constant worrier. If people were paid to worry, she'd be a millionaire many times over.

Then Rory's toes moved, imperceptibly at first, but then the movement became more noticeable.

"Very good, Aurora. Now you just take it easy. We'll have you up in no time, but there is no reason at all to hurry. Conserve your energy, all right?"

Aurora nodded weakly, opened her eyes, and looked at each of us individually. A smile spread on her face, and then she closed her eyes again and her face relaxed.

"Oh, I wish Neil could see this. He's still at work and can't free himself until later this evening. He'll be so relieved," Catherine gushed. She pulled out a smart phone and opened the camera app. "Rory, luv, if you can hear me, can you just open your eyes for a moment? I'm going to take a picture and send it to Neil." We watched her eyes open, and Catherine quickly snapped the shutter. She leaned over and gave Rory a kiss on the forehead. "Thanks, luv. He'll be very happy." She sat down and with some quick keystrokes sent the picture off to Neil.

The doctor had been looking at the chart, making some notes. Then she turned to us and suggested that we give Rory some time to herself. "Even if you aren't talking, the mere fact that you're here might make her want to speak and push herself. She's still very weak. Why don't you go to the cafeteria, have a cup of coffee, and come back in an hour? I'll put a 'Do Not Disturb' sign on the door. If you come back and it's still there, take a seat at the Nurses Station. All right?"

We both nodded, said goodbye to Rory, and headed to the cafeteria in another part of the hospital.

I expected an institutional place with linoleum floors and plastic tables. It was nothing of the sort. In fact, when I first saw it, I thought that we'd walked into a Starbucks.

Catherine ordered tea, while I ordered a latte.

"Isn't it exciting that she's come out of the coma?" Catherine said happily. Her words came out like a waterfall. "Not that she's out of the woods, but at least it's a good sign. In fact, it's the best sign we've had since her accident. I can't tell you how relieved I am."

She covered her eyes with her hands, and tears oozed out from between her fingers. She reached for a tissue from her purse, blew her nose, and wiped her eyes with her hands. "Well, now that's out of the way. I've been very strong since all this happened. I kept telling myself that it was going to all be okay. I never gave myself permission to cry - that would be admitting defeat, wouldn't it? Now that she's coming to, though .... now I can cry. Can't I?" she asked, still wiping the tears away.

"Yes, you can. You most certainly can," I said. Actually, my tears weren't far behind. But I held back. There were too many thoughts were running through my mind.

Catherine picked up her coffee. She took a long sip and leaned back in the chair, her eyes closed. It looked as though a huge weight of worry had been lifted off her shoulders.

After a few minutes of silence, she opened her eyes again and looked at me. "I'm sorry, Aurora. I'm not good company, am I? I've been so worried about my wee sis that I just have this wave of relief sweeping over me."

"I know how you feel. I've only known her for a short time, but for some reason I feel really connected to her."

"She felt that too, luv. She told me so. That's why she did this research for you."

171

"Did she tell you anything about Emeline at all? How she knew of her? Was it through Cecil Flanagan?"

"No, she didn't tell me, but whatever it was got her all excited. I haven't seen her like that in a long time. Usually her jobs are quite boring, you know, tracking down long-lost relatives and so on. Eventually she finds them and it's very satisfying and all that, but she just viewed it as a job. But when she called me about her research for you, she was just beside herself with excitement. What did strike me as odd, though, was that she didn't want to tell me on the telephone just what it was that she'd found. Was she afraid of being overheard, do you think?"

"You did hear what she said, didn't you?" I asked.

"You mean that she was pushed?"

"Yes. What do you make of that?"

"Well, I just assumed that she was jostled or pushed by someone accidentally," Catherine replied, looking at me in a quizzical way.

"What if it wasn't accidental?" I said, almost afraid to admit to that possibility.

Catherine opened her mouth in surprise. "You mean she was pushed deliberately?"

I nodded my head.

"But why? Who would do that? And if they did, do you think they meant to kill her?"

"I really don't know. But I think we should contact the police. If someone did try and kill her, how do we know they won't try again?"

"Oh, my God!" Catherine cried. "We'd best do something." She opened her purse and fumbled through the contents. Finally, she pulled out a card and set it down on the coffee table in front of us. The she fished out her cell phone and called the number on the card.

"Is that Inspector Little? This is Catherine Weeks. Do you remember my sister Aurora, who was found at the bottom of the stairs at the library a week ago? She's been in a coma ever since, but today she came out of it, sort of, and stated very clearly that she had been pushed on the stairs. No, she didn't say anything else. The doctor told us to let her rest for a bit." She listened intently for a bit longer. "All right, see you then."

"She said she'd pop by a bit later. She's going to pull the file." Catherine looked at her watch; we hadn't been gone that long. "Now I'm worried. Grab your coffee, luv. We're going back to the room."

With a jump, she stood up and marched out of the cafeteria, juggling her coffee in one hand, her cell phone in the other. When we arrived at Aurora's room, the 'Do Not Disturb' sign was clearly visible.

172

Catherine ignored it and barged into the room. Aurora was sleeping quite soundly. I detected the faint sound of snoring.

"I'm going to sit right here beside her until Inspector Little comes. I am not going to let her out of my sight," Catherine said, closing the door behind her. We sat in silence for a while, finishing our coffee. Aurora's breathing was the only noise in the room. I wanted to get back the hotel and jot down some notes from the conversation Patrick and I had had with Tomas Kensella while it was still relatively fresh in my mind. With Rory sleeping, it seemed like a good to do that. I quietly told Catherine that I was leaving, and that I would see her later. Neil was expected to arrive at any minute anyway, so it was probably best to leave the three siblings alone for a while. I gave Rory a gentle kiss on the forehead, which thankfully did not disturb her.

To say that I was greatly relieved was an understatement. But my relief was offset by a new worry: had someone deliberately pushed Aurora down the stairs, and if so, why? Could it ever be determined what had happened? I wished Dave was there, if for no other reason to be someone to talk it over with. Well, that wasn't the only reason, the nights were getting a little lonely. It felt as though I'd been gone for a month.

It was mid-afternoon, and for once the sun was shining brightly. In the sunshine, Dublin was a beautiful city. The combination of the architecture, the river, the curving streets, the Georgian mansions, and the centuries of history made it a unique place.

The trek back to my hotel now seemed like a well-trodden path. The election was three days away. Malcolm had sent me an e-mail earlier in the day asking if I could extend my trip until the election results were announced. At first, I thought he was kidding. Could I be that lucky? He wanted some on-the-street reactions to the results, and possibly a follow-up interview with O'Neil, particularly if he'd won. Malcolm had already arranged for a cameraman through Meredith, and asked me to contact her. This was really good news. Now I was going to be here for at least three or four more days, on Malcolm's tab.

Despite what Patrick had said, I really did want to track Emeline down. But it could wait for a day. Hopefully by then Rory could shed some light on what, if anything, she'd found out about Emeline.

A small white car pulled up alongside me with a flashing blue light on top. The car stopped and a uniformed man stepped out.

"Miss Weeks?" he said.

I turned to him, wondering if he was Inspector Little. Then I remembered that Little was a woman.

"Could we have a word with you for a moment?" The officer motioned for me to step into the car, which I did. He closed the door, went around the other side, and also got in. As soon as the door was closed, the car nosed into traffic again. I noticed that the driver reached out of his window and pulled the blue light inside.

"What is it you want to talk about?" I asked, after there seemed to be no effort on the part of the officer to make conversation. In fact, he was staring out of his window, not even looking at me.

More silence.

"Can you tell me where we're going?"

"To the station. We'll be there in a minute," the officer replied, still staring out of the window.

The car pulled into the driveway of an underground parking garage. I looked around for other police cars, but there weren't any. In fact, there were no other cars at all.

We pulled up beside a lone white van parked in front of a door that I assumed led to the elevators.

"Here we are, then," the officer said, opening his door and stepping out.

I opened my door, and as I stepped out, a hand came up from behind me, covered my mouth with a cloth, and the last thing I remembered was the white van doors opening and being shoved inside.

CHAPTER 47

A trout in the pot is better than a salmon in the sea.
- Irish proverb

When I came to, my first thought was to wonder why I was lying on a hard surface in an awkward position, bouncing along what could only be described a very bumpy road. My second thought was, 'Am I blind? No, I'm blindfolded.' And then, 'Why are my hands tied behind my back? WTF?' I tried to move my legs, but they were bound as well.

For a minute, I stopped struggling, trying to assess the situation. Other than getting into a police car, I couldn't remember anything. If I hadn't had a gag in my mouth, I would have asked whoever was driving the car if this was some standard procedure of how to treat foreign guests, but as it was, I decided I'd have to ask that question at another time.

The van slowed down and then came to a stop. The driver's door opened, and then it shut again. Moments later, the side door of the van slid open and something bulky was put beside me. Then the door closed, and the driver got into the van again. I could hear another car pulling away.

We continued along the bumpy road for some time until we came to another stop, which was a relief. At least the bumping was over. The side door opened, and I felt a pair of hands untying my feet. I tried to sit up, but it was too difficult with my hands tied behind my back.

A strong set of arms dragged me out of the van and made me stand up. I assumed we were not at a police station. Judging by the cool air and the absolute quiet, we were in the country. One of the men removed my gag. I sputtered and took a deep breath. Then I said something which was a combination of "Help", "What the fuck is going on?" and "Where am I?".

There was no response as they led me up some steps and through a door. And not too gently at that. Did I struggle? Not really. When your hands are tied behind your back, you feel groggy, and there's a burly chap on either side of you, there doesn't seem to be much point. I would save my strength until later.

The men led me further into what I assumed was a house or a cabin. Inside, one of the men untied my hands. While I was rubbing my wrists, I heard a door close behind me and a latch being secured. Not a word had been exchanged.

Removing my blindfold proved more difficult than I expected. Whoever tied the knot had definitely not flunked whatever knot-tying course he'd taken. With some difficulty, I was able to push the blindfold up the back of my head and fling it off. My eyes were blinded momentarily by the light coming through the window, but they adjusted quickly.

I was in a small room furnished with a single bed, a small writing desk, and an adjoining one-piece bathroom in what must once have been the closet. It was in desperate need of a remake. In fact, having a door would have been a good start.

The room only had one window, and the three heavy iron bars placed across it convinced me that this was definitely not a quaint Bed and Breakfast. I sat on the bed, taking deep breaths. Momentarily I would get my voice back and ask nicely, "WHAT THE FUCK IS GOING ON?" Too bad there didn't appear to be anyone around to answer the question. On a happy note, they'd tossed my suitcase into the room before leaving me here. Very thoughtful of them!

So there I was. Me and my Mary Tully scarf. I took it off and wondered if it was strong enough to strangle one of the bastards who'd brought me here. I noticed some plastic bottles of water sitting on the writing desk. That, and a heap of granola bars. Too bad there was no chair or a pad of writing paper so that I could do a quick review of this little hellhole. Desperately wanting a drink, I stood up to get one of the bottles. A wave of nausea swept over me, and I quickly sat down again.

I don't know how long I sat there. The daylight was quickly fading, and I guessed that it must be early evening. There was a solitary light bulb hanging from a makeshift fixture in the ceiling. I looked around and saw a switch on a wall. With slow steps, I walked across the room to turn it on. No such luck. There was no electricity.

I put an ear to the door and listened for any outside noise in the house. Nothing was stirring, not even a mouse. My full faculties were beginning to return. In the fading light, I quickly opened my suitcase. Whoever had packed it could have taken more care. My clothes and personal effects were thrown in without any due care. Fuckers! I looked around for my purse, which had my cell phone in it, but it was nowhere in sight. Neither was my laptop. The suitcase also was devoid of anything that would help me get out of this room. I supposed that I could tie the sheets together to escape out the window, but the iron bars would make that a tad difficult. Besides, I was on the main floor. I didn't need a rope, for God's sake.

After rummaging through my clothes for a magic key to get out of this hellhole, I put it all back as neatly as I found it.

I looked out the window. It must have been facing west, because I could see the faint glow of the setting sun. There was no sign of life anywhere outside. No other houses, no roads, no bus stops, no 'Welcome to Ireland' visitor's centre. Nothing except green rolling hills. Actually, in the fading light, the hills weren't green, they were grey. A dark grey, like my mood at the moment. My supportive inner voice said, Don't lose your sense of humour. But my louder, outer voice said, Don't lose your sense of humour? For chrissake, I'm trapped in an abandoned farm house, in the middle of Ireland, with no food except for granola bars and some stupid plastic bottles of water! And a bathroom that has no door on it! And you think I shouldn't lose my sense of humour? Show me one thing that's funny. C'mon, I dare you.

The hopeful part of me that constituted my inner voice looked around the room. Then I looked at the ceiling. Then I looked for an escape hatch on the floor. Then I tried the door knob. Then I flushed the toilet. And guess what? It flushed. WTF? Still, what was so funny about that? Was I going to repeatedly keep flushing in the hope that some township by-law enforcement officer would come by and give me a citation for depleting the local reservoir?

My inner voice conceded quietly that there was nothing funny about this whatsoever.

I sat on the bed, my knees drawn up as close as possible to my chest in order to curl myself into a ball. And I cried. *Go ahead, why not? I heard my inner voice say. No one will see your tear-stained cheeks, or the fright in your eyes. Go ahead and cry - it will make you feel better.*

Or more hopeless, that loud, outer voice of mine said. I shook my head and yelled at the top of my lungs, "FECK OFF!". There, take that you Irish bastards.

With some hesitation, I lifted up the cover on the bed to see if it had sheets. I was in luck, although it looked as though the sheets had seen better days. The cover, which was a poor excuse for a quilt, seemed like it just might be warm enough for the approaching chilly night air. It had a terrible musty smell, but, as Mom would have said, beggars can't be choosers. I decided to sleep in my clothes. I put my suitcase against a wall so that I wouldn't trip over it during the night should some magical fairies appear to help me make an emergency escape. And in case I had to get up and pee.

With nothing else to do, and now in complete darkness, I crawled under the covers. There was no pillow, so I pulled some clothes out of my suitcase and used them as a substitute. From my prone position, I could make out the moon through the bars. It was playing hide and seek with some scary-looking clouds. I thought about many things, not the least of which was the roof.

I hoped it didn't leak.

CHAPTER 48

It's for her own good that the cat purrs
-Irish proverb

I woke up early the next morning to the sound of absolute quiet. The room was damp and chilly, and the musty smell of the blankets had invaded my clothes. I lay in bed for the longest time, waiting for this stupid dream to end.

Reluctantly, I pulled back the covers and made my way to the window. Mist was rising from the fields, and it was eerily quiet. If I had a volume control, I would have immediately turned it up. Where were the birds? Or the cows, or the sheep, or the crows, or any other living creatures? This was Ireland after all. Wasn't it supposed to be the land of pastoral beauty?

With the mist, the scene outside was reminiscent of a movie I'd seen not long ago. It was a science- fiction thriller, and in it, the aliens were about to land. The heroine watched in horror as these weird indistinguishable shapes came floating across the landscape to where she sat, strapped to a chair, naked.

I quickly checked to make sure I was still dressed.

And that there were no aliens lurking outside.

I opened a bottle of water and had a drink, nearly draining the bottle. Then I splashed some on my face. One bottle down, only three to go. I opened a granola bar and ate it greedily. Then I belched. What had happened to my manners, I wondered? Not that it mattered. I could be prancing around the room naked and farting up a windstorm for all anyone cared.

The morning light became brighter, and as the mist burned off, it looked like it might actually be a nice day. My mood improved immeasurably.

I took inventory. One suitcase. Lots of underwear, sweaters, pants, skirts, two pairs of shoes, three bras, several Old Navy t-shirts, and, ahem, tampons, and the requisite amount of jewelry. If there was going to be a fashion show, I was ready. Other than my clothes and the

179

suitcase, there was nothing else in the room. Oh, I'd forgotten to include the water bottles and the granola bars.

If there was a survival manual that came with this room, I wondered what it would say? Check all exits. The door was still locked, and the window was still barred. Check for secret exits and entrances. I meticulously examined the floorboards, the ceiling, the walls, and the bathroom. Draw attention to yourself. I went to the window, which was nailed shut. Nonetheless, I shouted at the top of my lungs, "HELP ME!!" No response. I sat down on the bed and wondered if there was a Plan B. No answer was forthcoming to that question.

Slowly the sky changed from a light grey to a light blue, and then to a very deep blue. The fields became green, and I saw the shadow of the house in front of the window. Still no sounds, but every once in a while, a bird did make itself known.

I didn't think I'd ever experienced this kind of silence before. It was one thing to shut yourself off from the outside world, but it was a totally different thing when someone else shut the outside world off from you.

I paced the room, looked out the window, did some more pacing, and did some more looking. None of it helped my anxiety whatsoever.

I moved the bed so that it faced the window and sat there, contemplating my dilemma. Why have I been kidnapped? Am I a hostage? Does this have anything to do with the Flanagans? Everything else seemed to lead back to them, so why not this? Are these the same people who pushed Rory down the stairs? If so, why? Will I be left there to starve? How long will it take anyone to realize that I'm missing? It was kind of frightening to see what stupid thoughts could run through your head in a situation like this. Everything from indignation and outrage to fears of starving to death. I still had water and a stack of granola bars, so I wasn't at my wit's end yet. But I needed a plan. You need more than a plan, sweetie, said my inner voice. You need a shining knight galloping across the fields. Or a Dave Fullerton. Hell, I wouldn't even care if he arrested me for murder again, as long as he showed up.

Minutes passed. Then an hour, then two, and then three. I watched the shadow of the farmhouse shorten and then disappear as the sun finally made an appearance. The silence was driving me bonkers. How could I have wound up in such a godforsaken place? Ireland wasn't that desolate. Wasn't all the land carved up for small freeholds? Why, then, was there this vast farm, untended?

I paced the room. That felt weird, so I did Pilates. I closed my eyes and pictured Roseanne, my instructor back in Toronto, going through the routine. What a godsend. It calmed me right down. By the time I was finished, I was sweating profusely, so I downed another bottle of water without thinking. Then, for good measure, I ate an entire granola bar. Boy, would I be in trouble on a deserted island.

My watch said 3:05. How the time flies when you're having fun. I looked around the room for the umpteenth time. Was there possibly a magazine that I'd missed before? I checked every inch of my suitcase in case I'd forgotten about a secret cell phone that I might have planted and forgotten about. Alas, no matter what diversion I came up with, nothing worked. The only good thing was that the toilet continued to work. So if I ran out of drinking water, I could always take some from the tank. But where had that water come from? A scum-filled pond? A poisoned well? That rumination led me to wonder why the pump still worked when the electricity didn't. Or did it? I stood on my suitcase and unscrewed the light bulb. When it was safely out, I shook it. Sure enough, there was the telltale rattle of a burnt-out bulb. 'Let me just go to the supply cupboard and get a new one,' I thought. I placed it carefully on the writing desk. You never knew when the shards of a broken bulb might come in handy. Great, my first weapon. A used 60-watt bulb. Could things get any better?

Or worse?

CHAPTER 49

Pity him who makes an opinion a certainty

-Irish Proverb

To: Aurora
From: Dave

Hi Aurora – I've been back from my fishing trip for a couple of days. So what gives? No e-mail, no messages. Are you that busy? Can you send me some kind of sign? I had some time to think on my fishing trip (by the way, I caught lots of fish, and yes, I released them all except for one lake trout which is sitting in my freezer and which I will cook upon your return). I'm going to talk to the RCMP investigators tomorrow. You're right, of course .... I need to tell them, regardless of the implications. I've also decided to resign from the force. No big deal. Wasn't planning to go back anyway, and my pension is locked in. Maybe that house on St. George will still be for sale. Do you plan to come home in the near future? I'm almost tempted to go to Angelo's by myself, but you'll be happy to know that I've been tinkering with my curry recipe and can now make it perfectly. Its spice rating is one beer per serving. Enough for now. Call me, dammit.

D

CHAPTER 50

A buckle is a great addition to an old shoe
-Irish saying

I must look like hell!

That was my first thought when I woke up the next morning. The room was as chilly as it was the previous morning. Actually, it was dank. I had always associated that word with a prison, which, hey, was actually what my little room was. A prison cell. Now there's a cheery little thought to get you through the day, said my inner voice.

I lay there for the longest time, staring at the ceiling. In truth, I was trying to stop myself from going to pieces. But no matter what I thought of, I always came back to my predicament. How is this story going to play out? Have they left me here to starve? I glanced at the desk. There were still at least four or five granola bars. And water, well, unless I rationed it, I was going to be drinking out of the toilet tank soon.

I wondered how many people knew where I was. Two for sure, but how many others? Am I a part of a grand conspiracy? Am I being held for ransom? I mean, that happened a lot these days in the Middle East, but not in Ireland, surely. I suddenly remembered the look on Michael O'Neil's face at the end of the interview when he was leaving. In his heyday as an IRA commander, he would have been ruthless enough to kill me. Was he still? Hell, if Tomas's story was to be believed, O'Neil killed Emeline's boyfriend, so why not me?

I sat up in my bed. TOMAS. Oh, Christ, was he in danger? Did they know that I'd talked to him? Was that why I was being held there? And what about Patrick? I got up quickly. Something had to be done. Someone had to warn both men, if it wasn't too late already. I grabbed the handle of the door, and surprise, surprise - it was still locked. And the bars in the window were still securely in place. I stood in the middle of the room, fists clenched, and screamed as loudly as I could. It didn't serve any purpose, but it made feel a wee bit better.

I ate breakfast in bed and carefully rationed my water. At this rate, my weight should be dropping like a stone. Water and granola. Could I sell this as a new diet plan? Oh, and in order for it to succeed, you needed to be locked up in an isolated farmhouse somewhere in Ireland.

My mom was notorious for her little bon mots - I wondered what gem of wisdom she'd come up with for today. 'Don't let the bastards grind you down' might be an appropriate, one except she would never use the word 'bastard'. 'Be realistic, dearie' might be another. Okay, I'll be realistic: I'm going to die. Didn't Lorne Green once play a famous Indian chief who said, "Today is a good day to die."?

"Well," I said in my loudest voice, "today is not a good day to die. Do you hear that?" And that was the end of that conversation.

I paced the room, thinking of what horrible punishment I could inflict upon my captors with my 60-watt light bulb if they ever showed up again!

By noon, the sun was hidden behind clouds, and the wind was picking up. I could feel it through the cracks in the walls. By three in the afternoon, dark clouds had moved in, and a light rain was falling. The wind whistled through my room, and suddenly the skies must have opened, because the farmhouse was deluged with rain. I was sure the ceiling was going to cave in at any moment. I sat huddled on my bed, up against the wall, praying that the storm would pass. There was a fierce crack of lightning at one point that illuminated the room and scared the pants off me. Not a second later, there was an ear-splitting roar of thunder. I wondered which death would be worse: to be shot by some IRA goon, or to be fried by lightning? The light-and-sound show went on for some time. I swear it would have shaken the farmhouse off its foundation, if it had had one. And if it did have a foundation, did that mean there was a basement? I could hear that loud, outer voice of mine laughing. What if there is? There might be an attic, too. And maybe a kitchen somewhere. So what? You can't get out of this room. Point well taken. Where was a crowbar when I needed one?

The wind died down, and the rain stopped almost as quickly as it came. I tentatively stood up and went to the window. If there was a soundtrack to this bad movie right now, it would the part in the 1812 Overture, after the cannons have gone off and there was the pastoral sound of church bells ringing to signify peace and tranquility. If I wasn't mistaken, I even heard birds chirping. And so the day came and went. No knight came across the fields on a white horse. I just sat on the bed, knees up to my chest, thinking good thoughts, thinking bad thoughts, thinking nothing thoughts. I counted things: the number of boyfriends I'd had (16), how many times I'd been really drunk (3), the number of times I'd had sex in a car (4), how many pairs shoes I owned (18), how many weddings I'd attended (8), how many times I'd been a bridesmaid (4), how many men had tried to kill me (4), how many women had tried to kill me (0), and lastly, how many children I had (0). That's when I lost it. I sobbed hysterically. I wanted to get out of this alive and have children, whether Dave wanted them or not. The time had come, for me anyway.

In the end, I cried myself to sleep.

CHAPTER 51

If the knitter is weary,
the baby will have no new bonnet.
- Irish saying

I need a plan for when they come back.

That was my first thought of the day. You don't need a plan, you just need a gun or a cannon, said my inner voice, who must have just woken up too. And I also needed a plan if they didn't come back. Good luck with that, muttered that loud, outer voice of mine.

Another day, another chilly morning. I was out of bottled water. The toilet tank was next. There were just two granola bars left. I smelled. I needed to wash my hair. I needed to go for a run. I needed a bath. I needed some hope.

I wondered if the headline in The Irish Times today screamed 'CANADIAN JOURNALIST ABDUCTED'. Was anyone searching for me? Surely Patrick must have wondered why I hadn't called him. Catherine, too. I mean, why would I pack up and leave just as Rory was coming out of her coma? And what about Dave? At what point would he get concerned because I hadn't written? Today was Monday. Election day. Meredith would wonder why I hadn't contacted her regarding the cameraman for the on-the-street interviews. Would she make enquiries? I concluded that all of them had plenty of reasons by now to call the police. And if they had, why weren't there police cruisers barreling down the driveway? Surely there must be some clues left behind, somewhere.

I got out of bed, made sure that no one was peeking in the window, and took off my clothes. God, the room was chilly. I dunked one of my t-shirts in the toilet tank and gave myself a body wash. Soap would have been nice, but even without it, I felt cleaner. I quickly got dressed again, ready to face the day. Why don't you go out and vote? my inner voice said. 'Don't be a bloody eejit. I'm not Irish,' I replied.

Pilates was next on my agenda for the day. I was a minute into my routine when I realized that I had grown considerably weaker. There was just no energy left in me, or so it seemed. I sat on the bed and wrapped Mary Tully's scarf around my neck. Having it with me was almost like comfort food. Speaking of which, scrap the granola bar and water diet. Let me go and pick some nice little cucumbers. I could cut them up, and then throw in some pieces of grilled chicken. I mentally pictured what I wanted in my salad, the type of dressing, and what kind of cheese I wanted sprinkled on the top. Comforted by those thoughts, I closed my eyes and fell asleep again.

I must have woken up because of the hum. I'd become used to the sounds outside, and this was definitely a new one. It was a low hum that was slowly getting louder. Was it an approaching car? The hum stopped. Silence again. Two thuds. Sounded like car doors were being closed. YES, the cavalry was here.

I heard the voices of two men, having an argument.

"I told you to bring it," one said.

"No, you didn't. You didn't mention it."

"Well, one of us has to go back. You go and get it, and I'll make sure our friend is still alive."

I heard the footsteps of the one man leaving, then the car door slamming and the engine starting. Within moments, it was out of earshot.

I grabbed the light bulb, put it in a sweater to muffle the sound, and smashed it against the wall. As expected, there were tiny shards of glass embedded around the rim. I looked at it and wanted to laugh out loud. This was my weapon? A 60-watt bulb? Couldn't it at least have been a tri-lite?

Footsteps approached the door. The latch was undone, and the door handle turned. I sat on the bed, hands in my lap, holding the metal rim of the light bulb. If the situation hadn't been so serious, I would have said it was laughable.

The door opened, and a man stood there with a hood on his face. There were holes for his eyes, and his mouth. I'd seen pictures of men like that. They were usually ruthless terrorists. Pretending to be In a daze, I stared vacantly at him.

"Wake up, miss," he said gruffly. One hand held a gun, which thankfully was not pointed at me. It was just hanging at his side; I guess I didn't look that threatening. He walked around the room.

"Need some water then?" he asked, noting the empty water bottles. "Guess we didn't leave you enough, did we?" Nice of him to notice.

"Miss, I'm talking to you," he said, standing in front of the bed. I looked up at him, but didn't dare move. His free hand grabbed my scarf and lifted it up.

"You're right pretty, you know. You look just like an Irish lassie. We have some time to kill, you and me. Me mate had to go back and fetch something. So we have a bit of time. I'm sure you're starved for some company, aren't you?"

He let go of the scarf and slowly moved his hand down my body.

"You're not wearing a bra. I like that in a woman. Very sexy." His hand started to massage my breast. I desperately wanted to move, but I was afraid he'd see what I was holding. I was also conscious of the gun in his hand. Not to mention the sudden bulge in his pants.

"Aye, I think you and me are going to have a good time. A real good time."

He pulled up my sweater and fondled my naked breast. Then he took his hand away and undid his belt. He opened his jeans and let them drop on the floor. His willy, a wee willy at that, was practically bulging through his underwear, which he then pulled down with his free hand. I was eye level with his crotch. He stepped out of his pants, kicking them off to the side. His other hand came up, and he pointed the gun at my temple.

"Now then, lassie, why don't you and I get to know each other a little better?" he said, breathing hard.

I didn't move.

His free hand grabbed the back of my head and pulled me towards him. I put my hand on his shaft and moved my head towards it.

"Aye, now that's more like it. Be quick about it. And when me mate comes back, not a word." I nodded my head, and he stopped pointing the gun at my head and lowered his arm.

Now that I had a firm grip, I slowly brought my other hand up, and with as much force as I could manage, I ground the light bulb rim directly into his crotch.

He screamed with pain. His free hand went down to cup himself, while his other hand still held on to the gun.

The rim of the light bulb was embedded in his crotch. Doubled over with pain, he wobbled unsteadily on his feet, trying to extract it. The pain must have been intense, but it wasn't crippling. He raised the gun and aimed it at me. I jumped up, grabbed his hand with both of mine, and aimed the gun at his foot. Then I squeezed his trigger finger and the gun went off.

This time, his scream must have been heard throughout the county.

He dropped to the floor, and the gun fell out of his hand. I quickly scooped it up and ran out of the room as fast as I could. I stood in the hallway, panting. My heart was beating so fast that I thought it was going to come right through my sweater, which was still around my neck. I pulled it down and waited for my heartbeat to go back to normal.

I edged back along the hallway, pointing the gun at the doorway. Not a sound came from inside the room. The door was ajar, and I kicked it open. With both hands on the gun, arms outstretched just like they did in the crime shows, I stood in the hallway and stared into the room. The body on the floor was definitely not moving. I probably should have gone inside and frisked him to see if he carried a cell phone, but I was taking no chances.

A pool of blood was forming at the bottom of his feet. For a while, that was going to be his problem, not mine. I had no intention of playing Florence Nightingale.

I closed the door, figured out how the latch worked, and locked it securely.

Then I took a deep, deep breath.

One down, one to go.

CHAPTER 52

What's good for the goose is good for the gander.
- Irish saying

Inside the front door of the house was a satchel. I opened it and found my purse, my cellphone, and my laptop. I quickly rifled through my purse, and it all seemed to be in order. My credit cards were still there, the passport was in the 'secret compartment', and there was still cash in the wallet. I pressed the power button on the phone, but it was dead. I searched for the charger, but came up empty. It was probably still in the wall plug in my room. I took the passport and money out of the purse and stuffed it in my jeans pocket.

I didn't know how much time I had to get ready for the next guy. Should I stay in the house? Make a run for it? The latter wasn't appealing, since I wouldn't have known what direction to take. Besides, I'd be a sitting duck in the open fields. Staying in the house seemed to be the best plan, especially since I had a gun. Before I had time to really debate the options, I heard the hum coming down the driveway again. It was the white van.

I left the front door partway open and stood in a corner out of sight.

The driver's door opened and closed. I heard footsteps approaching the house. So far, so good .... there was only one person. My heartbeat was accelerating a mile a minute, and I really was afraid it might give me away. A man stepped through the front door, carrying a satchel in one hand and a face mask in the other. He dropped the satchel and yelled, "Conor, I'm back."

I eased my way out of the shadow, pointed the gun directly at his head, and said, "Conor is indisposed at the moment. Don't move an inch."

The man froze, and I circled him.

"Pull out your gun very slowly," I said.

"I'm not carrying a gun. Only Conor has one."

"Correction. He had one. What weapon do you have, then?"

"Don't have one. I'm just the driver."

"Put your hands against the wall and spread your legs."

He did so with the slow movements of a man who doesn't want to get shot by a nervous woman. I patted him in the places where I thought he might carry a gun, including his socks, but there was nothing.

"Okay, stay like that."

I knelt down, and with my free hand opened the satchel he'd brought with him. I didn't take my eyes off him once. My hand felt coils of rope and tape. I pulled out the rope and shook it so that it uncoiled.

"Sit on the floor facing me."

When he was seated, I threw the rope to him. "Tie your ankles together, really tight." I watched him and concluded that he was good at following orders.

"Now, lie on the floor, face down, and put your hands behind your back."

"Look, Miss......"

"DO IT! NOW!" I screamed. The anger in my voice was enough to scare anyone, including me.

He quickly obeyed, and I took another coil of rope, knelt on his back, and made sure that he could feel the muzzle of the gun pressed against the back of his head. Then, with my free hand, I managed to tie his two hands together. When that was done, I put the gun down, took another coil of rope, and this time really made sure that his hands were tied. I had no idea if my knotting skills were up to standards, but it didn't look like he was going anywhere.

I backed away, pulled up a nearby chair, and sat down, waiting for my heartbeat to stop racing. I placed the gun in my lap, and found its weight there oddly comforting. I leaned over and picked up the satchel. All that was left was another coil of rope and a roll of duct tape. There was also a bandana, presumably to fashion a gag with. I moved the contents around some more, hoping to find something else, like maybe a sandwich, or a slice of pizza, or a yogurt.

"Do you have any food in the van?" I asked.

"No, Miss."

"Do you have a cell phone?"

"Not with me, Miss." Polite chap, he was.

"What's your name?"

"Donegal. Charlie Donegal, Miss," he said, turning his head to look at me.

"Okay, Charlie. Let's have an honest little chat. Your friend Conor is in need of medical attention, if he hasn't bled to death already." Charlie's eyes opened wide with alarm. "Tell me what's going on."

191

"I really don't know much, Miss. Conor doesn't tell me much, and I don't ask. All I know is that there was a change in plans and that we were supposed to take you back to Dublin and leave you in a parking lot."

"What was the original plan?"

"I don't know Miss. And I didn't want to know." Charlie looked frightened now.

"Okay, so you were going to leave me in a parking lot. Were you going to leave me there alive or dead?"

"Oh, alive, Miss. We were told not to harm you, I swear."

"Who told you?"

"I don't know the man's name, honestly. Conor would. He's the one who made the arrangements."

"Then what?"

"Then we get paid."

"How were you going to get paid?"

"The man is going to meet us in the parking lot and give us cash."

"How much?"

"Three thousand pounds."

I smiled and wanted to say "I'm worth that little?". Instead, I asked when this exchange was going to happen.

"Tonight at 8, Miss."

I leaned back in the chair. I needed to think. Ideally, I wanted to see a police car coming down the driveway, followed closely by a pizza delivery van. Without a cell phone, though, that was going to be hard. I wondered if Conor really was bleeding to death. I grabbed the bandana from the satchel and told Charlie not to move.

I made my way down the hall and looked into the bedroom. Conor was still in the same position as when I'd last seen him. His chest was rising up and down. Good, he was still alive. His face was hidden because of the mask, and I wondered if it affected his breathing at all.

Approaching him carefully, I pulled off the mask. He was not a good-looking man. His face was ragged, and he had an oversized nose, outdone only by his bushy eyebrows. He looked better with a mask. The pool of blood around his ankle hadn't spread, so I assumed the bleeding had stopped. Another good sign. Regardless, I took the bandana and carefully wound it around his foot. It was so bloody that I couldn't really tell where the bullet hole was, but I did the best I could. Mom always said 'You can only do your best.'

I looked out the door to make sure Charlie hadn't moved. Then I stuffed all of my clothes into the suitcase, closed it, and wheeled it into the hall. Finally, I picked up Conor's jeans and brought them out to the chair. Charlie stared at them, and then up at me.

"If you're wondering how I got his jeans off, Charlie, Conor took them off himself before you got here. He wanted a little romp in the hay, as we say."

"He's a bit of gob shite sometimes."

"A gob shite? What's that?"

"You know, an eejit, Miss."

"You really should pick your friends more carefully, Charlie." He didn't respond, but I was sure he was thinking the same thing.

I went through Conor's pockets. No cell phone, just a wallet containing some pound notes, Euros, and a driver's license. Conor obviously didn't believe in loyalty cards.

"Tell me something, Charlie. Did you push a woman down the stairs a week ago at the library?"

"No, Miss. That was Conor."

"Why?"

"I don't know, Miss. Conor doesn't tell me much."

"Let me guess - you were just the driver."

"I was, honestly. Conor can't drive."

"How so? He has a license."

"That's before they found out he was colour blind, Miss. He uses it for I.D. It's not legal anymore."

"And you don't know who hired him to do that?"

"No, Miss, and I didn't want to know. I just want to drive, Miss, and get paid. That's why I don't carry a gun, Miss."

There was a kitchen off the vestibule where we were sitting. I went in and looked around. I had stupidly thought that it might have a well-stocked fridge. Wrong. It didn't have a fridge at all. There was a wood stove, a rickety table, two chairs, and cupboards without doors. Aside from some old plates and cups, the cupboards were bare.

I went back to the front door to get some fresh air. I thought that it might help me figure out what to do next. The easiest thing to do would be to get in the van, find the nearest village, and go to the police. But if I did that, would I ever find out who was behind all this? The police could set up a sting, couldn't they? But would they have time?

I turned around and sat in the chair again. "How long is it to the nearest village?"

"About fifteen minutes, Miss."

"Is there a police station there?"

"No, miss. That's at least half an hour away, if not longer."

"How long will it take to get to the place where you were going to drop me off?"

"Exactly forty-three minutes, Miss."

It was now 7 o'clock. We had seventeen minutes to spare.

"Okay, Charlie we're going for a drive. But I warn you, if you make one wrong move, you're going to see how well I shoot. Understand?"

"Yes, Miss."

I undid the ropes on his ankles first and then his hands. Once they were untied, I quickly backed off, my hands on the gun at all times. Charlie slowly stood up, rubbed his wrists, and stood there looking chastised. Or humbled, if such a thing was possible for a small-time hoodlum. Whatever, he had a vulnerable look to him that almost made me want to trust him. The operative word, though, was 'almost'. His cooperation so far hadn't lulled me into a false sense of security, not by any means. I just had the feeling that he knew he'd made a bad career choice.

"Charlie, go into the bedroom, get Conor's jacket off him, and bring out his mask. It's on the floor."

Charlie looked a bit apprehensive. Maybe he didn't want to see his mate lying on the floor, badly injured. After a brief hesitation, he walked down the hall and entered the room. I stayed close enough behind him to watch his movements.

When he saw Conor lying on the floor, I thought for sure that he was going to vomit.

CHAPTER 53

Forgetting a debt doesn't mean it's paid.
                                        -Irish proverb

We drove in silence for most of the trip. At first it was all country roads, but then Charlie pulled onto a paved highway. Throughout, I kept second-guessing myself. So did that louder outer voice of mine. Go to the police, you fool. You'll get us both killed. I knew it was right, yet I wanted to see this through. I didn't want there to be any chance of the guilty party behind all of this managing to just fade away.

Was I risking my life for a story? Maybe. No, there was more to it than that. I was following the truth, which was what people like me did, regardless of the risk. When you left it to others to find the truth, they would often come up with a version of it that suited them best. And if no one challenged them, their version became accepted fact, right or wrong.

My stomach growled. So much for deep thoughts.   More than anything, I was really hungry. Several times we passed signs for fish and chips, and I almost made Charlie pull over. Then I remembered that we didn't have much time to kill. Maybe the parking lot we were heading for was in back of a McDonald's, and while we were awaiting the arrival of Mr. Scumbags, Charlie could nip over and pick me up a Big Mac and fries. Nutrition be damned! Maybe if Charlie really stepped on it, we'd have time to go through the drive-through.

"We're getting close, Miss. It's about five minutes away," Charlie said, as if he'd read my mind.

I looked out the window. It was well past sunset and the landscape was dark, but it didn't look as though we were close to the city.

"I thought you said it was in Dublin," I said, trying to get my bearings.

"I did, Miss. We came in on a back road to save some time, and we're just at the outskirts of the city now. You'll see in another couple of minutes." He made a right-hand turn onto a deserted street. "We're going to an industrial area just at the edge of Dublin. That's where the drop-off was arranged to happen."

"How is it supposed to work?"

Charlie looked at me questioningly.

"The drop-off. What's supposed to happen in the parking lot?"

"I really don't know, Miss. Conor's the one who made all the arrangements. From what little I heard, our contact wanted to make sure you were still alive. You were to be blindfolded and tied up. Once he was satisfied that you were okay, he'd give us the satchel of money. Then we'd leave you in the parking lot and take off."

"Do you have any idea what this man looks like?"

"No, Miss."

"What kind of a car does he drive?"

"That I know, Miss. A black BMW."

I couldn't help but ask, "And how would you be knowing that?" Sometimes my sense of humour just comes from out of nowhere.

Charlie had a startled look on his face. Maybe, in the back of his mind, he'd just heard his mother's voice.

"I saw the car once before, Miss. After Conor pushed your friend down the stairs. I drove him to a meeting place to get paid. The man never got out of the car, but it was a black BMW, I'm certain. Conor talked to him through the window."

We were now passing through an area of low-level industrial buildings. Charlie turned on his right-turn indicator and pulled into a driveway, past a large building, and into the rear. It was a large lot, fenced in at the back with a high chain-link fence. There were no other cars in the lot except for a tractor-trailer backed up to a loading ramp. This was definitely not the back of a McDonald's.

"Is this the place?"

"Yes, Miss."

I pulled on Conor's mask and nearly gagged. It had the odor of sweat and cheap cologne or aftershave lotion. The image of Conor standing in front of me, waiting to be serviced, flashed into my mind. So did the light bulb. I doubted that he'd ever try that again, assuming that he lived.

There were no lights in the parking lot except for a small one over the rear door of the building. It was pitch black, and we sat there in silence. I wanted to ask Charlie if he could hear my heartbeat. Or was it his?

"Charlie, was that a real police car you used when you abducted me?"

"Aye, it was. Conor nicked it from a police repair station. But it wasn't a real uniform."

"And how did you get my suitcase?"

"Conor has a girlfriend who helps him sometimes. Conor got her to go into your hotel room and then phone the front desk to check out. Since it was being charged to your credit card, she didn't need to go down in person. Then she threw your clothes into your suitcase to empty the closet and make it look like you'd left, and took the back stairs to leave the place."

A light appeared in the driveway. Then the headlights of a car became visible. The car had halogen lights, too bright to look into. It was impossible to see anything but the lights, and I regretting having Charlie back the van up against the fence and park facing out onto the lot. The driver could see us clearly, while we were looking directly into his lights. Charlie and I might as well have been on stage, under the glare of spotlights.

The car slowly made its way across the lot, and then stopped. It was now angled slightly, which reduced the direct glare. The driver's door opened, and a man stepped out. He pulled the seat forward and took something out of the back. It was a satchel similar to the kind Conor had brought with him to the farmhouse.

If the man was armed, he didn't show it. I opened my door and stepped out. The gun was in my coat pocket, my finger wrapped tightly around the trigger.

"Open the side door," the man said as he approached.

I started to open the door, and he came closer.

"C'mon, hurry up," he said, impatiently.

I recognized the voice. I should have known it all along.

I turned to face him.. "Hello, Pierce. Come to take me home?"

He froze.

I pulled out the gun and took off my hood.

"Did O'Neil win?" I asked. "Was this all to protect him? To make sure there was no bad publicity? Did he order you to do this? Was this part of your job? Murder and kidnapping? Who else have you had to silence?" My questions were coming out fast and furious, but Pierce just stared at me.

"He doesn't know about this. He had nothing to do with it," he finally said in an even tone, having recovered from this initial shock.

"I'll bet. Once a murderer, always a murderer. Isn't that right?"

"You're wrong." Anger crept into his voice. "Michael's a good man now. He fought long and hard to get this far, and he deserved to win. I couldn't have that jeopardized because of some fanciful notion about an event that occurred forty years ago."

197

"Forty-two," I corrected him. "I wonder what Emeline would say about it?"

"Emeline's been dead for a long time."

"What, did he kill her too?"

"You bitch," he spat out, taking a step forward. I was so focused on his face that I didn't really see him swing the satchel at me and knock the gun out of my hand. It clattered to the ground as the weight of the satchel knocked me against the side of the van, and then Pierce and I were struggling with each other. It was times like these that I wished I'd taken karate when I was younger. Or self-defense classes. Where was another light bulb when I needed one? Pierce didn't seem to be much of a fighter, either. He just flailed away, trying to punch the shit out of me. As we fought, I heard the van's engine start up and then the van lurched forward, laying a strip of rubber on the pavement as it shot out of the parking lot. I guessed that Charlie had gone off in search of better friends.

Pierce and I were on the ground now, both struggling to get the gun, which was just out of reach. Unfortunately for me, Pierce was stronger, and he managed to get one hand on my face and bang it hard on the cement. I saw stars, figuratively and literally, as I lay there, looking up at the sky. There were lots of stars to be seen, actually. I was conscious of Pierce crawling over to get the gun and then slowly getting to his feet. I blinked up at him, the shooting pain in the back of my head was becoming one great big giant headache.

"I should have had you done away with," he said flatly. "It would have saved me a lot of trouble. Now, I guess, you leave me no other option."

I wondered if he was ruthless enough to harm me. What are you, nuts? that loud, outer voice of mine said. He's got the gun, and it's either you or him. Too bad you didn't go straight to the police instead of trying to play hero. Gee, thanks for those encouraging words.

I stared defiantly up at Pierce. He stood with his back to his car's headlights, and his face was in darkness. All I saw was a looming figure in front of me. I watched his arm come up, and I could see light reflecting off the barrel of the gun.

I could also see a pair of approaching lights as a van drove into the parking lot at full speed. Pierce turned his head around to see who it was, which gave me enough time to reach out and grab one of his legs. He tried to shake me off, but I was hanging on with all my strength. I guessed he wouldn't try and shoot me as such close range. The van

198

screeched to a stop, and the driver's door flew open. I caught a brief glimpse of a man running towards us with a crowbar.

"Leave her be!" the man yelled. It was Charlie.

Pierce turned around and fired. He might have been a good chief of staff, but he was a lousy shot. Charlie ducked sideways, which caused Pierce to completely turn around in order to follow his movements. Another shot, and this time Charlie went down.

"Charlie!" I screamed, as Pierce moved toward him. Charlie lay immobile, and I watched in horror as Pierce aimed the gun at him. Without warning, Charlie's hand holding the crowbar came around and smashed Pierce's kneecap. Pierce crumpled to the ground, still holding onto the gun. I was behind him, looking around for some sort of weapon. During the scuffle with Pierce, Mary Tully's scarf had been ripped off me and was lying on the ground. I grabbed it with both hands and came up behind Pierce. In one swift motion, I put the scarf around his neck and twisted as hard as I could. Pierce struggled violently, knocking us sideways, but I held on. Nothing was going to make me let go of the scarf. Then, finally, he went limp.

Charlie came crawling over to me and sat up, holding his shoulder.

"I think you can let go of him, Miss. Unless you want to kill him."

CHAPTER 54

A long stitch, a lazy tailor.

-Irish saying

"I couldn't leave you, Miss," Charlie said, as I removed the scarf from around the neck of Pierce Foley. I lifted Pierce's hand and felt for a pulse. To my relief, he was still alive.

"At first, I just wanted to get away, but then I thought about what you'd said, you know, about choosing better mates. I've done that a lot in my life, chosen the wrong mates. I thought about what might happen to you in the parking lot, and I thought how wrong it would be for me to leave you. He would have killed you for sure. That's why I came back."

"Thank you, Charlie," I said gratefully. "I'm glad that you did. You saved my life. I'm not much of a fighter. My sword has always been the pen."

"You seem to have done all right for yourself. Not many get the upper hand on Conor. Don't know about this bloke, though," he said, nodding at Pierce.

"Are you badly hurt?" I asked, noticing the blood seeping through his shirt.

"I think it's just a graze. When he shot me, I was more stunned than anything, and it sort of knocked the wind out of me, if you know what I mean, Miss. What about you? The back of your head is bloody."

"I'll be all right. Do you still have some rope in your van?"

"Aye, that I do. And your suitcase, too."

"Bring the rope, and let's tie him up before he comes to. Can you check his car to see if he has a cell phone?"

Charlie stood up very slowly and shook his head several times. Then he walked to the van, opened the back door, and brought out some rope. He stopped at Pierce's car, turned off the ignition, and came back holding a cell phone in his hands. He gave me the cell phone, and started tying Pierce's hands and then his feet.

"Charlie, will you call the emergency operator and tell them where we are?" I asked, handing the cell phone back to him. "And ask them to send an ambulance and a police car."

Charlie powered up the phone and dialed 311. "Operator, I'd like to report a shooting. We're in a parking lot at the rear of the Reddy Printing

Factory on Belfast Road. No, he was taken down and is unconscious. Yes, a woman has a head wound. It happened about ten minutes ago .... " Charlie was about to end the conversation, and I asked him for the phone.

"Operator. Is there a way you can connect me with Inspector Little of the Dublin Police? Yes, I'll hang on."

There was a lot of crackling on the line and then a female voice came on. "This is Inspector Little."

"My name is Aurora Weeks. The Canadian one. I believe you were the investigator in the case of the Irish Aurora Weeks, who was pushed down a set of stairs...."

"Are you all right? Where are you?" she interjected.

"Sort of. We've just called 311 to get an ambulance. There's been a shooting. I wondered if you could come. The shooting is related to the other incident."

"Are you sure you're all right?" she said. "We've been very concerned about you."

"Other than a bruise on my head, I'm fine. I'm in the parking of lot of the Reddy Printing Press on Belfast Road."

"I'm on the way. Is there anyone else with you?"

"Yes, the man who tried to kill me, but he's unconscious and tied up."

"I'll get there as quickly as we can."

The line went dead. I looked at Charlie. In spite of the fact that he'd helped kidnap me, I felt sorry for him. As far as I was concerned, he had redeemed himself. "You can still leave, Charlie," I said. "And take the money with you. I won't try and stop you."

"No, Miss. I'm not leaving you again. I'm done with running."

I reached over and squeezed his hand. "Thanks, Charlie."

We remained silent, lost in our own thoughts about what had just happened. Mostly, I was relieved that it was over, and hoped that nothing had happened to Patrick Mahoney and Tomas Kensella.

I still had Conor's jacket on, despite the fact that I couldn't stand the smell of it. I was feeling more chilled by the minute and needed its protection from the cool night air. I started to shiver, and drew my knees up to my chest to try and stay warm.

"Are you all right, Miss?" Charlie asked, looking concerned.

I found it hard to speak, so I just nodded and started to cry. He sat down beside me and held me really tight. Through my tears, I saw two flashing blue lights pull into the lot, followed by several more. Cars screeched to a stop, and footsteps approached.

A woman knelt beside me as Charlie stood up and backed away. "Aurora," she said. "I'm Inspector Little. Let me look at your head." I could feel her moving my hair aside. "Paramedic," she called out. "Over here."

The paramedic quickly came over, cleaned up the blood around the abrasion on my head, and dabbed on some antiseptic. Another paramedic took Charlie aside and assessed his injury.

"Are you hurt anywhere else?" Inspector Little asked.

"No, I'm not, but one of the kidnappers was shot in the foot at the farmhouse where I was being held. He's in bad need of medical attention. The man over there, Charlie, can tell you where to find him."

Paramedics were working on Pierce Foley. They had untied him and were preparing to transfer him to a stretcher. "Secure the area," Little said to one of the uniformed policemen, who seemed unsure as to what to do.

"How about we take you to the hospital and get you checked out, and you can tell me what happened on the way. That all right?" Little asked, returning her attention to me.

"Can you arrange for me to go to St. James Hospital?"

"I'm sure we can. Can you stand, or do you need a stretcher?"

"I can stand. Just give me a hand up." She called a paramedic over, and they helped me up. Charlie's wound was being dressed, and he smiled at me.

I smiled back. "See you later, Charlie."

Pierce was just being secured onto the stretcher. I stopped beside him and turned to Inspector Little. "Do you know who this is?" I asked her.

"No, who is he?"

"Pierce Foley, chief of staff for Michael O'Neil."

Inspector Little let out a low whistle. "Really?" She called over a policeman and asked him to help me to the ambulance. "I'll be right with you, luv," she said to me.

As we walked to the ambulance, I looked over my shoulder and saw Inspector Little lean over the stretcher and look at Pierce closely. Then she took out her cell phone and made a quick call.

In the ambulance, I was asked to lie down. At first I resisted, but then I gave in. I wanted to eat, and I wanted to see Rory. I wanted to ask Inspector Little a million questions. A few moments later, she came into the ambulance, sat on an empty stretcher opposite me, and nodded to the driver. The rear doors closed, and the ambulance started moving slowly out of the parking lot. A moment later, the siren went on and we sped off.

"If you want to talk now, go ahead, or we can wait till later," she said. "Considering who we're dealing with, it would be very helpful to me if you could give me a quick outline of what's happened. There will be lots of attention on this, as you can imagine."

I smiled. "Yes, I can well imagine. But can you tell me how the election went? Did O'Neil win?"

"You haven't heard?" she asked.

I shook my head.

CHAPTER 55

There are finer fish in the sea
that have ever been caught.
                                    -Irish saying

"O'Neil had a massive heart attack yesterday. He's in intensive care and may not make it," Inspector Little said bluntly.

I was speechless. In a way, I'd been looking forward to confronting him again.

"Is he involved in this?" she asked apprehensively. I could feel her discomfort; it was one thing for Pierce Foley to be responsible for the attack on Aurora and for my kidnapping, but if O'Neil had been behind it all, it would be a whole different ballgame.

"Not according to Pierce," I said, "if he's to be believed."

"Did he tell you that?"

"Yes, he said he was trying to protect O'Neil. He felt that we were trying to implicate O'Neil in a murder and that it would ruin his chances of getting elected."

"Are you talking about the bombing in Belfast that killed a man named Fergus Flanagan forty years ago?"

"Forty-one," I responded.

Little looked at me with bemusement. "Your brain obviously hasn't been damaged. Want to give me a quick outline of what happened? We'll be at the hospital soon."

"How's Aurora?"

"She's doing fine. Out of intensive care and talking up a storm."

I laughed. "That's the best news I've heard all day. Okay, so here's the five-minute version."

I told her about being hustled into a car and then a van, and then being left in a deserted farmhouse for four days with only water and granola bars. I told her about Conor and his obsession with oral sex, and my obsession with a 60-watt bulb. I could swear that she laughed as she took notes. Then I related the trip to the parking lot, the confrontation with Pierce, Charlie making his getaway, losing the fight with Pierce, Charlie making his reappearance and saving my life, and, finally, wrapping Mary Tully's scarf around Pierce's neck.

I paused for a moment while Little was busy scribbling in her notebook.

"Has Patrick Moore been in touch with you, by any chance?" I asked.

"Yes, daily. Patrick is a very influential man, by the way."

"Did he mention anything about an old man named Tomas Kensella?"

"Yes, he did. He told me about your visit with him."

"And is he all right?"

"Yes, he is. I don't think he was ever in any danger. No one would have taken him seriously. Regardless, we put a watch on him."

"I took him seriously," I said soberly.

Inspector Little and I made eye contact and held it for a few seconds until I finally broke it by looking at the ceiling.

"My name is Nancy, by the way," she said. "I'd prefer if you called me by my title in public, though."

"Okay, Nancy....." I didn't get to finish the sentence. The ambulance pulled into the emergency bay at St. James Hospital, and I was whisked away on the stretcher into the bowels of the hospital.

I was examined by two doctors who looked at the abrasion on my head, poked and prodded me in various places, took my vitals, and then suggested that I be given some IV fluids to get back to normal. It was late, nearly 11, and to be honest, I just wanted to sleep.

Inspector Little waited to talk to me again until the doctors were finished and I'd been wheeled into a private room.

"We're going to have a guard outside the door, just to make sure you don't have any unwanted visitors," she explained. "I'll be back in the morning, and we can talk some more, all right? I think the nurse is going to put the IV in now. See you tomorrow."

I nodded and closed my eyes. The last thing I remembered was a needle being inserted into my arm. Then the lights went out, figuratively and literally.

CHAPTER 56

A silent mouth is sweet to hear.
-Irish saying

That was the best sleep ever.

I dreamt about heaven. Actually, I think it was about the Garden of Eden. I was walking through this incredibly vibrant garden filled with the most amazing flowers, while birds were chirping and singing and flying around. Once in a while, little bunnies would sit on the path, and I would bend down to pet them. There wasn't a cloud in the sky, and the sun's rays felt warm and comforting on my skin.

I was sitting on a wrought-iron bench with my eyes closed when an angelic voice came floating out of nowhere. "Hello, Aurora."

I opened my eyes, expecting to see Gabriel. Instead, I saw Rory. Hmm. She hadn't told me she was an angel.

"I've been sitting here, watching you. You had the loveliest smile on your face. How are you, luv?"

I blinked, coming fully awake, and realized that Rory, the real Rory, was standing beside the bed, wearing a hospital gown. She had gotten some of her colour back, and her bruises had mostly disappeared. What a change. Not long ago, she had been the patient and I'd been the visitor. Now the tables had turned.

I sat up. Surprisingly, I felt really good. The headache was gone; so was the fatigue.

"Never mind me. How are you? I've been so worried about you," I said, reaching out for her hands.

"Oh, I'm doing better every day," she said, linking her hands with mine. "The doctors say I may be able to go home any day now. But we were all so worried about you. You just disappeared. Gave us all a right fright, I must admit. Thank God, you're safe. But what happened? Inspector Little didn't say much other than that they found you in a parking lot in the company of two gentlemen."

"One gentleman, anyway. The other one tried to kill me." I sat upright. "Where's my scarf?"

Rory looked at me as if I was crazy.

"Are my clothes in the closet?" I asked. "Can you check and see if there is an Irish scarf there?"

She turned and opened the closet. Most of the clothes I'd been were hanging up, including Conor's jacket. I wished that they'd burned it. But my pants were sitting on low shelf, and the scarf was neatly folded and lying on top of it.

"It's here," she said.

I breathed a sigh of relief. The scarf and I had been through a lot in the last few days, and I would have been distraught to lose it.

A nurse walked in. "Good afternoon," she said. "How are you feeling?"

Afternoon? Did she say afternoon?

"How long did I sleep?" I asked, all confused.

She looked at her watch and said that it had been about fourteen hours. No wonder I felt so good.

"I'm going to take some blood, then we'll run a little test, and I'm sure you'll be set to go in no time. You look pretty fit, from what I can see. I'll send some food around as well. You must be starved."

"Did someone force-feed me pizza while I was sleeping?" I asked. "Because I don't feel all that hungry."

The nurse quickly inserted the needle, drew out blood which, thankfully, was still red, and then left.

"Pull up a chair," I said to Rory, "we have lots to talk about. Actually, wait a minute." I pulled the covers back and swung my legs out of the bed. "I'll just sit like this, it's more comfortable."

"What are the odds of two women with the same names being in the same hospital?" Rory said, as she pulled up a chair and sat down. "And for the same reason," she added.

"I guess that was the problem, wasn't it? So let's trade stories. You first." I said.

"Well, you know that I tracked down Cecil Flanagan. He was a downright nasty one, he was. From my research, I knew that he had a brother, so I tracked him down as well. He was much more talkative, and he told me the story about Emeline O'Neil. After my conversation with him, I did some research on Emeline and found that she'd died a year after Fergus. Suicide, I think. There was an obituary in the paper. That's when I decided to call one of the O'Neils. I figured I'd never get to Michael, so instead I called his brother, Joseph. He was easy enough to track down. I told him who I was and that I was doing family research. He was cooperative enough until I mentioned Emeline and her engagement to Fergus. That's when he abruptly stopped the conversation. A couple of days later, I went to the library to do some unrelated research, and that's when the man pushed me down the stairs. He was behind me when I was nearing the top of the stairway. I remember him quite well because I held open the door for him, but he told me to go ahead. I hadn't taken two steps when he gave me a big push. And that's all I remember."

"You've just filled in a blank for me," I said.

"What was that?" Rory said.

"Pierce Foley mentioned that Emeline was dead, which I didn't known. Wait, maybe I'd better start from the beginning." I told her about the interview with Michael O'Neil, and meeting Pierce Foley. Then I told her about my visit with Cecil Flanagan, and going with Patrick to see Tomas.

A hospital worker came in with a tray of food and set it on the moveable table. I positioned it over my lap so that I could talk and eat at the same time. Mom would have told me that it was bad manners to do so, but it worked for me.

I had a spoonful of yogurt and then some applesauce. My God, I thought I'd died and gone to heaven.

In between bites, I related the kidnapping saga. By the time I finished my story, I'd polished off the entire tray of food while Rory sat there wide-eyed.

"Let me see if I get this straight," she said, as I was cleaning out what was left in the yogurt container with my finger. "Joseph O'Neil called Michael and told him that someone named Aurora Weeks was enquiring about the relationship between Emeline and Fergus. Michael tells Pierce Foley, who tracks me down and has someone push me down the stairs to silence me. Then he meets you at the interview and realizes that they'd gone after the wrong person. In a panic, he has you kidnapped to keep you quiet until after the election. Does that make sense?"

It made perfect sense, and I was glad to see that Rory hadn't suffered any brain damage.

"Yes, it does, except that Joseph O'Neil might not have spoken with his brother. He might have talked to Pierce Foley instead. It's not all that unlikely, Michael was a busy man at the time. So Pierce took matters into his own hands, without Michael being aware of what was going on. How is Michael, by the way? Have you heard?"

"From what they say on the telly, the doctors removed a large section of his skull because of the swelling. They say that he has irreversible brain damage and is on life support. He's not expected to last long."

"That's not good. How did he fare in the election?"

"Came in a distant fourth. They said that if he hadn't had the heart attack, he might have had a good shot at it."

The nurse returned with a doctor who asked me some questions, looked at the back of my head, and said with a smile that I could be discharged. As she was leaving, she looked at my empty plate. "Good to see you haven't lost your appetite."

The nurse finished writing some notes on my chart, and then said to me, "Although she said you can be discharged, we're not to do so until we get permission from the police. I'll place a call to the inspector right now. But first, let me take out your IV."

"Is it Inspector Little?" I asked, while she was taking out the needle and putting a band-aid on my arm.

"Yes. I think that's the one. I'll be back shortly." She secured all the tubes and then wheeled the IV trolley out of the room.

I stood up carefully, walked to the window, and looked out. It was a nice sunny day, just as it had been in my dream.

"You know what I really need?" I said to Rory. "A shower."

"Why don't you have one, then? I believe there's one right in there," she said, pointing to a door. "And I should get back to my room before they send out a search party for me. Come and see me when you're done. I'm in 1105. B wing."

Rory turned to go. Just before she reached the door, she stopped, looked at me, and came back to where I was standing. "I'm so glad you're safe. Give me a hug."

"I'm glad we're both safe," I said, choking up.

We hugged for the longest time.

And then I had the best shower ever. I don't think I even washed myself. I just stood under the hot water and let it wash away the unpleasantness of the last few days.

Aside from confession, nothing is as good for the soul as a long, hot, shower.

When I came out of the shower, Inspector Little was sitting my room, writing in a notebook. I sat on the bed and she finally stopped writing, put the pen away and looked up.

"How are you feeling now?" she said.

"Much better. It's amazing what a difference a good night's sleep and a trouble-free mind can make."

"You look much better," she said, putting the notebook away in her purse.

"Yeah, I know. I must have looked like..." I paused for the briefest moment, trying to find the right word. It came to me in a flash. " .... shite."

Both of us laughed.

"The doctor said I can be discharged, but that I need to talk to you first."

"I need to arrange a formal interview at headquarters with you, if that's all right," she said. "I've scheduled it for tomorrow morning at 9:30. In the meantime, I've taken the liberty of booking you into a hotel under an assumed name. I assume that's okay. We don't want you to be bothered by the media. Your suitcase has been sent there and should be in your room by the time you arrive."

"You've been very kind. Thank you for everything, Inspector Little." I caught myself. "Nancy, I mean. I'm very grateful."

"Don't mention it. By the way, you might not be able to leave Ireland for a couple of days, just in case we have any more questions with respect to what has happened. You will also be asked to come back for the trial."

"Yes, I understand. I'd just like to spend a quiet evening getting caught up. Tell me, how is Pierce Foley?"

"He's fine. You didn't kill him, if that's what you're worried about."

"What about Conor?"

"You didn't kill him, either. He'll live, though he may have some problem walking properly in the future. Though I suspect that the only walking he's going to be doing is in the prison yards. Oh, and he might have some lingering damage to his, er, privates."

"Good. And Charlie?"

"He was lucky. The bullet only grazed him. No real damage done."

"You know he saved my life, don't you? He could have left me, twice. Yet he came back. I shudder to think what would have happened if he hadn't."

"He's cooperating with out investigation, which will help. With your good words, he may escape serious punishment, especially if he continues to be cooperative."

"That's good to hear. I think that, deep down, he's a good man. Have you talked to Foley at all?"

"Aye, I have. He's not saying much of anything. We'll hold off charging him until after our interview tomorrow."

"Can I get dressed while we're talking?"

"You sure can. I'm going to give you a lift to the hotel. I want to make sure you don't get diverted again," Inspector Little said with a smile. "We can talk some more on the way."

She handed me a bag. "I took the liberty of getting some fresh clothes out of your suitcase. I thought you might want them."

How thoughtful. I must ask Dave if he would have done that under the same circumstance.

I signed a form at the nurses' station, and we made a quick detour to Rory's room. There was a policeman stationed outside her door.

Rory was nodding off to sleep, and I promised to come back and see her the following day.

"How long did it take for anyone to realize I might be missing?" I asked Inspector Little as we got into her car.

"It started late Saturday when Patrick Moore called the hotel and found that you had checked out. He telephoned St. James, thinking that perhaps you'd gone to see Rory. Catherine was there and told him that you hadn't been seen since the previous afternoon. She thought it was a bit odd, but was sure you'd turn up soon. He then asked for my phone number. He called, but I was off-duty. I returned his call the next morning, and he was very agitated. He told me that your disappearance was suspicious, and that it might be linked to the IRA because you had some damaging information about Michael O'Neil. Incidentally, he didn't know that Rory had been pushed down the stairs."

We were stuck in traffic, and after a few moments, Little opened the window, put the flashing light on the roof, and the traffic parted.

"I said that we would start making some enquiries," she continued. "But since there was no evidence of foul play, and his story did seem rather farfetched, it wasn't treated with any real urgency. There was a suggestion that you might have gone back to Belfast. We deliberately tried to play it low key for fear it might become a feeding frenzy for the media, which might have endangered you if indeed you had been kidnapped."

We were getting close to the hotel, and Inspector Little removed the blue light from the roof. "Now that we have Pierce Foley in custody, though," she said, "it will hit the front pages for sure. Be prepared. I'd prefer it if you didn't talk to the media until you and I have had our chat."

She pulled into the hotel driveway. "You're registered under the name of Keri Delaney. Oh, and by the way, I've spoken with Mr. Moore and told him you were safe. You might ring him soon, he was anxious to speak with you. I'll see you in the morning .... say 9:30? I'll send someone round to pick you up."

"Thank you, Nancy. I appreciate everything that you've done."

"You've been through a lot, Aurora. Have a good rest."

I stepped out of her car. It was just over a week ago that I'd first set foot in Dublin. Now it felt surreal. So much had happened in the intervening period that I wondered if I was actually the same person.

"Welcome, Miss Delaney," said the desk clerk, after I gave him my name and he checked his computer.

"Good to be here," I said. In more ways than you can imagine. "Oh, I wonder if you could help me. I left my cell phone charger behind." I pulled the dead phone out of my purse. "Would you happen to have a spare one I could use?"

He looked at it, turned around, opened a drawer, rummaged around, and pulled out a cord. "Here you go." Things were looking up.

I was happy to see my suitcase in the room. Much to my surprise, my laptop was right on top, along with the battery cord. It wasn't at the farmhouse, so I could only assume that Charlie had put it there afterwards. Maybe it had been in the van the whole time.

I plugged the phone charger into a wall socket, and attached my iPhone to it. I was anxious to call Dave, but I didn't want to use the hotel telephone for fear of a huge long-distance bill. As I waited for the phone to get a partial charge, I had an overwhelming and maybe irrational desire to have another shower. And so I did, spending a long time just letting the hot water wash every little vestige of the last few days out of my pores.

I wrapped myself in one of the hotel bathrobes when I was done, and looked closely at myself in the mirror. I looked pale and tired despite the good sleep I'd had the night before. Maybe a day at the spa would help. I wanted to weigh myself, but there was no scale. Surely the pounds had melted away at the farmhouse.

The iPhone now had enough power to make some phone calls. I piled the pillows high behind me on the bed and called Dave.

"Well, well, if it isn't Aurora come lately," he said, in a rather clipped tone. "When I didn't hear from you on the weekend, I was beginning to think that you'd been kidnapped by the IRA and was about to call Interpol."

"I was."

"Was what?"

"Kidnapped by the IRA."

"Lame excuse. Try another."

"I was held in an abandoned farmhouse for three days, and I managed to get away by grinding a light bulb into the kidnapper's crotch. Then I strangled one of the others with my Mary Tully scarf."

"Aurora, stop kidding. How's the election coming? I've been so busy hitting the books, I haven't had time to check the news." A plaintive tone entered his voice. "You coming home soon? I haven't had a good meal since you left."

"Well, Inspector Little said I might have to be in Dublin for another couple of days, until they wrap up the investigation. Tomorrow morning, I'm going to the police station to give a statement."

"Wait a minute," he said slowly, realizing that I was serious. "Aurora, is this for real?"

"As real as I'm sitting here, under the assumed name of Keri Delaney, in a hotel called Jury's Inn in downtown Dublin."

We talked for an hour. Actually I did most of the talking and only stopped because the power was getting low again on my mobile. Dave showed the appropriate amount of concern and relief, and made me promise to come home as quickly as possible. He'll make a good father, my inner voice said, and I agreed. I decided I'd wait to tell him that in person.

His talk with the investigators had gone well, whatever that was supposed to mean. But he sounded upbeat, so I took that as a positive sign. His final words to me were, "Hey, maybe you should write a book about Ireland."

My Dave. Ever the kidder.

Next, I called Patrick. He answered so quickly that I wondered if he was sitting by the phone. When I said hello, he let out a big sigh of relief. "Yes, it's her," I heard him say to Mary. I quickly filled him in and promised to have dinner with both of them the following day. Lastly, I called Meredith, but only reached her voice mail. I asked her to call me at the hotel under the name of Keri Delaney. I didn't tell her what had happened. Her voice mail box wasn't big enough.

I turned on my laptop and checked my e-mails. Among the many messages in my in-box was a crisp e-mail from Malcolm, asking me to contact him immediately. I assumed he wanted an explanation for my absence on the day of the election. I decided to save the conversation until tomorrow. I'd done enough talking tonight. My body was craving food, and I opened the mini-fridge. There, nestled among the wine and beer, were two granola bars and two bottles of water. I laughed out loud, got dressed, and went downstairs to eat in the hotel dining room.

CHAPTER 57

May you live to be 100, and a year extra to repent.
-Irish saying

At 7:45 the next morning, I was awakened by the incessant ringing of a telephone. I opened my eyes and looked around the room. Nothing seemed familiar. Had I been kidnapped again? No, my hands weren't bound, nor were my feet. Finally the light bulb inside my groggy head went on, and I picked up the handset.

"Hello," I said tentatively.

"Aurora, this is Inspector Little. Did I wake you?"

"Sort of. But I should be up anyway."

"I'm sorry," she apologized. "I just wanted to let you know that the story is slowly leaking out. Rory has been tracked down by the media, so we've moved her to a different room. They don't know about you yet, so you should be left in peace. That may change after today, though."

"Not to worry .... I can handle it."

"I'm sure you can. I'll have someone pick you up at 9:15. That all right?"

"That's fine. How long will the interview take?"

"I should imagine a couple of hours."

"Okay."

I hung up the telephone and lay back on my pillow. The thought of having to face the media didn't phase me. I just didn't like it.

I remembered seeing Michael Flatley dance in a performance of "Riverdance" in Ottawa once. God, that man could dance. The way his feet moved was magical, and the cast behind him was choreographed to the nth degree. And that's what I felt like all of a sudden. Like Michael Flatley, standing on stage, looking at all the dancers behind with their feet tapping in a rhythmic crescendo that rose to a climax. Then they all stopped. Not a sound to be heard anywhere until Flatley tapped one foot, then the other, then faster, and before long, he was dancing across the stage like a man possessed.

I couldn't dance like that. Not even remotely close. But facing a media circus would be a little like Michael Flatley trying to keep step with all those dancers behind him.

215

I sighed. I'd rather be in the audience and not on stage. With that happy thought, I forced myself to get up.

I made myself a cup of instant coffee, and, for old times' sake, ate one of the granola bars in the mini-fridge. Then I turned on the news. O'Neil was still on life support and not expected to survive.

I was just heading to the shower when I heard the announcer say, "An arrest has been made in the attempted murder of a young woman from Galway who was pushed down the stairs at the National Library a week ago. The woman, Aurora Weeks, had been in a coma ever since her fall, but has regained consciousness and was able to identify her attacker. Two men have subsequently been arrested and charged with attempted murder. In a related story, Michael O'Neil's chief of staff, Pierce Foley, is under police guard at a local hospital. Details are not available from the Garda, but a well-placed source said that he is rumoured to be connected with the men who attempted to murder Miss Weeks. A police spokesman would only say that the investigation was still ongoing."

Well, maybe I wouldn't have to do much dancing after all. I'd just assume Keri Delaney's identity for the rest of my stay in Ireland and quietly slip out of the Emerald Isle. Good luck with that, said that louder, outer voice of mine.

The telephone rang again.

"Hello," I said, again tentatively.

"Keri Delaney?"

I recognized Meredith's voice immediately. "Hello, Meredith. It's Aurora."

"Aurora? I thought you'd gone back to Canada. Have you been here all this time?"

"Indeed I have."

"Then you've heard that Pierce Foley's been arrested. Can you believe it? I always knew he had a dark side to him. They haven't released any details, so I don't know anything at this point."

"Have you got a minute to talk?" I asked, knowing that I could trust Meredith.

I gave her an abbreviated version of my kidnapping. When I finished, she let out a low whistle and said "Oh my God." And then she repeated it about five times.

I asked her to keep the details to herself at this point, since I hadn't formally had my police interview. I didn't think Inspector Little would appreciate me leaking the story ahead of that.

Meredith asked if she could come down from Belfast to talk to me before I left, and I agreed. As a journalist, she knew that there was a larger story here. I saw no harm in that, in fact I welcomed it.

CHAPTER 58

You'll never plow a field by turning
it over in your mind

-Irish Proverb

Sitting on the airplane heading back to Canada gave me a definite feeling of déjà vu. It wasn't that long ago that I was making the same trip back from Berlin, having escaped from the clutches of a madman. Maybe I should just stop taking trips to Europe. I mean, who would have guessed that my simple interest in family history would lead to my imprisonment in an isolated farmhouse where I was left to ponder my fate.

I'd been trying to anticipate Dad's reaction, not to mention Aunt Fionola's. Both of them had warned me that I should essentially let sleeping dogs lie. But if I did that, I wouldn't be much of a journalist. Not long ago, I'd read an Irish proverb that stuck with me. All sins cast long shadows. If we ignored the shadows, who were we fooling?

O'Neil died the same morning that I was being interviewed by Inspector Little and another Garda official, who had the impressive title of Deputy Commissioner. For me, O'Neil's death was a blessing in disguise. The media put the Pierce Foley story on the backburner, and I escaped any media scrutiny. Aside from the fact that there weren't many details available yet, I suspect that the media thought it would be indelicate to start throwing dirt around about O'Neil before he was even buried.

Meredith did come down from Belfast. She told me that she didn't want to be part of the tabloid frenzy, as inviting as it may sound. She planned to do some research, and then talk to Rory and probably the Flanagans as well. Maybe Cecil would be nicer to her; after all, she was a local. Then she would write a thoughtful opinion piece. We planned to stay in close touch.

Rory had been discharged from the hospital. She was even more determined now to find the missing ancestral link between us, if indeed there was one. As for the media attention, she could handle it. "Can't hurt my business, can it?" she said, with an impish smile.

Dinner with Patrick and Mary was delightful. Patrick knew much more about O'Neil then he'd let on, and shared some confidences with

218

me. In his view, he didn't doubt that Michael O'Neil deliberately murdered young Fergus Flanagan. At the same time, he firmly believed that Michael had played no part in my kidnapping. I told him that now I really wanted to write a book, and he promised to give me all the help I needed. I was looking forward to that. His help would be invaluable.

Now, watching the clouds roll by at 35,000 feet and enjoying a glass of red wine, I was making a mental list of things to do when I got back home.

The first thing was to talk to Kim Gordon, my publisher. I had an outline in my head for my next book, whether she wanted it or not. The working title would be "*Two Weeks*". My great-grandfather's death had cast a long shadow, on that had stretched almost ninety years. In that shadow lingered the birth of a nation, a civil war, terrorism, murder, and despair. But at the same time, others had stepped out from under that shadow and gone on to forge new lives in a new world away from violence and strife.

Next on the list was a heart-to-heart talk with Dave about our future. I wouldn't emulate Marisa Tomei, but the message would be the same. The time had come, and I couldn't wait any longer.

Again, my family-planning thoughts were interrupted, this time by the man in the seat next to me. Earlier, we had exchanged pleasantries as the plane taxied out to the runway. He'd confided that he hated take-offs and landings. As the engines roared and the plane picked up speed, I saw him gripping the arm rests very firmly, eyes closed, teeth clenched. When we reached a cruising altitude, he finally relaxed his grip and slumped back in his seat. It took about half an hour before he regained his composure. When the drink cart came, he tersely ordered a double rye and coke. I ordered a glass of red wine.

"My name is Donald Anderson," he said, reaching over to shake my hand.

"Nice to meet you. My name is Aurora Weeks."

"Yes, I know who you are. I'm with The Irish Times. I wonder if you'd care to chat about your involvement with Pierce Foley?"

Time to start dancing!

Author's Note

The shooting at the Shannon View hotel in Castleconnell, county Limerick, is a documented historical event which occurred on April 17, 1921 and is a matter of public record. In the event, a company of British Army Auxiliary, also known as Black and Tans, exchanged gunfire with patrons in the hotel bar. Two RIC Constables were killed, as was the innkeeper, Denis O'Donovan. According to an eyewitness, O'Donovan was murdered by the soldiers after the shooting had ceased. A subsequent military inquiry absolved the British Army Auxiliary soldiers of any wrongdoing, especially in the shooting of the innkeeper.

Sgt. William Joel Hughes, one of the two RIC constables killed, was posthumously awarded the Constabulary medal of the Royal Irish Constabulary, its highest award.

The innkeeper in this novel, Richard Mahoney, and his family, are fictitious characters which have been invented for purposes of this story.

Acknowledgement

I'd like to thank the people who helped me along this Irish journey in one way or another - Don Anderson, Susi Delaney, Joe Sexton, Monica Hofmann, Joanne Ingrassia, Roy Beresowsky, Allison Buck, and Sue who did her usual outstanding job maintaining a consistent story narrative. Lastly, I'd like to thank Fionola Meredith, a freelance journalist in Belfast whose columns on politics and life in Northern Ireland inspired me greatly. Thank you one and all.

I should also acknowledge my grandson, Brody. He didn't help in this book whatsoever. In fact, at times he could be an immense, but pleasurable, distraction. However, he knew that I was writing a story about Ireland and it led him to write his own little story called Aliens in Ireland. He thought it was a much better title. His story needs a bit more polishing but one of these days - look for it on the book shelves.

www.ingramcontent.com/pod-product-compliance
Lightning Source LLC
Chambersburg PA
CBHW072050170626
46813CB00004B/1291